Return of the Eagle

Other Books in the Reclamation Saga

Rachel
VanZandt

Return of
the Eagle

The Reclamation Saga, Book I

Cover and interior designed by Nicole Klungle.

Hardcover ISBN: 979-8-9855884-0-8
Paperback ISBN: 979-8-9855884-4-6
Ebook ISBN: 979-8-9855884-3-9

To my mother, who ofered insi ghtful edits and lots of ~~them~~ LOVE.

Contents

CHAPTER 1

Last Day of School

Classroom doors flew open, and empty halls began to flood with students as the final bell of the school year rang through Washington High. The corridors that only moments before had been quiet were now filled with teenage boys and girls yelling out to friends or boisterously cheering the end of exams and the start of summer vacation. Teachers trailed behind their students leaving the classrooms and lingered in their doorways, giving them final high-fives until the next school year.

Sage melded with the sea of students flowing toward the main entrance of the school and the freedom of summer on the other side of the doors. With one strap of her nearly empty backpack slung over her shoulder, she smiled and waved to friends calling out their goodbyes as they rushed for the bus. Sage was in no hurry, though. Every day after school, she and her brother, Douglas, met at the same place on the steps outside the school. They chatted with friends who were coming and going while waiting for their mother to pick them up on her way home from the elementary school where she taught second grade.

Warm breezes rustled the leaves of the trees lining the sidewalks and the main courtyard. After a grueling winter that had seemed to have spilled over into the spring, the trees and flowers had finally awoken throughout the city. Strands of Sage's long, wavy auburn hair blew across her face, momentarily hiding her bright blue eyes as well as the slight frown creasing her delicate features. Exams were over, it was a beautiful day, the family trip she looked forward to each year was only a day away, and yet she was troubled.

"Hi!" a familiar voice called out. "How did your exams go?" Sage's best friend, Wendy, skipped down the first short flight of stairs to where Sage was already sitting.

"Fine, I think," Sage replied, twisting the stray hair away from her face. Wendy had been her best friend since the end of elementary school and had never been an all-A student like Sage. She had to work hard for decent grades and usually worried her hard work still wouldn't be enough.

"Don't be ridiculous! I've known you too long to believe *fine* is all you did," Wendy replied, blowing off Sage's attempt to downplay the easy exams. "Mine were *fine* too, by the way."

Sage opened her backpack and pulled out a bag of M&M's to share with her friend. "To celebrate," she announced ceremoniously, pouring half the contents into Wendy's hand.

"You *know* me!" Wendy sighed happily. "When do you leave for your grandfather's?"

"Either tomorrow afternoon or early the next day," Sage answered, smiling broadly. Her grandfather's cabin, on the outskirts of a national park, was a favorite family destination. Every spring, when school first let out, her family traveled the long seven hours to the cabin for an extended vacation. Their grandfather would visit them once in the fall or at the holiday season, but this was always their longest time with him and, even more importantly, it was out of the city. There were advantages to living in the city, especially a city within an hour's drive of Chicago. A short drive from their suburban home provided access to every variety of cuisine imaginable, entertainment, museums, the lake, and Navy Pier. So many of Sage's friends, including Wendy, loved the lights, noise, and life of the city and couldn't imagine themselves anywhere else, but it was not where Sage's heart longed to be. That would be the forest. "I should be back in about two weeks," Sage continued, though she wished the visit would be longer.

"Oh, there it is. You have that far off look again," Wendy grinned. "Listen. After every visit to your grandfather's, I ask what you did while you were there. All you ever say is that you hiked in the park and read. Boring! There is *everything* to do here—especially in the summer! When you get back, we can go downtown shopping or go to the movies or ..."

"Douglas is life-guarding at the city pool this summer," Sage interrupted in an attempt to change the subject. "He starts right after we get back."

"Ooooo! I may just have to take up swimming," Wendy said, glazing over into her own dreamy look and twirling her short brown hair.

"Oh, brother!" Sage rolled her eyes.

"Yes?" a deep voice teased. Sage's brother, Douglas, snatched a few M&M's from her hand before reclining against the railing. Sage turned to face the direction her brother had come, knowing that following closely behind him would be a tall, lanky young man—who was today trying, almost successfully, to twirl a basketball on his finger.

"Rosy!" Douglas's friend exclaimed while snatching some M&M's of his own from Sage. He sat down next to her, draped his arm around her shoulders, then cleared his throat and wiggled his eyebrows up and down. When he spoke, it was in a dramatically deep and persuasive voice.

"What do you think about me and you getting together at the pool this summer? Maybe a movie on a *hot* night?"

"You are too smooth, Demo," she said playing along with him. "How *do* the girls ever resist your charms?"

"Hey," he sulked. "I was being serious, and there you go toying with a man's feelings."

Sage laughed, knowing that he may have been serious about the date, but he was certainly not feeling hurt by her teasing. Though she was not the prettiest girl in school by far, she did draw her share of attention. Much to her brother's dismay, this more and more often included some of his own friends.

"And how many times do I have to ask you to stop calling me Rosy?" she said, bumping him with her shoulder.

A silver four-door sedan pulled to a stop along the curb in front of the school. Sage and Douglas grabbed their bags, said goodbye to their friends, and started down the last few steps to the car.

"Hi, Mom," Douglas said, slipping into the front seat.

"How were your exams today?" their mother asked them.

"No problem," Douglas told her with a shrug.

Sage smiled at her brother's easy manner. There was no doubt in her mind that Douglas had indeed breezed through his tests and would be starting his senior year the following fall in the running for valedictorian.

"Me, either," Sage told her mother.

"Wonderful! I'm going to try to finish up my grades tonight. That way, I will just have to clean up the rest of my classroom tomorrow morning, and we can hit the road," their mother said excitedly. "Oh, Sage. When I talked to

Grandpa last night, he asked me to remind you to bring that book with you—you know, the one he sent you for your birthday."

Sage and her grandfather loved to walk or read together in the forest. A trail, worn from years of daily walks, led right from his home into the national park and to its largest lake. Since they were small children, Douglas and Sage would walk with their grandfather in the cool shade of the forest. Many a day were passed with Sage and her grandfather sitting on the rocks bordering the lake with their feet dangling into the water, while Douglas swam—his favorite activity outside of basketball. In the birthday card her grandfather had sent with the book, he had told her the book was special and they would find some time together on their next trip to go through it.

"I already have it packed," she answered with a smile. She had been looking forward to some special time with her grandfather ever since their last visit together.

At dinner that evening, Sage listened to her brother talking about his summer plans. She felt off tonight—heavy and still troubled, like something was wrong or maybe she had just forgotten to do something important. While she half-listened, she wondered if maybe it was because this would be the first summer in as long as she could recall that she and Douglas wouldn't plan their activities together. Sage didn't know too many families where the siblings, especially a brother and sister, got along with each other as well as she and Douglas. She went to all the home basketball games to cheer for him, they played in the high school band together, and they shared the same circle of friends. She hadn't thought of having a summer without him or given a thought to what she wanted to do with her own time.

"Penny for your thoughts," her mother said, watching Sage with her fork full of pasta stopped halfway to her mouth.

"Oh, I just was thinking about what my plans might be for the summer. With Douglas working, I'm not sure what there is for me to do. It is a strange feeling." Sage mused. "Wendy and I could get together, I suppose."

"You could come out to the pool, though it would be better for everyone if Demo didn't know when you were going to be there," Douglas laughed. "And I won't be working all the time. We'll still have plenty of time for a summer adventure."

Sage shrugged, not feeling any better.

"You could help me with the garden, too," her mother suggested. "You have much better luck than I do."

"Yeah, that would be fun. I'm sure there will be lots of things to keep me busy."

After dinner was cleared, their mother got to work on finishing grade reports for her class, and Douglas took off for a game of basketball at the park with Demo. Sage grabbed her backpack and took it upstairs to her room. She dumped the remaining contents onto her bed. Just as she began sorting through a stack of school papers, the phone rang.

Sage smiled. She knew it would be her father calling to let them know he had gotten to the cabin safely. Douglas and Sage hadn't seen their father all week. His work as an environmental consultant for several large firms kept him traveling. In addition, he served on the council of a large organization that worked on environmental protections. Sage thought it was ironic that he chose his career because he loved being outdoors enjoying the natural surroundings but was so sought after as an environmental expert that he spent much of his time on airplanes or in city boardrooms.

The heavy feeling from dinner was suddenly much stronger than earlier. She kept herself from running down the stairs, her mind racing to Douglas. *Something is wrong,* she thought. *Where is Douglas?* At the bottom of the stairs, she turned to her right, looking into the family room. Her mother was alone, sitting on the couch with the phone to her ear.

"I don't understand, Avery," she stammered. "No, I just talked to him last night! I don't believe this. This just cannot be happening...."

Her mother began crying in earnest, still trying to listen to her husband on the other end of the line. Sage could feel the weight of her mother's pain and sadness—and was beginning to piece together the reason. Crying so hard now that she gasped for air, her mother handed Sage the phone.

"Dad?" she asked quietly.

"Hi, honey," her father said. He sounded fatigued from traveling, and his voice trembled with emotion. "I have some ... news," he began. "When I got to the cabin tonight, I found Grandpa on the floor ... not breathing." Sage sucked in a breath. She felt like she had been kicked in the stomach. "I called

5

the paramedics, but it was too late. There was nothing left they could do. He's gone, Sage. He's gone."

"W-what happened?" she asked trying to catch her breath.

"I don't know. They think maybe a heart attack. I just don't know," he answered sorrowfully. "You and Douglas need to help your mom with whatever she needs tomorrow—at home or at school. And I'm afraid you will all need to pack for a longer stay. There will be some things we'll have to take care of here, and I have some business in the area over the next few months," her father rambled. "Sorry.... Sorry. I have so many things running through my head.... I'm just thinking out loud." There was a long pause. Sage could hear her father sniffle. "I need to talk to Douglas. I'll tell him myself. I don't want your mother to do it. Is he there?"

"No, he— Oh, wait," she replied despondently as the front door opened. Douglas ran inside in such a rush that he forgot to close the door behind him. His eyes widened as he looked at his mother crying on the couch, tissues clumped in her hand, and Sage's shocked, white face.

"What's going on? I thought I heard you calling...." He stopped as Sage, unable to speak, held out the phone for him to take. "What is it?" he asked her uneasily, not really certain he wanted the answer. He slowly took the phone from her outstretched hand and put it to his ear.

"Hello?" he gulped.

None of them got much sleep that night. Sage had left her bedroom door open in case her mother needed her in the night. Sage still felt heavy, weighed down with the burden of her own sadness and that of her mother. Now, after hours of lying awake listening to her mother cry in her room across the hall, the realization hit Sage that all of the grandparents were gone. She and Douglas were lucky to have had such a close relationship with their grandfather. They knew very little of their other grandparents; all of them had died long before she and Douglas were born. Tears streamed down her cheeks and dampened her pillow. She wouldn't be going on long walks on the forest trails with her grandfather anymore or listening to him read his favorite stories and poems to her as she watched the sunlight through the trees above. It was because of him that she knew the plants of the area and had such a deep appreciation of the power of nature. The only other person who felt the way she did about the forest was gone from her now. She closed her eyes and let her tears continue to fall.

"Good morning," her mother said softly, her voice hoarse from crying.

She was holding a cup of hot coffee and looked as if she had been up for some time. There was a list of things to do on the table in front of her and another list of people she needed to call with the news of her father's passing.

"Good morning," replied Sage, trying not to sound exhausted.

"Did you manage to get any sleep last night? I'm sure I kept you and Douglas awake for quite a while," she said in an apologetic tone.

"You didn't. I was sad, too," Sage said. She didn't want to make her mother feel any worse than she already did.

Douglas slunk into the seat at the table next to his mother. He didn't even try to hide his exhaustion. He put his head down on the table and groaned. "Ugh! It can't really be morning already." To Sage's surprise, their mother chuckled a little and slid an empty bowl and a box of cereal toward him.

Sage and Douglas spent the morning packing boxes and taking down bulletin boards while their mother concentrated on finishing the grades she had been interrupted from completing the previous night. Before noon they were leaving the elementary school and taking care of details for an unexpectedly extended trip.

Their mother checked items off her to-do list, making plans for the mail to be forwarded to the cabin and having the son of one of her friends take care of the lawn until their return. Douglas talked to his boss at the pool, who was very understanding and assured him he would be put on the work schedule whenever he returned. After finishing phone calls, double checking lists and packing up the car, they were finally ready for the next day's trip. Sage stood for a moment, watching as Douglas closed the trunk. She was heartbroken. They should have been excited, packing for an eagerly anticipated visit, but instead, news of their grandfather's death had filled them with immeasurable sadness. *How quickly our plans have changed.* She sighed. Sage turned to go back into the house. The same terrible feeling that had ebbed and flowed over her in small waves throughout the day was back again. *What exactly am I feeling?* she thought. Sage opened her bedroom door and sank exhaustedly onto her bed. There was grief for sure—and a bit of anxiety, too. This was more the sense of foreboding. Sage sighed again. Foreboding seemed like a rather bleak description—yet it seemed to fit, too. Her grandfather's death was going to change everything—for their family, for the summer, and in ways she could not yet imagine. For now, she was just too tired to try to figure it all out. As soon as Sage's head touched her pillow and her eyes closed, she fell asleep and slept without moving until the alarm went off the next morning.

After taking care of some last-minute details, they were finally ready to leave. Sage settled into the back seat as the car pulled away from their home and moved through the city. Time passed quickly for Sage as she watched the changing scenery from the backseat windows. Soon the yards around the houses were growing larger and farmland was replacing city blocks. Sparse patches of trees turned to dense woods. The drone of the road beneath the car, the green landscape, and the smell of the fresh air relaxed Sage, and she rested her head against the back of her seat. Soon the rolling hills would begin to rise and fall more sharply at the foothills of the mountains.

The sound of the rough gravel crunching beneath the tires as the car left the paved road and climbed the cabin's steep drive woke Sage from her needed rest. As she attempted to shake the weariness from her body, she saw her father step onto the porch. He looked tired but pleased to finally see them there. Her mother pulled the car up near the cabin, and all three passengers pulled their stiffened bodies out for a long stretch.

CHAPTER 2

The Memorial Service

Their father reached out for their mother, drawing her close. "Oh, Adel," he said. "I'm so sorry." They held each other in a long embrace while he lovingly rubbed her back. Sage and Douglas had done their best to comfort their mother, but she, in turn, was staying strong for them. Now, with their father, she could finally show her own pain and lean on him for comfort. Adel had managed to make it through the last two days with a great deal of composure—too much composure, in Sage's opinion. With so much to be done, her mother had stayed focused instead of allowing herself to cry or to grieve. Even in a brief conversation with their father about the plans for the memorial service the evening before, she had shown no signs of breaking down. Sage knew that after the service, her mother would be able to rest and begin the long grieving process.

Sage and Douglas each greeted their father with a hug before everyone turned their attention to unloading the car. Entering the cabin without their grandfather was unsettling. It was usually their grandfather's sparkling blue eyes, broad smile, and joyful laughter that welcomed them after the long drive. Instead, it was quiet and dull, even with four people moving in and out of the door carrying loads from the car. The scent of their grandfather's pipe tobacco still lingered in the air, and his recent book and magazine readings were where he had left them on the coffee table in the living room. It was more than their mother could bear, and she excused herself to the porch when at last the car was empty.

Sage, Douglas, and their father stayed inside the cabin to discuss the room arrangements for the time they were there. The cabin had been renovated into a year-round home when Adel was about the same age as Sage. The once one-bedroom cabin was now a two-bedroom home with a loft study that doubled as an extra bedroom when needed. Their grandfather had one bedroom; their parents always took the second. That left Sage and Douglas to split the loft. Each summer, they alternated who was going to get the privacy of the loft and who was going to end up on the couch.

"I think that we should leave Grandpa's room empty until your mother is ready to have people use it," their father recommended. "That leaves the couch and the loft."

"Douglas has gotten too tall for the couch," Sage said. "He should have the loft. I'll take the couch. I don't mind, really."

Sage joined her mother on the porch and sat quietly, viewing the wooded landscape. It was into the late afternoon hours when the heat of the day was heavy and still. There was a breeze only substantial enough to give freshness to the air and a gentle wave of movement to the trees and grasses. Adel finally spoke without turning her eyes to her daughter.

"You're a lot like your grandfather. He always took me out on the trails, hoping I would love the forest like he did. I appreciated the beauty of the sur-roundings—but I loved the beach and my summer friends a bit more," she said lightly. "When your brother was born, your grandfather could see he wanted to be near the water. He taught Douglas how to swim when he was still so small that I just knew the lake would swallow him right up. Your grandfather was right: He was a natural," she said, lost in a memory and with a smile brightening her face. "He was right about you, too," she said with a pause. "When you first started walking, you were fast! If we weren't watching you closely, you were heading into the forest before we knew you were gone. You would go for evening walks with him on the trails into the park. Sometimes, your father and I would wonder if we should go after you because you were gone so long. As you got older, he would start taking books along with him on your walks and you would be gone even *longer*," she paused again, looking at the wooded mountains that surrounded the cabin. "Now that I am older, I realize how much this place means to me and why Grandpa loved it so much." She stopped, turning to fi-nally look at Sage.

"We have—*had*—a special place," Sage said quietly, still watching the trees. "It's covered thick with moss, just like carpet, and it's under a canopy made from some overlapping branches in the trees. It's the perfect place for reading," she continued as she pictured the spot. It had always seemed so mag-ical there as she was growing up. "When I was little, we pretended the trees were kaleidoscopes and looked up into the tops when the sun was shining through the leaves," she explained. Sage looked up through her raised hands as if seeing it at that moment. "It was best when the wind was blowing a little. The leaves would move around and change the light patterns and shapes."

She lowered her hands and had tears on her cheeks now but still didn't look at her mother. Sage didn't want to talk about it any longer, either, and was more than a little relieved when Douglas and their father came out to the porch. They brought out a tray of cold drinks and a large salad for dinner. As the family ate, they all began to feel more relaxed, and conversations turned to final preparations for the memorial service the next day. Memories of their grandfather were shared across the table, and ideas for displaying family photos at the funeral home were discussed. They went through stacks of pictures their mother had brought from home and created a simple board displaying photos of their grandfather. There were pictures of him as a boy growing up at the cabin, of his life as a landscape architect in the city, and of his retirement years with friends and family. Much of their grandfather's adult life had been lived hours away in the city. Sage knew his friends and colleagues from there would not likely travel so far for the service, but he had many friends in town, and they would probably fill the small funeral home.

Sage made up her bed on the couch and unpacked her dress clothes for the service the next day. Her parents had gone off to bed, and with Douglas settled in the loft, the cabin was quiet again. She was surprised how tired she felt even after having slept in the car on the way there. Sage lay down on the couch and reached over to the end table to turn off the lamp. The cabin went black. She had forgotten that there were no streetlights near the cabin. In the city, when the lights went out, there were still streetlights, security lights, the headlights of passing cars, signs on buildings....

The next morning, her father was the first out of bed. The aroma of the pot of coffee he started along with the eggs, bacon, and toast woke the cabin. Soon everyone had gathered at the kitchen table for a hot breakfast as they discussed the day ahead. The mood was surprisingly light and easy, though Sage knew there would be nothing easy for the family in the hours ahead. Their father had made all of the arrangements for the service. Being so close to his father-in-law, Sage was sure he had tried to consider exactly what their grandfather would have wanted. He had always been considered humble and down to earth by those who knew him. *It will be a very simple service*, Sage thought.

Everyone took turns showering, and Sage couldn't help but think that her grandfather should have planned a second bathroom in his renovations. He loved when she wore anything blue to match her eyes or anything emerald green, like her dress for the service, to complement her skin and hair. She adjusted the loosely tied belt of her dress, turning to double check herself in the bathroom mirror. Then, satisfied, she tucked a stray curl behind her ear before going to join the others in the living room. Her grandfather would have smiled at her when she came down the hall, flattering her by saying something about being able to look beautiful wearing a burlap bag. But he wasn't in the living room when she came down the hall—no one was.

Her soft footsteps barely made a sound down the hallway to her parent's room, though the same could not be said of Douglas as he thundered down the stairs and across the living room. Sage waited outside of the door, wondering what her brother was in such a hurry over.

"Are you sure you want to wear a suit, Avery?" she heard their mother whisper as their father fastened her pearls around her neck.

"It's just easier this way. That's all," he whispered back.

"I think you two look great," Sage said, startling them. Both were smartly dressed, their mother in a simple navy-blue dress and their father in crisp navy-blue pants with a sharp crease down the fronts and a tailored grey suitcoat.

"We didn't know you were there," Adel said. She was flustered, though Sage wasn't sure why, and she instantly regretted interrupting their moment together.

"Oh, my. Time is getting away from us!" Avery said just a little too loudly. He turned his attention to Douglas, looking helpless with a silk tie clutched in his hand. "Let's work on that tie, shall we?"

Avery joined his son near the full-length mirror hung on the bedroom wall. With them standing together, Sage could clearly observe how her brother had not only outgrown the couch but had also lost his boyish features. Douglas looked remarkably like their father, matching his height, lean build, and broad shoulders. Each had light brown hair that bleached out to blonde during the summer months while, unlike Sage, their skin easily turned a golden bronze.

They were both handsome, smart, and charming—*and*, Sage thought, *nothing like me.*

She turned her eyes to her mother, who was putting in her last earring. Sage had her mother's fair skin and her reddish-brown hair, but she was quite a bit taller than her mother, and her build was much more slender. She and Douglas did have one feature they both shared with their parents: their bright blue eyes. Sage thought for a moment and supposed that, unlike Douglas, she looked a bit like both of her parents but still not very much like either.

"Hey there." Her mother's voice broke her thoughts. "I was just asking if you were ready to go."

Her mother, father, and brother, handsome with his crisply knotted tie, stared at her.

"Oh. Yeah, I guess," Sage lied.

The family drove along the two-lane highway twisting through the forested mountains. The cabin was only a short drive from the nearest town. A large carved and painted wooden sign on the side of the road read: WELCOME TO GRACE, with smaller letters underneath reading: THE TOWN OF GOOD WILL. It was a small town except for the summer months, when tourists crowded the small shops and inns on their way to and from the national park. There were special events planned all summer, including a huge Fourth of July carnival and street party, which had become a birthday tradition for Douglas. With the tourist season already in full swing, the t-shirt and mug shops on the main road were crowded. On the next block, people gathered at one of the corners, listening to a man playing a hammered dulcimer.

Like many tourist towns, there were the main streets for those traveling in and out of town, and then there were the side and back streets for those who lived in the community year-round. Those streets held the grocery, florist shop, library, auto parts store, post office—and the funeral home. They turned into the large, blacktopped parking lot. People were already gathered at the entrance of the funeral home. Sage's stomach lurched. She wasn't ready for this.

The family entered into a quiet lobby with rich, velvety drapes framing the tall windows and deep, soft chairs upholstered in muted floral prints grouped comfortably throughout the space. The family had not yet reached the room where the service was to be held when they were greeted by the owner. He smiled sadly, being sure to acknowledge each member of the family before speaking.

"Spencer and I knew each other for most of our lives. He was a wonderful person, and I will miss him very much," the man said sincerely. With a respectful nod, he turned slowly and led them down a hallway to a much larger room filled with chairs, calm music, and places to display the many pictures they had organized. They worked silently until every board overflowed with their grandfather's life through pictures and every table was ready to welcome friends to browse through family photo albums.

Even with the sadness of the other people wandering throughout the room, Sage could feel the grief and pain flowing from her family most. She stayed close to her mother as she admired the beautiful plants and flowers the funeral director said had begun arriving almost immediately after news spread of Spencer's death. Her mother was surprised to find many arrangements sent from those who had known her father from his work in the city and took time to read each card accompanying the flowers. Soon, the family moved to the front seats, signaling for others to take seats of their own until the room was completely full of people both seated and standing. Quiet music continued to play in the background as people spoke softly or sat silently in thought. Sage had not been to many funerals or memorial services during her life and didn't know exactly what to expect. She thought a pastor of a local church might hold the service, or maybe someone from the community who had known her grandfather well, but it was her own father who stood and addressed the gathering first.

"Welcome, everyone," he began emotionally. He closed his eyes for a moment, taking a long slow breath before continuing. "As you know, we have assembled here today to remember a dear friend, Spencer Douglas Baker. He was a man of integrity, kind to all and adoring to his family. Many of you had known him since he was just a boy, vacationing here at the same cabin in which he spent his last days. Others of you knew Spencer as a business owner or as a man who freely gave his time and money to help those less fortunate than himself. Still others of you knew him as a person who took great responsibility in maintaining our natural surroundings, whether through his work in the city or in retirement here at his cabin. Stories of his life here, from a boy to adulthood, as a man who served the needs of others and as a naturalist, have been told to me from the moment people were informed of his early and unexpected passing. At this time, I would like to invite anyone with a special thought or memory of Spencer to share it with the rest of us."

Moments like this made Sage very uncomfortable. She had only been to one other service where the mourners were asked to share their thoughts and, whether through grief or fear, nobody stood to speak. She squirmed now in her seat, flushed from the overwhelming emotions buzzing through the room. *What if no one says anything?* she thought nervously. The thought had no sooner entered her head when several people stood at the same time to speak. Her father, pleased with the response, directed a nice-looking older man to speak first.

"Spencer and I grew up together. I am a permanent resident here, and during the summers, he and I spent our time in the woods between his family's cabin and the lake. Since he decided to make his stay here permanent, we haven't gone too many Saturday mornings without meeting for breakfast down at Marge's Coffee Shop," the man paused, his chin quivering. "He talked about his family and how the grandkids were doing in school so often, I feel as if I know you. I am terribly sorry for your loss and want you to know how much I am going to miss him." With tears in his eyes, the man sat slowly in his seat.

The next to speak was a much younger man wearing the uniform of a forest ranger. He stood silently for a moment, rotating his green hat in nervous hands.

"Mr. Baker and I met in the forest when I was fresh out of ranger school. He introduced himself to me one day when I was still learning my way about on the trails and he was out for a walk. We had a nice conversation, and it became obvious to me that he knew a great deal more about this forest than I did," he said. Many people who knew Spencer chuckled at the truth of the man's statement. "Once, I was leading a group of elementary students on the trails on the east side of the lake, just off of the most popular hiking trails. It was right when school started at the end of summer and, as most of you can imagine, the trails that were less maintained were overgrown. We were discussing safety in the forest, the importance of staying together, and that you should never leave the trails. I went to show the kids a plant with ripe red berries that the animals like to eat but they should avoid, and ..." He paused. "I lost the trail." Everyone laughed. To Sage it was a wonderful reprieve from the sorrow. "I spent several minutes searching for the trail, trying not to show them I was panicking by pointing out several plants as I searched. Mr. Baker must have been out on his daily walk around the lake and spotted me with the kids. I'm pretty sure he knew I was lost, but he certainly didn't let on to the children—or to me. He yelled out, 'Good morning! Oh, I see that you are learning about poisonous plants,' and continued to entertain the kids by pointing out poison ivy and poison oak while leading us all safely back to the trail. I learned a lot from Mr. Baker. He was a caring steward of the land, and I am going to miss seeing him in the forest he loved so much," he said respectfully and took his seat.

Many stories and thoughts followed until Sage's father decided everyone who had something to say had spoken. A sense of relief filled Sage when he rose from his seat. Her head was spinning, and she felt quite light-headed from the flood of emotions. Her father gave his grieving wife a gentle smile before looking around the overly filled room.

"Thank you all for coming today. Your thoughts have meant more to our family than we can say. Spencer would have been honored and probably a little embarrassed to have had so many people here to say goodbye. I would like to add one final thought to those already shared. I will be forever grateful that Spencer came into my life. I was just a teenager when my father passed away, and I was left on my own. Spencer offered a room for me at the cabin, and in doing so he gave me so much more than a place to live. He was an encourager, a mentor, and a friend." His eyes were wet and his voice shaking, but he continued. "Farewell, Spencer. You were an amazing man, dearly loved by your family and respected by your friends and colleagues. You will be greatly missed."

People began to rise, many coming to share condolences with the family. Slowly the room cleared, and the emotionally drained, mourning family headed into the hall. Nearing the main lobby, a figure stepped in front of the family, blocking their path down the hallway. He was dressed strangely in flowing, dark blue silken pants and a silky white shirt with a narrow band collar. A leaf embroidered in gold thread adorned the left breast of his flowing robe. He struck Sage as someone who was overly conscious of his image, standing tall, almost stiff, with his chin angled upward. His shoulder-length gray hair was pulled smoothly into a ponytail at the base of his neck. Not a single strand dared to stray out of place. He did not smile, although his expression could not be described as unpleasant, either. The muddle of feelings Sage sensed coming from the man revealed an obvious dislike for her family. He nodded curtly at Sage's father, who returned the nod.

"Very sorry to hear about Spencer, Avery," the man said. "My family and I held him in the highest regard."

"Thank you," her father replied. "I think you will remember Spencer's daughter, my wife, Adel?"

"Yes. It is a shame to meet again in this way," the man said. He briefly took Adel's hand. The gesture lacked sincerity and seemed only a politeness he could not avoid.

"Thank you for coming. It is nice to see you again," Adel replied.

"I don't believe you have had a chance to meet our children, Douglas and Sage," Avery said, motioning to Sage and her brother.

"No, I have not yet had the pleasure. Your grandfather and I knew each other since we were boys, and he often spoke of you both." The man nodded at each of them, though his gaze remained fixed on Sage.

His cold, narrowed grey eyes sent a shiver down her back. Sage sensed a surge of emotions from the man and thought for a moment she might become ill. The man continued to study Sage, making her visibly uncomfortable.

"You look *amazingly* like your grandmother," he said slowly and distantly.

Avery cleared his throat loudly to redirect attention away from Sage.

"Douglas. Sage. This is Evron. His son, Frayne, and I grew up together," indicating a much more pleasant-looking man waiting in the lobby with two others, a young man and a young woman. "I spent many a day playing at Evron's home, especially before I met your mother," their father added with a small chuckle.

"Nice to meet you," Douglas said politely.

Sage only managed to smile slightly and nod in his direction.

"Avery, if you need anything, please do not hesitate to ask," he said with a slow bow of his head.

"Thank you, Evron. We will. And please tell Frayne I will catch up with him when things have settled down a little," their father said as Evron turned to join his family and leave.

The hall and lobby were now empty except for Sage's family. Mistaking Sage's nausea for sadness, her mother wrapped an arm around her shoulders and walked slowly with her to the car. Now they would be heading back to the cabin to begin the hard work of sorting through their grandfather's papers and belongings.

CHAPTER 3

The Special Place

Condolence cards were still arriving daily, but the phone calls had slowed in the three quiet, solemn days since the service. Adel and Avery were spending several hours each day writing thank-you cards and handling legal papers. To busy and distract themselves, Sage and Douglas took on jobs around the cabin from cleaning to lawn care, but everyone was getting cabin fever. Emotionally exhausted and feeling cooped up himself, Avery suggested they all take the afternoon and evening off.

"Why don't we each find something we would like to do for a couple of hours, then I will treat you all to dinner and an ice cream in town," their father said, receiving only enthusiastic responses from the whole family.

Douglas and Avery decided on a game of basketball by the garage, and Adel chose an uninterrupted nap. Sage did not have to think for long before asking, "Dad, can I go for a walk on the trails?"

"Of course, but be sure to stay on the regular trails. And don't go too far," he told her.

Sage took her first step into the forest that had been calling to her since her arrival five days previous. The earthy smells of the moist ground and decaying wood, the shadows and light, and the calm aliveness of the forest filled her senses. She let her eyes adjust to the filtered sunlight before focusing on the trail leading from her grandfather's cabin into the park. She had walked this trail countless times with her grandfather and had taken it to the secondary trail leading to the lake as well. Most of the trails in the park were on the other side of the lake, near the campgrounds and swimming areas. They were wide, maintained, and well-marked. Benches for resting during a hike dotted those trails. It was different on this side of the lake. If her grandfather hadn't walked these trails almost daily, the narrow path in the foliage would not be visible even this early in the summer. Sage strolled and stopped and strolled again for several minutes, just listening to the birds and breathing in the smells. When next she stopped, she smiled to herself.

Here it is, she thought. Off the trail about twenty feet to her right was a large patch of deep green moss. She walked through the ferns on the forest floor and sat down on the dense green carpet, running her hands over its softness. With a contented smile she lifted her eyes up to the treetops. *Here is our special place*, she thought again to herself. The changing pattern of light above her was just as she always liked to picture it in her mind. Sage's eyes lowered back to the landscape around her. She sighed and reclined against the closest tree.

The faint sound of the river could just be heard from where she sat. The trail from the cabin meandered through the forest before turning off to the left, heading to the lake. That was the trail they most frequently walked. Rarely had Sage continued on the trail beyond the turn. That section of the trail ended abruptly at a place along the river just before it emptied into the lake. There were other trails, too. Some of them they walked on rare occasions, usually when wild onions or mushrooms were to be found. Other trails she had no memory of ever taking with her grandfather, like the one that forked from the trail that met the river, running parallel with it and deeper into the forest. That trail was well maintained, but when she had asked her grandfather about it years before, he had told her it was not accessible.

Relaxed and pensive, she lost track of just how long she had been sitting there. No matter how long it had been, she knew it was beginning to get late and she should start heading back to the cabin. Sage stood, took a deep breath, and sighed. Just as she took her first step back to the trail, she caught sight of something moving where the trail bent toward the lake. Sage turned to get a better look, surprised to see a man leaning against a tree, silent and still. It was very unusual to see a hiker on this side of the park. *Maybe he is lost*, she considered. She decided to follow the trail to take a closer look. As the trail brought her near where he stood, she tried to make eye contact. He glanced over his shoulder, looking behind him as if trying to avoid her or maybe to see what it was she saw.

"Hello?" she said, still studying him. Again, the man looked around, seeming confused at her addressing him.

"Are you hurt?" Sage asked, stopping on the trail directly in front of him.

"Uh … no. I was just resting," he said, flustered.

He looked familiar to her, and it took a moment for her to place his face. He had been one of the people standing in the lobby waiting for Evron after the memorial service.

"You were at my grandfather's memorial service, weren't you?" she asked.

"Yes, I was there," he said taking a step toward her. "My father thought it would be best if we didn't all crowd your family with new introductions that day. It was my grandfather, Evron, you were speaking with after the service. My father said there would be plenty of time to introduce ourselves after your family had time to mourn. Your grandfather was a good friend to many. I'm sorry for your loss."

Although he was approaching her, she felt no need to be concerned for her safety. His genuine smile and laid-back manner set Sage at ease. He was, in fact, a young man not much older than she. Though not quite as tall as Douglas, he was built with the same slender physique and broad shoulders. His blonde, wavy hair fell loosely across his forehead. He absent-mindedly brushed it from his blue eyes.

"Allow me to introduce myself properly," he said, offering his hand to her. "My name is Terran. You're Sage, right?"

"Yes, I'm Sage," she said flushing a little as she released his hand. "And my brother's name is Douglas."

"You two must be getting a bit stir crazy," he said with a nod. "A few of my friends and I are going to go to the lake tomorrow, if you guys would like to come along."

"That sounds great! Well … I suppose I should check with my parents first. Do you have a … number? Oh, I don't have anything to write on—or *with*, for that matter," she said, checking her pockets and laughing nervously.

"I'm heading back that direction." He pointed up the path toward the cabin. "How about I just walk with you, and you can ask when we get there?"

"Do you live around here, then?" she asked him.

"My family is here year-round," Terran replied. "I spend most of my time in the park. Um … in the summer, I mean."

"I don't see people on this side of the lake very often," she told him. "I thought you were a lost hiker or something."

"No … no," he laughed. "I've never been lost in here. The forest is my favorite place to be." He did truly appreciate the forest; she could see it on his face as he talked.

"Mine, too," she smiled.

They found Avery and Douglas relaxing on the porch, drinking lemonade, when they reached the cabin. The basketball was left abandoned in the driveway under the basketball hoop as if waiting for the next game.

"Good game, Dad? Who won?" Sage asked when they were close enough.

"Douglas, of course," her father began. He turned toward her and was surprised to find she was not alone.

"Terran. How are you?" her father asked warmly.

"Very well. Thank you, sir," Terran responded.

"Douglas, this is Evron's grandson, Terran."

Terran jogged up the steps and shook Douglas's hand as Avery introduced him.

"Did you find Sage wandering around in the forest?" Avery asked jokingly.

"No, sir. She found *me*," he said.

"Oh, I, um, well, I see." Avery turned away quickly, awkwardly arranging drinking glasses on the porch table. "Would you two like a glass of lemonade?"

"No, thank you, sir. I should be heading home now. I wanted to see if Douglas and Sage were free to go to the lake with me and a few friends tomorrow," Terran asked.

"Well, I don't think we have any plans made." Avery turned to his children and shrugged. "I guess it's up to you."

"Awesome!" Douglas exclaimed.

The next morning, just as planned, four teenagers came off the trail to the cabin. Sage and Douglas were on the porch, waiting, excited to be spending time with people their own age. Terran greeted them before beginning his introductions.

"This is Sage and Douglas," he told his friends. "They are Spencer's grandchildren. My best friend, Anila," he said indicating a strikingly beautiful girl with long black hair and smooth, olive skin. Her deep green eyes complemented her bright, warm smile. "This is my cousin, Jason," he said, slapping his hand on the shoulder of a thin, awkward-looking boy with sandy hair. It was hanging in his eyes, and Sage suspected he would probably be more comfortable if it hid him completely. "And Lamar," he continued, pointing to a tall, handsome boy with very dark skin and sparkling amber eyes. Sage couldn't help but smile, sensing instantly he was the fun-loving prankster of the group. *This just may turn out to be a great vacation after all,* she thought.

The group chatted casually on the way to the lake. Even this quickly, it was clear Douglas and Lamar seemed to be cut from the same cloth. Watching them ahead of her on the trail, Sage marveled that they were built alike, had the same mannerisms, and were lost in conversation more like old friends than new. Sage walked alongside Anila, already enjoying her company and energy. She asked Sage about school and about things she liked to do, about places she had been and about Chicago. She told Sage she had never been to a big city and, by the number of questions she had, Sage could tell she was very curious about it.

The lake sat in a valley, bordered by the rolling mountain range and surrounded by forest. Rivers and streams fed into the lake from the mountains. There were other lakes in the park and the surrounding area that were more accessible to boats and kayaks, so it was rare to see more than a paddle boat near the opposite shoreline. The side of the lake that the group had come in on was very rocky, with large, rough boulders and the sharp edges of mountain faces falling straight into the deep water. The soft, sandy beach was far on the other side of the lake, brought in for the tourists to spread their beach towels. From here, the few people on the far shore were barely visible. Though she didn't much care for the water and was frightened by the darkness of the deep lake, the wildness of its surroundings suited Sage. She preferred climbing on the rocks or dangling her feet into the chilly water while taking in the breathtaking views.

With their shirts and shoes stripped and left on a rock to be warmed by the sun, the boys wasted no time getting into the water. Anila and Sage watched the horseplay with amusement as they continued to talk and get to know each other. Anila was sixteen, only months older than Sage.

"I have an older sister, Delaney. She is going to have a baby this summer," she told Sage proudly. "We have always been really close." Anila frowned, suddenly saddened. "But now she may be moving away."

Sage didn't know what to say just then, especially not knowing Anila very well. She waited, giving Anila the chance to continue if she wanted to share more. Anila remained quiet, though, focused on a mountaintop barely visible above the trees. It became obvious that Anila was trying not to show Sage how upset she was.

"How long have you known Terran?" Sage asked, trying to help Anila by changing the subject.

"We've never not known each other!" she replied with a laugh. "We have been friends all of our lives. He is a great guy," she said sincerely.

Both girls suddenly screamed. Lamar had come from below the surface, grabbing their feet dangling in the cool water. Anila was the first to start laughing. It was joyful and infectious, and soon everyone had joined in. The entire day was enjoyable and, instead of worrying about what the summer would bring, Sage began to look forward to it.

For the next several days, Terran and Anila met Sage and Douglas at the cabin in the morning to plan a day of activities either there or at the lake. Lamar often met them at the lake, and on occasion Jason would join the group as well. As for the girls, Anila had confessed she could not swim and, like Sage, she also feared what could be moving in the depths of the lake. So, while the boys enjoyed their swims, Sage and Anila would walk the forest or climb the rocks surrounding that part of the lake. When they stayed near the cabin, Douglas found Terran to be quite a match on the basketball court, and Anila enjoyed relaxing on the porch with Sage and Adel, playing card games and talking. Sadness was still awakened with every letter received, every cupboard opened, and every story made with new friends that wouldn't be shared with their grandfather. But the new friends were healing for Sage and Douglas, just as being at the cabin was healing for their parents.

"I found this box when I was sorting through some of your grandfather's things," Adel said one evening at dinner. "It's marked for you," she said handing Douglas a shirt box wrapped in bright blue paper. "Grandpa must have gotten your birthday present a little early so it would be here when you came to visit. You can open it now … or save it till your birthday next week if you like."

"I'd like to open it now, I think," he responded quietly after some consideration. Douglas sized up the weight of the box. "It's too heavy to be clothing." He popped the tape at the ends and top of the box, and the paper fell open. He paused for a moment before lifting the top, and Sage knew he was thinking how strange it was to be opening a gift from their grandfather when he was no longer with them. He pulled the top off the box and removed a wonderfully hand-painted wooden shield about the size of a dinner plate.

"What is it?" he wondered, touching its surface.

"It's a crest!" Avery declared, admiring the craftsmanship.

The left half of the shield was painted in glossy black, and the right in an indigo blue of the same sheen. There were several rows of a wave pattern going between both halves of the crest in a matte silver paint.

"Look! There's writing on the back," Sage told him.

"Douglas ... Dark Water," he read. He smiled broadly. "Huh! It must be what my name means. Cool!"

"That's really neat, Douglas," Sage told her brother, squeezing his arm.

"Yeah," he agreed. "Grandpa always did find gifts that were unique. *Special.*" He turned the crest over in his hands once more before carefully returning it to the box.

"Oh, I also found a box of pictures you might be interested in," Adel said to both children. They began to lift albums and loose photos from a banker's box. Some of the albums had been filled with pictures of Sage and Douglas at the cabin as they were growing up. There were a couple albums of Adel from the time she was very young and of her teenage years. Many of the photos in the albums of Adel as a teenager also included Avery. They were all fun to look at and laugh over, but the older pictures were the most interesting to Sage. Black-and-white photos of people she didn't recognize began to pile in front of her.

"Those are your great-grandparents, my grandparents," Adel said, flipping through a few of the photos in Sage's pile. Sage picked up the next picture in the pile. It was her. "That's ..." Adel began.

"... our grandmother," Sage interrupted.

"Wow!" Douglas exclaimed as he swiped the photo from Sage's hand. He stared at it and then looked back at Sage. "That Evron guy was right!" he remarked. "She does look like you! I mean you look like her!"

This was not the first time she had seen pictures of her grandmother, but she was a young child the last time the box of pictures was opened. Now she was much closer in age to the teenage girl she saw in the photos. There were more pictures of her in the box, and each one captivated Sage's imagination. She had heard stories of her grandmother and knew that she had died after giving birth to her mother there at the cabin. Adel asked questions about her mother as she was growing up, and Spencer had done his best to describe the kind of person she was. He would tell Adel stories about how they had met at the cabin when they were teenagers, fallen in love, and gotten married. They had both been overjoyed they were going to have a child, but the news she had died shortly after delivering Adel had devastated their grandfather. The loss was too much for him to bear in the cabin surrounded by memories of her, so Spencer took his newborn daughter to the city where he had grown up and began a life for the two of them there. Her mother didn't know much more than that, and her grandfather never offered anything further.

Adel sorted the loose pictures as they talked and placed them in the protection of another album. The time had passed quickly with stories from Adel and Avery about the people in the pictures. They had been sitting around the kitchen table looking at the photographs for hours when, finally, their father stretched his arms above his head and gave a long, drawn-out yawn. One contagious yawn turned into many.

"I can't believe how late it's gotten," Adel gasped when she glanced to the clock on the kitchen wall. "But, oh, it was nice to see those old pictures again." Adel began placing the albums back into the box, pausing at a small, framed black-and-white photo of her mother. She held it up a little and smiled at her daughter. "Those pictures of my mother— How much you look like her! She was a young woman then, just like you are now. You've grown up too quickly," she said, placing the last album in the box and picking up Douglas's birthday gift. "Both of you."

CHAPTER 4

The Fourth of July Celebration

I t was unseasonably hot in the days leading up to the Fourth of July. The only places to be were in the shade of the forest, in the water, or in air conditioning. With the rising humidity, Sage wasn't even sure her love of the forest would get her to leave the cool, dry air of the cabin. The water had been so inviting that Douglas and Lamar had become somewhat inseparable during the daytime. Sage saw her brother in the morning at breakfast and again when food hit the table at dinner. Most of her own time was spent with Terran and Anila. The three of them tried to find ways to entertain themselves that required the least amount of physical exertion. Soon after Douglas left each morning, Sage would gather up a blanket and a board game in a bag and head into the forest to meet her friends. They would always already be there, waiting for her at the place she had first met Terran, just off of the trail she had never taken along the river. The trails to the lake, the cabin, and along the river converged at that one spot, making it the perfect meeting place.

"You two always seem to beat me here," Sage commented as she approached her friends along the trail.

"We're just so excited to see you, we can't wait to get here," Terran said jokingly.

"Ha ha," she managed to moan.

Anila helped Sage spread the blanket over the soft moss, and they all made themselves as comfortable as they could. "Ahhh," was the only response they could manage when Sage pulled three ice-cold bottles of water from her bag.

"I hope it isn't like this for the Fourth," Sage grumbled.

"That's still two days away," groaned Anila as she wiped the icy bottle on her forehead. "I can't take too much more of this, and Terran and I are going to … um … a family reunion. On the fifth. If it is this hot …" She faded out as she reclined backward.

"Isn't Douglas's birthday tomorrow?" Terran asked, trying not to let the heat get him down.

"Yeah, and every year for as far back as I can remember, he makes my parents take us to the celebration in town because he never gets a birthday party," Sage replied.

"Maybe we could all go together," Terran suggested, looking more refreshed.

Anila jerked straight up and began bouncing in place as if she had forgotten about the heat altogether. "That would be fun!" Anila said, her eyes lighting up at the idea.

"I'll ask Lamar and Jason if they want to come along," Terran continued. "Jason usually doesn't like to go, though—too many people for his taste. But I'll ask him anyway."

"That would probably make my parents' day!" Sage said. "They only like to go to the celebration for the cotton candy—and I can bring them some back."

"All right! It's settled!" Anila exclaimed. "Are you sure your parents won't mind?"

"Yeah, it should be fine. I'll double check, but we'll probably have a family celebration tomorrow with cake and presents, so I doubt they would mind us going without them on the Fourth," Sage assured them.

"Great! Now who wants to get beat by me again today?" Terran teased as he opened up the lid of the game box and everyone helped to set up the board.

It was just too uncomfortable to stay out any longer, even in the relative cool of the forest. The group walked back to the cabin and sighed when they opened the door and the cool air hit them.

"Oh, I don't know," Avery teased after Sage talked to her parents about their plans for the Fourth. "I do so enjoy being herded like cattle on an overcrowded street with loud teenagers."

"I suppose we could get over it," Adel pouted, "if you bring us back some cotton candy."

They all laughed and, after another cold drink, Sage opened the door to walk her friends out.

"If it's like this tomorrow, we may just stay near home. So, we'll either meet you here tomorrow or on the Fourth for the celebration," Terran said, drawing his arm across his forehead to wipe the dripping sweat away from his eyes.

Sage waved goodbye to Anila and Terran, and as they entered the forest, a tall, dark figure with bleached blonde hair stepped out toward the cabin.

"Mom, Douglas is home," Sage said.

"Of course, he is," Adel laughed. "It's dinner time!"

The next day was equally as hot and sticky as the day before with promise of the same for the Fourth of July. As expected, Terran and Anila did not come to the cabin, and although she completely understood, Sage missed her friends. Since their first meeting, she had spent nearly every day with them, and, were it not for the weather, she would be with them now. But it had been a while since Sage spent a day with her mother, and she could admit it was relaxing puttering around the cabin helping her mother with small tasks.

"Whoa! It feels wonderful in here!" Avery exclaimed as he entered the cabin.

"How was your, um, phone conference?" Adel asked. She poured him a glass of lemonade and set it in front of him at the kitchen table.

"Unfortunately, there were lots of people gone for the holiday, so we didn't get through much," he replied, thanking her for the drink.

"You had a meeting? Today?" Sage asked with surprise.

"The world still turns! Even around the Fourth of July!" Avery joked. "Where's Douglas?"

"He's at the lake for a swim. He won't be out long because Lamar had … other plans … and couldn't stay late," replied Adel, licking frosting from her finger.

"Great! Because that cake looks ready to eat!" Avery teased as he too swiped a taste of frosting.

Soon enough, Douglas was home, dinner was devoured, and chocolate cake was being set on the table with seventeen blazing candles. After the traditional Happy Birthday song, sung as terribly off key as they could manage, Adel reminded Douglas to make a wish. With one big blow, all the candles were extinguished. Several brightly wrapped gifts were brought out and set before Douglas on the table. His eyes grew wide with excitement when he opened the box with new basketball shoes, the very ones he had wanted for his senior year of high school.

"Thanks, Mom and Dad," he said after opening the last box with some new swimsuits and beach towels. Sage slid a very small box across the table to him. She knew her brother wasn't fond of jewelry and usually wore only his class ring from school, but this she thought he would like. "Wow, Sage. Where did you find it?" he asked as he pulled the silver chain and pendant from the box.

"Do you like it?" she asked apprehensively.

Douglas held the miniature black and indigo blue crest up to examine it more closely. He smiled at her. "It even has the little silver wave markings," he said, impressed with the detail.

"Look at the back," she told him.

"Douglas ... Dark Water. Very cool." He fastened the chain around his neck. "Where did you get it? I mean, I only opened the crest from Grandpa last week," he said.

"I remembered seeing something like it in a catalogue, and Mom helped me order it," she replied, sounding very pleased with herself. "We weren't sure it would be here in time."

"It's great, thanks. Really. Thanks, everyone," Douglas said appreciatively.

"We meet with Dad's lawyer on Friday," Adel said, making a note on the calendar. Everyone sat together at the small kitchen table for breakfast, discussing the plans for the day and for the upcoming week.

"I am going to have to be out of town for a couple of days. I'll need to pack tonight so I can leave early in the morning, but I should be back before the meeting with the lawyer," Avery said. Adel added his trip to the calendar.

"What about the Fourth of July celebration in town tonight?" Douglas asked. The expression on his face showed how surprised he was that they had forgotten about the yearly tradition.

"Oh, that," Avery said with a sigh. "I'm really sorry, but your mother and I can't take you this year," he said with sincere regret. He watched the expression of disappointment spread cross his son's face. "We've decided that you are too old ..." He paused dramatically. "... to have your mom and dad following you around at the carnival." He finished with a smile, handing Douglas spending money and the keys to the car. "Sage and your friends will be in charge of keeping you out of trouble from now on."

"No way!"

"Happy Birthday, Douglas! Well, yesterday. Sorry, Lamar couldn't come. He had other plans tonight," Terran explained when he and Anila arrived just after dinner.

"Yeah, he said he had a family reunion thing to go to for a couple of days. Ready to go?" Douglas asked everyone.

"Does everyone around here have their family reunions at the same time?" Sage remarked, remembering that Terran and Anila would be gone the following day. Douglas only shrugged and headed for the door.

"Be home by eleven, please," Adel shouted after them.

The heat hadn't kept too many people from enjoying the celebration. Lights from the rides and on the vendors' trailers flashed. Smells of popcorn, sweets, and fried foods filled the air. The lines for the Ferris wheel and the bumper cars were lengthy, so the four friends decided to go through some of the air-conditioned shops along the main road before they closed for the evening. The ice cream shop, no matter how appealing, was out of the question, as it was full inside and had a line of waiting people clear out the door. They wandered through a few of the t-shirt shops, mostly to cool down, and were about to head back toward the carnival attractions when Anila saw a sign she had never seen before.

ANA'S EVER-SEEING EYE

"Let's go in there," Anila said with her usual curiosity, pointing at the sign. "That place is new. I haven't seen it before, and it might be fun."

"Yeah, this wasn't here last summer," Sage agreed.

"It's someone pretending to be a psychic or something, Anila. She's only here for the tourists," Douglas complained, shaking his head at what he considered silliness.

"It could be fun, Douglas. Come on, let's go see what this Ana has to say," Anila said. She looped her arm through Sage's and led the way across the street.

"Oh, all right. Then we're going back to the carnival and do something that isn't so girly!" Douglas yelled to their backs.

The front room of the small store was awash with richly colored silken fabrics draped on the walls and windows. Shades of purples, blues, and reds in shimmery and iridescent materials created a very exotic and mysterious mood in the dimly lit room. Light from clusters of fragrant candles flickered throughout the space, and crystals in all colors and sizes decorated a high ledge that bordered the shop. Sage imagined that this dark, shadowy room was probably quite cheery and inviting when the morning sunlight poured through the large front window. There was an oversized, comfortable-looking couch along one wall with deep red, velvety cushions. A table dressed with the same shimmery materials as the walls and drapes sat between the couch and an overstuffed chair.

"Where's the crystal ball?" whispered Douglas sarcastically.

"Ssshh!" Anila scolded, but there was laughter in her voice.

"Welcome. I will be right with you," a smooth, kindly voice said from the other side of a beaded curtain that separated the front of the shop from other rooms.

A tall, slender, aging woman stepped from behind the beaded curtain. Sage already knew Douglas would think her clothing to be cliché and way over the top. She wore a long silken gown of oranges and reds, weighed down in the front with large beaded necklaces. Her graying hair was barely visible under the multicolored silk scarves tied securely around her forehead. They were pulled back, covering her hair and trailing down her back. The woman took in a sharp breath as she got her first clear look at the four friends. She tried to cover her gasp by pretending to cough, but Sage had seen the surprise in her eyes and felt the anxiety in her reaction. At that moment, wondering what vision the woman may have seen, Sage began to regret stepping through the door.

"Oh, I am sorry. I was just getting ready to close for the night, so I will have to be very brief. I do apologize," the woman said in the same kind voice. "Who will be getting their reading first?" She directed the question to everyone, but her eyes avoided Sage's. The friends took a seat on the couch as Ana eased herself into the overstuffed armchair.

"I will," Anila said adventurously.

The woman took Anila's hand, closed her eyes, and took a slow deep breath.

"You are as kind as you are beautiful," she complimented, causing Anila to blush slightly. The woman spoke very slowly and deliberately, choosing her words carefully. "But you are worried about something that should have happened already ... and you fear the decision you may be forced to make. The solution to your problem will be found by a friend." Ana's brows furrowed in thought. "I also see many other challenges and discoveries in your future over the next few summers." She opened her eyes as she finished and looked at a very shaken Anila.

Anila gladly moved over, allowing Terran to slide into the seat she had occupied. Sage watched the woman, the shadow of her features in the soft light, even her hands as she reached for the one Terran offered her. Again, Ana closed her eyes and prepared herself with a deep, cleansing breath.

"You are not like others in your family, and you will cross one who has chosen another path. Your future will be entwined with the one who sees through your eyes. You will be led by your inner strength and convictions." She paused for a moment, considering her words. "Though I see many of the same challenges and discoveries as your friend's in your own life over the next few summers," she said slowly.

She opened her eyes and observed Terran's bewildered stare. Sage knew from Douglas's large eyes that he had also seen their friends' reaction to the woman's readings. She sensed his anxiousness as he reluctantly took his spot across from the old woman.

"I see you like to swim," the woman said softly, and although her eyes were closed, a smile was forming on her lips. Douglas gasped. "What you see and feel in the water intrigues you. You will find power in your love for another. You, too, will make discoveries and confront challenges with your new friends."

Douglas had lost his desire to mock the woman and, like the two before him, he rose to trade places with Sage without speaking. The woman had looked deeply into the eyes of the other three before giving their readings. But now as Sage sat before her, she continued to avoid meeting her eyes. Sage felt terribly awkward and shifted nervously in her seat. She could sense the woman's feelings of fear and sorrow, though she was doing her best to hide them and concentrate on the reading. The woman took a shaky breath and reached out for Sage's hand.

"I see you have some reading to get caught up on during the summer months," she began thoughtfully. "Your silent voice will be heard throughout the lands." Sage could feel her heartbeat quicken. "Each of your discoveries—even those that are about yourself—will lessen the burdens of others."

With a moment's pause and without looking at Sage, she rose from her chair. Ana requested only five dollars as payment and thanked them for coming. Without another word, she left the room through the same beaded curtain she had entered. The four friends quietly left the shop and began walking toward the carnival. It was clear they were all stunned by what they had heard, and they walked in silence for a minute or so.

"That wasn't as much fun as I had hoped it would be," Anila finally said, breaking the tension and starting the group laughing once again.

"I see challenges and discoveries ..." Douglas said with renewed sarcasm. He wiggled his fingers in the air, pretending to do magic.

Sage joined in the laughter but couldn't shake her feeling of unease, not so much about what she had heard, but about the woman who said it. Her mind racing, she glanced back at the storefront in time to see the lights go out.

For the rest of the evening, everyone enjoyed the rides and carnival games. Douglas even won each of the girls a stuffed animal at the ring toss.

"It's a monkey, I think," Anila said turning the toy in her hands.

"It's a blue alien monkey," Sage added uncertainly.

"It's a blue alien monkey in a jumpsuit," Anila continued.

"It's a blue alien monkey in a jumpsuit holding a microphone?" Sage guessed.

"Oh, it's cute, whatever it is," Anila said happily, squeezing the plush toy.

They were eating their greasy and very messy cinnamon-and-sugar elephant ears when they heard the first roll of thunder. The noise of the carnival had let the rumbles of an approaching storm go unnoticed. Now lightning was visible in the sky, and the winds that had brought refreshing relief to the steamy night were beginning to pick up speed. They had all hoped to stay for the fireworks that evening, but it was clear the storm would be hitting soon.

"We'd better head for home," Douglas grumbled in disappointment.

The four began to walk from the carnival, hoping the rain they could smell on the air would hold off until they reached the car. Sage stopped suddenly in the street.

"Wait here! I'll be right back," she said. She turned around and ran back toward the carnival. Moments later she returned with a large bag of cotton candy, and they all continued toward the car.

CHAPTER 5

The First Discovery

T he storms had passed, and blue sky was once again prevailing through the white puffy clouds drifting over the mountains. The heavy rains carried cooler, more comfortable temperatures to the area, and Sage was eager to be in the forest again. Today was the day Terran and Anila were supposed to be back from Anila's family reunion, and they had already made plans to meet at their usual place that afternoon.

"Do you want to come along?" Sage asked Douglas as she prepared to leave.

"No, thanks," he said, shaking his head. "With all that rain, the grass needs mowing, and I want to get it done before Dad comes home tonight. I'll probably run into you later, though. I'm meeting Lamar at the lake when I'm done here."

How amazingly different it looks after a good rain, Sage thought, sighing contentedly as she entered the forest. A couple days of rain had fed the plants on the forest floor, and the trail was already grown over in places. Long, prickly wild raspberry stems stretched up to nearly the level of Sage's face, catching her clothes and causing her to stop occasionally to secure them safely out of the way. When she reached the point where her friends were to be meeting her, she was surprised to find that, for the first time, they were not already there. She stood waiting a few minutes for them to arrive, relaxing and listening to the sound of the rushing river. Another sound mingled with that of the water. There were voices coming from the trail she and her grandfather had always walked past when heading toward the lake. It was the trail that ran parallel with the river and deeper into the forest. Sage was certain her friends entered the park from that direction and decided to walk up the trail a bit to meet them.

The roar of the river grew louder, drowning out any sound of the voices Sage thought she had heard. She knew the river flowed down from the mountains to the lake and that the trail would continue to rise as it followed the river upstream. Deep, wide steps had been constructed in the earth, easing the difficulty of the climb. For the minuscule amount of traffic Sage expected the trail received, she was puzzled as to why it was so well maintained. She had been walking parallel to the river, admiring the newness of her surroundings, when the trail took a sharp curve around a very large, very old ash tree and straight toward the water. Moving cautiously around the huge tree, Sage came to a complete stop. Arching over the rain-swollen river was a wide wooden bridge—not a narrow, poorly built, or even crumbling bridge one might expect to find this far into the forest on a trail that no one was ever seen hiking and that her own grandfather had said wasn't accessible. What she saw seemed so out of place, no reasonable explanation made sense, so she hesitantly decided to go farther. Sage stepped onto the bridge and ran her hand over the beautifully carved handrails. As if the bridge itself wasn't strange enough, the details in the woodwork were astonishing. Oak leaves, ash leaves, pine needles, and maple leaves were carved into the railing, its surface smoothed by countless hands running over the deep golden-brown wood, just as Sage's did now.

Who could have made this? And why here? she thought. She slowly proceeded over the bridge with her hand still gliding on the carved rail. Another large ash tree marked the opposite side of the bridge, and again the trail turned sharply around it. Sage rounded the old tree to find yet another puzzle, gray stone steps laid into the sharply rising trail. She had long forgotten about meeting Terran and Anila. The only thing she wanted now was to discover where the path was leading. With each step she took upward, the sound of the river began to fade a little and the sound of voices could be more clearly heard. It was only now Sage realized it was impossible to have heard these same voices at the start of the trail. She had walked too far for the sound to carry, and the river alone would have drowned out these normal speaking tones.

Finally reaching the top of the climb, Sage stood before an opening in a wall of trees. Grape vines and ivy hung like drapes into the opening and were neatly pulled back like delicate lace curtains. Sage held back a stray vine brushing her arm as if it were reaching for her and moved through the opening into another world. Tucked neatly amongst old trees, stone and wood structures bordered a broad clearing. Flowering vines and ivy twisted up columns and around arched doorways. The homes were well kept, with flowers and vegetable gardens planted in interesting and intricate patterns alongside most of the dwellings.

Sage knew her grandfather had always believed there were people who, for whatever reason, had chosen to live in seclusion in the forests of the mountains—although, to her recollection, he had never mentioned the possibility of an entire village.

The stone pathway before her widened and wove between the trees and homes. The voices grew louder as the trail continued to lead toward what Sage could only presume was a sort of town center. She walked closer, far too curious to stop now. People flowed around her on the trail, moving between the homes and the town center. None of them seemed at all bothered by her presence, greeting her with a friendly smile or a nod of their head. She paused in the shade of a tree, trying to absorb everything she was seeing. They were dressed in clothing Sage could best compare to the medieval-style apparel she had seen in movies. Children played in dresses or pants and loose-fitting shirts instead of shorts and t-shirts. Many of the women were dressed in loose, silken pants of soft, cool colors. Matching shirts were fitted at the top but hung long and flowing to their knees, with slits up the sides to the hips. Sage thought they looked elegant, even noble. The men, she noticed, wore— Her heart began to pound in her chest. They wore the same style of clothing she had seen her father's friend, Evron, wear to the memorial service.

What is this place? she wondered.

Her eyes searched, still trying to take everything in. The town. The way people were dressed. There were many people gathered around one particular building in the village square. By far the largest of the buildings in the town, it, too, was made of stone, with ivy gracefully decorating the ancient entrances. Oversized arched doorways and windows gave the building the appearance of an open, airy gazebo. Voices projected from inside. Small groups of people stood at the doorways and windows or were seated on the grass under the surrounding trees, listening to the dialogue within. With her heart beating even more fiercely, Sage carefully walked through the people sitting on the grass and peered through an unoccupied window. Seats curved around the room, raised in levels like bleachers made of stone. Her eyes, like those of the men and women in the room, were drawn to the front of the space, where a man standing behind a podium was speaking.

"Dad?!"

She had called out, unable to stop herself. Her voice carried easily around the stone room and was loud enough to disrupt the speaker and everyone listening. All eyes turned to Sage, but she didn't notice; she was still staring at her father in utter confusion. People began to murmur as she and her dad held each other's eyes for a long moment. He opened his mouth to speak at the same time a man sitting on one of the stone benches rose. Sage's initial confusion turned to discomfort, even queasiness. She knew that feeling. She knew him, too. Evron.

"This is outrageous!" Evron bellowed, repeatedly pounding his walking staff on the floor. The sound reverberated throughout the room and to the people listening outside in the square. His glare remained fixed on Sage, still standing at the window to his left. Evron's expression was cold and hard, just as the stone surrounding him.

"Avery," he continued in a patronizing manner, returning his eyes to the podium. "Have your children never learned proper meeting etiquette? Under no circumstances are the meetings of the Elf Council to be interrupted." Though Sage did not understand why, it was obvious the venom in his voice was intended for her. Several older men and women dressed in the same dark robes as Evron crossed their arms sternly, nodding approval of his reprimand.

Sage turned back to her father as if to ask, "What does he mean?" but there was no need for him to answer. She saw the truth on his face. It was the look of someone who had been discovered in a lie or found to be hiding a secret. Confused, embarrassed, and still sick to her stomach, Sage wished only to flee. Yet she could not. Avery did not respond to Evron, a small frown the only hint of his frustration. Instead, Avery directed his attention to the man sitting in the chair to his right. The man nodded at Avery and stood, taking the papers quickly being handed to him.

"Jake has agreed to continue where I must leave off. I apologize for the disruption, but as Jake and I have worked very closely on this project, I can assure you he is most knowledgeable and quite prepared to answer your questions," Avery announced to the gathering, bowing his head deeply. He thanked Jake and walked hastily to the nearest doorway.

Sage turned her back to those inside and leaned against the frame of the archway. With her eyes closed, she concentrated on her breathing. Her nausea had subsided slightly now that Evron had taken his seat once more, but her own thoughts and emotions were still spinning violently in her head. Sage took another deep breath. The discussion inside had resumed, but it had not drawn back the attention of those outside of the building. She felt their eyes even before she reopened her own.

Panicking, Sage wrenched herself away from the window, scanning anxiously for a clear way back to the trail and out of the town. One of three teenage girls standing in the shade of a nearby tree giggled nervously as Sage began weaving around the blankets spread on the grass. Another, striking in her beauty—quite contrary to her nasty attitude—glared at Sage suspiciously, and the third girl, out of place with the other two, couldn't even manage to bring her eyes to meet Sage's. Only the young man standing with them spared Sage a sympathetic smile. He appeared to be contemplating whether he should help her somehow or stay out of the matter entirely. Sage hadn't believed anything could possibly get worse, but him coming to her aid was the last thing she wanted at that moment—another awkward situation, but this one involving a handsome young man trying to rescue her from complete humiliation in front of an entire town of strangers.

"We were running late to meet Sage." She didn't know if it was the familiar voice or the sound of her name, but she swung her head away from the group of teenagers and toward the front of the building. "We checked back at the cabin, and she's not there either," Terran was trying to explain between gasps. The man Sage recognized as Frayne, Terran's father, was trying to quiet him so as not to draw more attention. "I don't know where she is." Terran had not yet spotted Sage among the crowd, never thinking for a moment she would be there.

"She's here!" his father hissed, trying to quiet his son again. Terran's head whipped from side to side as he searched all of the small groups of people gathered outside the building. "Avery didn't want them to find out this way."

Too many feelings to discern poured over Sage until the moment Terran finally spotted her. Then she only wanted to run. His friendship had been a lie—and so had Anila's. Terran took hesitant steps in Sage's direction, but Avery's hand clasped his shoulder, stopping him.

This only managed to anger Sage more. She spun away from them, hurt by their deceptions, confused and embarrassed. Before Sage could get her bearings on how to get herself out of this strange place, a firm hand took hold of her elbow.

"Let's go," her father almost ordered. "We have a lot to talk about."

Terran ran up alongside Sage as they zigzagged through the small crowds and away from the town center. He was visibly upset, but at that moment she was too angry to care.

"Sage!" Terran pleaded. "I'm so sorry. We'll come … tomorrow … and explain everything."

"Don't bother!" Sage snapped crossly, yanking her elbow from her father's grip and running a few steps to get ahead of both of them.

"Tomorrow will be fine, Terran," Sage could hear her father call out even as he jogged to catch up with her.

The eyes of the people in the village were still following her; she could feel them. Sage lowered her head, watching only the pathway until they reached the entrance that led back to the stairs, the trail, and the security of the cabin. She said nothing to her father when he caught up to her and he said nothing to her until they reached the opposite side of the wooden bridge.

"Frayne was right. I didn't want you to find out like that," he said remorsefully, stopping her for only a moment. "I suppose it would have been quite a surprise no matter how it came out, but *I* really wanted to be the one to tell you and Douglas."

Sage was almost to the split in the trail before she spoke. With anger still perceptible in her voice, she asked, "It's true, then? Whatever that was back there? Whatever that Evron guy said?" It seemed so absurd to even be asking such questions. "This Council— You are one of them?"

"The Elf Council," he said slowly. "Yes. Elves do exist—though not like they are in fairytales. And yes, I am one."

Sage came to a complete stop and turned to face her father. She knew her father was telling her the truth, and, as angry as she was and as much as she wished it to be a joke, the idea of him having a secret life now made complete sense.

"You mean to tell me," she began again in a harsh, steely voice, "that every time we've thought you were away on a business trip, you've been right here all along?!"

"We have a lot to talk about. You and Douglas will have a lot of questions, I'm sure," he answered in his most calm and understanding voice.

"Douglas is seventeen now, and I'm going to be sixteen in a few months. You've lied to us this entire time! Don't you think this is something we should have—" Sage suddenly became silent, at last hearing what her father had just said. "Wait a minute," she said slowly, keeping her eyes suspiciously narrowed on her father. "You keep saying 'you and Douglas.' What about Mom?" Again, her father's expression gave her the answer. "She knows?"

Sage stormed past her father, half running toward the cabin. She leapt up the porch steps and burst into the house, slamming the door shut behind her.

"What on earth?!" her mother exclaimed as she jumped up, her book falling to the floor. "What's happened? Are you okay?" she asked seeing the expression on Sage's face.

Sage said nothing. She just stood stiff, furious that her mother, too, had kept her father's secret for all of these years. Sage folded her arms across her chest and turned her back to the both of them as Avery came in the door.

"It's time we had that talk we've been putting off," he told Adel in a strained tone of voice.

"What's going on? What's happened?" Douglas asked. He rushed from the bathroom, still rubbing his wet hair with a towel. "Whoa! What's wrong with you?" he said after reading the anger on Sage's face. He looked to his mother for an answer and then to his father. "I've never seen you wear anything like those clothes before." He stared wide-eyed at the forest-green silken suit their father wore. "Like that Evron guy."

Sage had been too confused and angry to pay attention to what her father had been wearing, but she knew it was the same as what the other people at the Council meeting were wearing.

"Oh, my," Adel said. She became noticeably uneasy, wringing her hands and shaking her head. "This is going to take a while. Oh. Well. Why don't we all have a seat in the kitchen, and I'll get some drinks."

Sage uncrossed her arms and scowled at her father, following her mother toward the kitchen. Avery took his usual seat at the table and sat quietly waiting for everyone to be seated before beginning. Adel brought glasses of lemonade for everyone, eventually sitting in the empty seat beside her husband. Avery took a deep breath and slowly, shakily began.

"Your mother and I have kept a sort of secret from you and your sister," Avery said, addressing Douglas. "We didn't feel it was necessary for either of you to know—that is, until Sage met Terran in the woods. Since then, we have been trying to find the right time and the right way to talk to you. I want each of you to know that I never meant any harm or hurt feelings to come of it." He paused to look at them both before continuing and received a gentle squeeze from Adel as she took her husband's hand in encouragement.

"Today, Sage took another trail through the woods. I am assuming she was waiting for Terran and Anila?" Sage nodded without lifting her head. The sincerity in her father's voice wasn't enough to lessen her anger. "The trail took her to a village not far from where I grew up. There are four of these villages in this mountain area that were established communities long before it became a national park, and there are countless others throughout the world." Avery paused to make sure Douglas was following along. "For thousands of years, there have been people who were charged with the task of caring for the earth and its creatures. They had powers gifted to them, powers that helped their people to better protect themselves and serve the needs of the environment that surrounded them."

"Huh?" Douglas was completely lost and squinted his puzzled eyes at his father.

"I am one of these people. I am an elf, a guardian of the earth," he said, again addressing Douglas.

"A what?!" Douglas barked, almost tipping his chair over backward.

"I am an elf," Avery repeated slowly, knowing Douglas would need some time to absorb what he was hearing. "And until this summer, I felt there was no reason to share that information with you. You see, the elves are leaving their communities and integrating with the human world."

Sage had refused to make eye contact with her parents and instead had been looking down at her clasped hands on the table. Now she could feel the sorrow from her dad for what he had just told them. For the first time since taking her seat, she lifted her eyes. He gazed at her sadly, his chin quivering slightly. Avery took a long pause from speaking to compose himself. Adel squeezed his arm tenderly, and he smiled weakly but gratefully at her before continuing.

"Many years ago, when my parents were young, the elves began to lose their powers. Some thought it was because the forests, waters, and mountains we lived in were slowly being used for city expansion or developments. More and more left their homes to live and work in the surrounding towns and cities. As more elves left, more of the power left with them. As more continue to choose to leave, the problem continues to worsen.

"As you know, I met your mother when we were just teenagers, and we eventually fell in love. When I asked your mother to marry me, I already knew it would not be permitted for me to bring her into the elf community. You see, elves have survived these thousands of years by remaining unseen and protected. Many believe that bringing a human into the elf world would make us more vulnerable to discovery. Now, elves and humans have married before. We weren't the first, and the children of those couples have always been human, showing no signs of elvish powers. That is why I have lived my life with you in the human world. It seemed inevitable that the powers of the elves would someday be gone, and I would have had to leave anyway. But having a human wife— and human children—pretty much made it necessary." He stopped for a moment to check the reactions of his two children. Adel smiled at him reassuringly, visibly relieved to have their secret finally revealed.

"Your grandfather knew I loved the land and that I wanted to do something with my life that involved working with the environment. He arranged for me to enter the human world, which is no easy task. You must remember that being an elf meant I didn't exist on paper in the human world. He also paid for me to have a college education studying environmental sciences. Since then, I have worked as a consultant for major industries across the country, guiding them to make responsible environmental decisions, decisions that directly impact my people. I am *proud* of what I do. It is a career that allows me to live in the human world with you, help improve the environment, and travel to the other elf communities as a council representative. When Sage found the village of Ashtyn today, she saw me sharing my discussions from the other elf communities with the Council. I was working, just not the work you know me to do," he finished. Everyone sat silently for some time just studying each other's faces.

"What did me meeting Terran have to do with you telling us the truth now?" Sage asked quietly and without the anger in her voice from before.

"Terran is an elf. As I said before, elves have certain powers in their natural environment. When you saw him, he was under the power of protection. Humans cannot see an elf that does not want to be seen," he said waiting for the meaning of it to sink in.

"You mean ... Sage ... is an elf?" Douglas asked in disbelief.

"No. Well, maybe. She saw Terran and the trail, which is also protected and seen only by elves. That means she has some elvish powers, but that may be all she has," he said. "Your grandfather always suspected she had some ability. He thought she had the gift of an empath," he continued.

"Because I can feel what others are feeling? But can't everyone do that?" she asked.

"Yes … and no. You've been sensitive to others' feelings since you were little," her mother told her. "And it is true that people can relate to or be sympathetic to the emotions others have, but not in the same way you are."

"Wait! You said Grandpa helped you enter the human world. He knew too?" Sage questioned.

"Yes. He knew of the elves from the time he was a teenager spending his summer vacations at this very cottage," Adel said. She hesitated before she continued. "There is a bit more to the story. Like your father and I, my parents met in this area, fell in love, and married. My mother was from Oakley, an elf village beyond the village of Ashtyn. I am the child of a human father and an elf mother. Your father and I have always known the time would come to tell you everything, but we thought you would be like me, and all others like me—without powers."

Both parents waited for any response from their children.

"What do Terran, Anila, and Lamar have to do with all of this?" Douglas asked.

"When you all met, Terran told me how everyone hit it off really well. I asked him to make sure that you didn't wander alone. There have been some, well, *unusual* events happening lately. Unexplainable things. All three of them said they would keep a look out for strange things when they were with you, but they *weren't* babysitting you. They genuinely like you both, and none of this is their fault. If you have anyone to blame for keeping secrets, it's me. Your mother has wanted to tell you everything for some time now," their father said sincerely.

"So, let me get this straight," Douglas said. He put his hands up in front of him to stop anyone from saying anything else. "Dad is an elf." He paused. "Sage might be an elf who can feel what other people are feeling." He paused again. "Our grandmother was an elf." Then he smiled. "Could I be an elf, too?" he asked hopefully. Sage smiled at her brother. Douglas had already forgiven their parents. He had always been quick to forgive. It was one of the things she loved most about him and a characteristic she did not have.

"Maybe. We just don't know yet," their father said, chuckling at him. "But I do know that there will be no more secrets."

It had been late afternoon when Sage and Avery had walked through the door. They had been talking through the dinner hour, and only as the sun was falling behind the mountain did they all rise from the table. Sage stood and moved slowly to where her father was now leaning against the kitchen counter.

"I'm sorry. I am still upset and pretty confused," Sage paused, "but I had no right to speak to you like that in the forest."

"Yes, you did," he said placing one of his hands on each of her shoulders. "I am the one who is sorry. You were shocked, surprised, and embarrassed, finding out like that. Almost sixteen years is a long time to have had a secret like this kept from you. Besides, your discovery today has taken a terrible burden off me. I am relieved that you two know, and wish I had been brave enough to tell you sooner." He drew her in and wrapped his arms around her. She leaned her head against his chest and hugged him back.

"Dinner is served!" Adel called as she placed the last bowl on the table. Hot fudge, caramel, nuts, and whipped topping hid the scoops of vanilla ice cream in each of the four dishes.

"Don't get used to it," she laughed, seeing Douglas's bulging eyes.

CHAPTER 6

Ashtyn

Early the next morning, Avery and Adel gathered all the important papers they needed to take to the lawyer's office. Not a word had yet been spoken of the previous night's events, but Sage was certain more would be discussed when her parents returned home later.

"We should be back around lunch time, but if you find other things to do, don't wait around for us. We'll just plan on seeing you here for dinner if you aren't here when we get back," Adel told her children as they said goodbye on the porch.

"And as for all those questions that have been brewing in your heads all night, you could wait until later or ..." Avery gestured to three figures moving slowly from the forest trail toward the cabin. "... you could ask some other experts on the subject." He kissed Sage on the forehead, then he and her mother stepped off the porch toward the car.

"Good morning," Adel and Avery said to the three friends.

"Good morning," Terran returned, his hands fidgeting nervously in his pockets.

Sage could see that they were all tired. Anila had red, puffy eyes, and the sight of Sage and Douglas started tears streaming down her already streaked face. She hastily wiped her face with the back of her hand and followed Terran forward. With his head hanging, Lamar chose to remain a few steps behind his other friends as they approached the porch. Sage moved slowly down the stairs, followed closely by Douglas, to where their friends were now standing. Not giving them the chance to speak or apologize, Sage cleared her throat and was the first to speak.

"I'm sorry for being so rude to you yesterday," she said, addressing Terran.

"I deserved ..." he began to reply, but she shook her head for him to wait.

"I—*we*—don't blame any of you for not telling us. There's no way we would've believed you anyway. Besides, it certainly wouldn't be safe for you to go around telling everyone ... *humans*, I mean." Sage spoke with sincere understanding in her voice.

"We thought you would be so *mad* at us," Anila said between sniffles. Whatever her reason, Anila was feeling especially guilty. Sage shook her head again and gave Anila a little smile.

"I was really mad at first," Sage agreed. "I thought that you guys were only being our friends to, well, keep an eye on us. My dad told us everything last night, and he made it clear that wasn't the case at all. He kept this secret, not you, and it is him I have to forgive—not you."

"I would have thought it was a big joke if you had told me," Douglas said, speaking more to Lamar than the others. "We do have questions, though. Maybe you guys wouldn't mind answering some of them for us?"

"Sure," Lamar said with a gleam returning to his eye. "Ask away!"

"Well, for one thing, I didn't get to go to the village you are all from, so I was wondering if you could take us and show us around a little?" Douglas asked.

"We don't all live in Ashtyn—the village Sage went to," Lamar explained. "Terran is the only one of us who lives in Ashtyn—well his cousin, Jason, does too. Anila lives in Oakley, farther up the river from Ashtyn, and I live in Layton, under ..." He paused and looked at Sage and Douglas as if to say *You aren't going to believe this*. "... under the water."

"You live under the water?!" Douglas asked, barely able to contain his excitement. "How do you get there? Is the entrance above the water or ... or maybe that cave down deep? Do you hold your breath, or can you breathe under—"

"Wait!" Lamar shouted. It was the only way of cutting Douglas off. "What cave are you talking about?"

"The one in the rock face that faces west—the one that goes straight into the water. It's better than twenty feet down, I'd guess," Douglas answered, observing the glances between Terran and Lamar.

"Yeah, that's the one I thought you meant," Lamar said slowly. "That is one of the entrances to Layton," he continued. "You saw it?"

"Yeah, I've always been able to see the cave. Wait a minute ... I saw the entrance! I have powers, too!" Douglas cheered. He punched his fists in the air over his head to proclaim victory.

Everyone smiled at Douglas's reaction. His fooling around even had Anila laughing in her joyful, carefree manner again.

"Take me there!" Douglas begged his friend.

"I can, sure. But I don't know if you can hold your breath long enough to pass the serpents and reach the entrance!" Lamar said with concern.

"SERPENTS?" Sage and Douglas asked together.

"Yeah, serpents! And they won't let you in if you aren't supposed to be there!" he replied, emphasizing his worry about the matter. "Listen, I'll take you there, but you have to stay right with me, and if you show any—and I do mean any—signs that you won't make it through, I am taking you straight up to the surface!" His voice was commanding, and he pointed his finger into Douglas's chest to make sure he understood.

"That's a deal! When can we go?" asked Douglas impatiently.

"Now, if you want," Lamar said with a shrug of his shoulders.

"Let me get my stuff. I'll be right back," Douglas said. He ran up the steps two at a time.

"Did you want to come, too?" Lamar asked Sage.

"No, thanks. The water is definitely Douglas's thing. I never really liked swimming on this side of the lake. I do better when I can see—or feel—the bottom," she said.

"Me, too," Anila agreed. She was looking more like her cheerful self.

"I can swim pretty well, but I'm certainly not the swimmer Douglas is," Sage told them. "I know I wouldn't make it down there," she added.

Douglas came flying out of the house wearing his swimsuit, a t-shirt, and sandals and carrying a beach towel. "All set!" he announced.

"Wow, Douglas! I don't think I've ever seen you move that fast," Sage laughed.

"You coming, too?" he asked her.

"We went through this while you were inside," Terran explained. "I think Anila and I will take Sage on a guided tour of Ashtyn. We'll walk with you to the split in the trail, though."

Sage could tell that everyone was relieved to have the secret out in the open. Apologizing to them had been the right thing to do. They were only doing what they had always done: protecting their people. It was something Sage now understood was simply a matter of safety. And, after feeling the strength of Anila's guilt, she thought it may have even been a harder night for her friends than it had been for her and Douglas.

"Is that the trail you took yesterday?" Douglas asked Sage.

"Yup," she said. "That's the one."

"I always wondered why we never took that trail. I guess it was because Grandpa didn't even know it was there," Douglas speculated.

"Well, he knew it was here *somewhere*," Terran said, staring down the length of the trail. "He'd been to Ashtyn before, as a guest. He was very well respected in our community."

"Can we go to the lake with them first to make sure Douglas can make it in?" Sage asked.

"Sure. I want to see," Anila said. She turned to Terran to make sure all three of them were in agreement.

"We're not in any hurry," Terran said with a smile. "Besides, I want to know if he makes it, too."

They reached the lake, the mountains and trees reflecting in the smooth surface. Even with the full sun and calm waters, they would not be able to see Lamar and Douglas once they entered the darkness of the lake.

"Is that the mountain the cave is in?" Sage asked, pointing to a steep, flat expanse of rock climbing thirty to forty feet straight out of the water.

Douglas nodded. He removed his sandals and t-shirt and set them in a neat pile with his towel on one of the low flat rocks at the edge of the lake. His new chain and crest pendant glinted in the sunlight.

"Cool necklace, Douglas," Anila said. She lifted it in her hand to examine it more closely.

"Thanks. Sage got it for me for my birthday. It's a crest of my name. See?" He flipped the necklace over to show the inscription.

"Douglas. Dark water," Anila read aloud.

"Well, that's quite fitting, isn't it?" Terran said with a chuckle.

"Assuming everything goes as planned," Anila teased playfully, "why don't we meet you guys here at the lake in a few hours? I can't see that we would be in Ashtyn very long."

"Okay. Sounds good," Lamar replied. He perched himself on the edge of a rock and got ready to dive.

"Be careful, Douglas," Sage pleaded with her brother. He was also on the edge of the rock, preparing to enter the water with Lamar.

"I will. Gosh, you sound like Mom when you're worried! See you in a while," Douglas said. Only Sage could tell he was not feeling as confident as he sounded. With a nod to Lamar, both the young men dove into the deep black lake. When they were out of sight, Sage looked to Terran and Anila.

"Don't worry. He's with Lamar, and you heard what he said back at the cabin. Nothing will happen to him. He'll probably have no problem getting in," Terran reassured her.

"We'll wait a little longer, Sage. If he needs to come back up, he'll do it quickly," Anila added warmly.

Minutes passed, and although Sage was still unsure, Terran and Anila were convinced that Douglas was fine. Sage glanced at the water once more before heading back to the trail with her friends. She knew every twist, turn, and bump in the trail between the cabin and the lake, but the trail to Ashtyn still looked unfamiliar. As she walked with her friends, she noticed things she hadn't noticed the day before. Berries and grapes, ripe, plump, and completely out of season, dangled from vines within arms' reach of the trail. Flowering plants, many that were very unusual, were attractively grouped as if they had been planted there purposely.

"My dad said that elves had powers gifted to them. He mentioned the power of protection. Are there others?" Sage asked, trying not to shout over the roaring river.

"Elves have powers to manage or control plants, animals, wind, and water. Before the powers started to leave us, all elves were able to do a little of everything but were strongest in the powers from the realm where they lived," Terran began. "The elves who lived in the forest were the ones who had the most power over the plants and animals of the forest. The elves in the water communities were strongest with the water and its creatures. And the same for the elves of the wind communities. They're the ones that live high in the mountain tops. They controlled the wind and the winged creatures. Since much of our power has left us, we only have the ability to do things in our own environment, and even that's become pretty limited."

"So, you have power over plants and animals because you live in the forest?" Sage asked with great interest. The three reached the bridge, and Anila paused in the center, leaning on the carved rail to watch the water below. Terran and Sage joined her. The water moved more gently here without interference from large rocks like at the rapids farther toward the lake.

"My parents have power over plants, but they don't do well with even the smallest woodland animals. There really aren't many large animals around anymore, not that they would be able to manage them if there were. And my grandfather—he's downright afraid of anything larger than a chipmunk." Terran chuckled to himself. "I don't have any power over plants—well, not that I know of, anyway—but I love the animals of the forest, and I come out to talk to them, feed them, you know ... play with them," Terran explained.

"Oakley must be a forest community as well, right?" she asked Anila. "Do you have the same power as Terran, or is yours over plants?"

"My family has a gift with plants. You should see my mother's garden. It's beautiful, especially from above, because it's laid out in a spiral design. My sister has her own garden, too, and uses many of those plants to make fabrics," she said, proudly modeling another one of her beautiful outfits.

She stopped there without another word about her own powers. Sage had sensed uneasiness from Anila when the topic came up, growing as Terran had talked. Now that Sage had asked her about her own powers, Anila's eyes avoided hers nervously, making it clear that Anila desired to avoid the topic entirely. Even Terran was at a loss for what to say.

"It's close now, right?" Sage said changing the topic. She continued across the bridge to the other large ash tree.

They climbed the stone stairs and stepped through the curtain of vines to the clearing Sage had found herself in just the day before. It was still amazing, even magical, to look at, but it now had new meaning for her. They walked along the trail and approached the first of the homes slipped in between the privacy of the trees.

"So many of these houses are empty now. So many people have left just this year," Terran said. His usually steady voice tensed, clearly expressing his disillusionment. "This one here," he said. He pointed to a tall, narrow stone building with the same arched windows and doorways as several others Sage had seen. "This is Jason's family's house."

Sage looked at him, confused. The house looked as if it had been empty for some time, but she had just met Jason this summer.

"Oh," Terran said, considering the expression on her face. "He lives with us right now. His parents are studying to be doctors in the human world. There isn't a need for two healers in our community anymore." He scuffed some gravel off the path to the house. "They don't get to come visit much, and they are too busy to have him live with them. He will probably go with them once they're done with their studies, but he has pretty much grown up in my house."

"Evron was really mad when they left," Anila added. "He still acts as if he never had a daughter to begin with!"

Sage looked at Terran, and he raised his shoulders, confirming that what she said was true.

"How horrible for her—and Jason. No wonder he always seems so unhappy," Sage said sadly. "I hope Evron treats Jason better than that. I mean, Evron can't always act so ..."

Sage caught herself just before she said something about Evron that might offend Terran. Anila realized what Sage was going to say and started laughing.

"Rude? Cold? Grumpy?" Terran asked. He was smiling at her. "Yeah, he's grumpy all right, but he's harmless, really. Just set in his ways. As for Jason, Grandfather is okay with him. We do our best to include him in things, but I know he misses his parents," Terran said sympathetically.

There were fewer people today, Sage noticed, and they were dressed more casually, in pants or shorts. Some people were tending their gardens or chatting with neighbors, but the town square was markedly empty in comparison with the previous day. Ahead of them, a fairly broad woman with a deep tan and short spiky hair was kneeling along the stone path. As Sage and her friends passed by, they could see that the woman was talking in a whisper to a plump black squirrel. Its tail twitched erratically, and it chattered happily as she handed the animal a small chunk of bread.

"This is where most of the action used to take place," Terran said, stopping in the center of town. "My dad said that when he was a small boy, before so many people started leaving, there were stands with fruits, meats, and vegetables every morning. He said you could smell the breads and roasting nuts before you opened your eyes and got out of bed. People from all three realms traded fabrics, food, metal work—all kinds of things—in the centers of the towns. He said it was always full of people. Very festive."

Terran became lost in his thoughts. Sage closed her eyes and could almost see what he imagined the place to have looked like. It sounded wonderful, and Sage could not help but smile at the thought of it.

"There were even entertainers that traveled around the communities," he continued as he began walking toward the council building Sage had spotted her father in the previous day. "During the evenings, people would gather in and around the council building to watch."

"Why aren't there as many people here today?" Sage asked. "Yesterday it was much busier, and everyone was dressed up."

"Yesterday was the closing of our yearly gathering," Anila explained. "Every year around the Fourth of July, elves from the four local communities and many others from around the country come here for several days of meetings. They discuss important projects, issues of concern, and the future of our people. There were lots more people here a couple of days before, but they began going home yesterday."

Anila turned to face Sage, looking suddenly very serious. Sage knew that whatever Anila had to say was important and was weighing heavily on her. Even so, the sober expression on her face seemed completely out of character. Sage had to fight to keep the corners of her mouth down and not break into a smile.

"I don't want to lie to you or keep any more secrets from you," Anila began. "We weren't at a family reunion. Neither was Lamar. We were here for the yearly meeting."

Sage waited for Anila to go on, expecting her to say something that would be devastating or painful to hear, but it didn't come. Anila stared at Sage with nervous anticipation. Finally, Sage could not contain herself any longer and laughed.

Anila pushed out her lower lip and scrunched her eyebrows, not understanding what she had said that was so funny.

"By the look on your face, I thought you had done something horrible," Sage explained, setting Anila back at ease. "Thank you for telling me the truth."

Together they walked across the rest of the open space toward another cluster of homes. Terran headed straight for a house larger than the others Sage had seen so far. A sizable garden grew to the side of the stone home. Tomatoes, corn, beans, squash, and carrots, in various stages of ripeness, grew weed free in their terraced beds. Lightly fragrant flowers were growing along the meandering paths through the vegetable garden and spilling over the stones to the front door.

They walked through the door and Terran excused himself to announce their arrival to his parents. Sage had expected the inside of the house to match the aged look of the stone exterior, imagining it would be quite rustic, maybe even cold and uncomfortable. But just the opposite was true. The home was quite normal looking on the inside with beautiful wood flooring covered with woven rugs, inviting furniture upholstered in bright fabrics and curtains she had not even noticed from the outside of the home.

The sound of footsteps running down the short flight of stairs near the entrance caught both Sage and Anila's attention. Jason turned the corner to the living room where Anila and Sage stood waiting. Being more than a little surprised to see Sage there, he abruptly lowered his eyes in shyness.

"Hi, Jason," Sage said cheerfully. "Douglas and I haven't seen you in a while. Maybe you could come with us to the lake sometime."

"Yeah! We need to get you out of the house more often," Terran said, re-entering the room and tackling his younger cousin. Jason fixed his mussed-up hair with a smile on his face and punched affectionately at Terran.

The man Sage recognized as Terran's father smiled warmly at Sage as he entered the room. Bright eyes, the same shade of blue as Terran's, set Sage immediately at ease.

"Hello, Sage. I am Frayne. It is good to finally meet you properly," he said genuinely as he clasped her outstretched hand in both of his. "This is my wife, Linaeve," he said as he stepped aside for his wife to approach.

A lovely blonde-haired woman wearing a flowing silvery gown seemed to glide toward her. She had warm brown eyes and a smile as inviting as her husband's. Terran's wavy hair matched his father's, but the color matched his mother's.

"Welcome to our home. I have heard so much about you and your brother, Douglas. Terran and Anila enjoy your company very much," Linaeve said, taking Sage's hand. "My husband and I want you to know that our door will always be open to you."

"Are you taking the tour of our fine village?" Frayne asked.

"Yes, sir. It's much better coming here ... well, now that I know. It's a beautiful place," Sage said. She sighed to herself. "I wish I had known about it sooner."

"Don't be too hard on your father," Frayne said in an understanding tone. "It's torn him up all these years, not saying anything. He really believed he was doing the right thing for his family."

"I know that's true. It's just been a lot to absorb, and it's going to take some getting used to," she replied.

"Well, you and Douglas are in very good hands," Frayne told her. "I'm certain these three will do their best to answer all your questions. But I'd watch out for Lamar," he added with a wink.

"That reminds me!" Terran exclaimed, suddenly remembering the exciting news. "Douglas went to Layton today!"

"What? How did he know how to get in there? Did he make it beyond the serpents?" Frayne asked. His concern was still clear to Sage—even through his attempt to appear excited.

"He saw the cave-side entrance when he was swimming, maybe even when he was a boy," Terran started to explain.

"We all think it's really weird that Douglas's name actually *means* dark water," Anila eagerly added.

"Lamar went down with him to make sure he could get in. We waited for a few minutes, but they didn't come back up, so we think everything is fine," Terran continued. This didn't appear to relieve his father's concern. "We're going to head back to meet them in a few minutes."

"Well, I'm sure everything is okay," Linaeve reaffirmed calmly. "I hope you will excuse me. I am working on some canning for my friend Daphne and her family."

"Did something happen?" Anila asked. The level of concern Sage sensed over something so minor caught her by surprise.

"She woke up this morning to find her garden dead—a complete loss. There is just no understanding it," Linaeve replied with a shake of her head. She then smiled at Sage once more. "I am glad to have finally met you, Sage. Please feel free to stop in any time you are here in Ashtyn." Just as she had seemed to glide into the room before, she left the room so gracefully she appeared not to touch the floor.

"And I'm heading out to meet your grandfather to go through the details from this year's gathering." Frayne addressed the two boys as he opened the door and paused dramatically. "You four have fun—because I certainly won't be having any—and I'll see you at dinner."

The door closed behind him, leaving the four teenagers standing in the living room. Jason fidgeted uncomfortably and eyed the staircase as if planning to make an escape from another outing with his cousin, but Anila was on to him. She slid her long fingers around his wrist before he managed his first step.

"Frayne is right," Anila's voice was silky, persuasive. "Why don't you come back to the lake with us, Jason?"

Jason flushed red as a sunburn and stuttered nervously, "I— I— I—" Before he was able to compose himself enough to offer an excuse, Terran put him in a headlock and led him, struggling, upstairs.

"Come on. There's no way out of it. Let's go get some suits!"

CHAPTER 7

Anila

Sage, Terran, Anila, and Jason squinted against the sunlight as they left the shade of the forest. It was early afternoon now. The sun was high in the sky, reflecting harshly off the lake. Lamar and Douglas, who'd been reclining leisurely on the sun-warmed rocks, sat up as their friends entered the clearing.

"Hey! How was Ashtyn?" Douglas asked Sage.

"Better now that I know what's going on," she answered, taking a seat next to her brother. Her story could wait for now. His could not, since she knew he was ready to explode from excitement. "Well?!"

"It was awesome!" Douglas exclaimed. His fisted hands punched the air as if he were declaring his victory. "There really are serpents! I can't believe I never saw them before! I mean, they're actually kind of hard to miss, and they let me through! So, after that, I didn't have any problem reaching the cave."

"What are they like? What is Layton like?" Sage asked, happily encouraging him to continue.

"Long. I mean, like, twenty feet long! They're dark, too. Uh, green or black, I'm really not sure. They circle around the entrances, but Lamar says that they are only there to protect the people of the town. He says they even like to play sometimes, but I didn't think I was up to trying that quite yet," Douglas told her. "Anyway, you have to swim quite a way into the cave before you come up out of the water into a cavern. There are lights all along the inside of the cavern that continue all the way down a set of stairs. You have to take the stairs to the bottom of the lake to reach the entrance of Layton. The whole town is covered by this huge, clear bubble thing. I could even see the fish and serpents swimming outside. It's totally cool!"

He was gesturing wildly, speaking so quickly his words began to run together.

"Slow down, slow down!" Sage laughed at her brother.

"Sorry," he sighed, still lost in his memories of the day. "It's— It's just really amazing! I guess if I could have imagined it being possible, I would have expected a town at the bottom of the lake to be dark and damp like a bed of seaweed. But it's not. Everything is so bright and cheerful. The main walkway is made of shale from the mountains. It reminds me of old cobblestone streets, and it's even lined with old-fashioned-looking streetlamps. They weren't on, though. There is some way they have of directing the sunlight down through the water, and it looks light as day," Douglas continued. "All the buildings were painted in different colors, with boardwalks connecting them like sidewalks do on our street back home. It was like walking down the street of an old seaport town. You know, bright colors but with that weathered look? It seemed as if everything was carved with fish or serpents or seaweed or shells. Everything! From the doors to the fence posts, you name it!" He paused for a breath, smiling at the images in his head before shrugging his shoulders as if returning to reality. "Other than that, it looks like any normal neighborhood, with houses, gardens, and a market area. Lamar told me the marketplace used to be busy all the time with people trading and talking." Douglas grimaced. "There were only a few people with baskets of vegetables while I was there. It's kind of sad, really," he said regretfully. "I would have really loved to have seen it busy like that." He sat quietly for a moment. Sage knew exactly how he felt, and from the looks on everyone's faces, so did they. "Anyway," he said, returning from his thoughts, "Lamar said there is a lot more to see, and I haven't met his family yet. He thinks I should try the main entrance at the bottom of the lake next time."

"Why don't we see other people coming out of the lake?" Sage asked Lamar. "I mean, you come out all of the time, and didn't anyone from Layton go to the ... um ..."

"Yearly gathering," Terran interjected helpfully.

"Yeah," Sage smiled. "Why haven't I ever seen anyone coming out or going into the lake?"

"Well, the cave entrance was built a long time ago, when the elves had a little bit of power from all the three realms. The ones that were going to Layton but were from one of the other realms would use that entrance. They had enough power to get themselves that far, but not all the way to the bottom. Now, some of the people of Layton don't even have enough power to make it to the bottom … to the main entrance. In the last couple of years, I've seen fewer and fewer people surface," said Lamar. "I think they are afraid they won't be able to make it back in. Most of the people around the same ages as our parents still do fine, and so do the older people who are still healthy. It's the younger ones like us that have trouble."

"You don't have any problem," Douglas commented.

"I practice every day," Lamar reminded him. "I'm determined to make it—powers or not. As a matter of fact, I was a little surprised you didn't have any trouble."

"I've always been a strong swimmer. My swim coach used to joke that other teams were going to think I was cheating if I didn't breathe more during a race."

"Well, we'll try the bottom next time," Lamar said almost as a challenge.

"You're on. Anyway, I'll tell you more about Layton later," Douglas said to Sage. "Hey! Jason, good to see you again," he added, finally noticing the shy boy sitting a bit off to his side.

"Jason and I brought our suits, if you two are up to another swim," Terran coaxed.

"Sure. Water's great," Lamar responded.

Terran and Jason threw off their shirts and shoes and jumped off the rocks, followed by Lamar and Douglas. Sage and Anila watched as the boys splashed each other and raced in the cool water. Sage took off her shoes and slid to the edge of the rock to dip her feet in. Anila sat lost in thought with her knees bent close to her chest, her arms wrapped around them.

"I'm sorry if I embarrassed you or made you feel uncomfortable earlier," Sage said, knowing the others could not hear.

"Embarrassed? Oh, that." Anila was again looking tense.

"I know how you were feeling," Sage said.

"How could you know?" Anila said. She was more curious than irritated.

"It is my power to feel other people's emotions. Apparently, my grandfather told my parents he suspected as much a long time ago. A gift, he called it. I don't notice other people's feelings as much when I am at home. When I'm here, I can't ignore them. I just knew you didn't really want to talk about your powers and that you were starting to feel really uneasy. I didn't want to pressure you then, but I know it's something about your powers that's bothering you, and I'd be happy to listen if you want to talk," she said, looking at her friend.

Anila was staring out over the lake, her dark, shiny hair spread smooth across her back. She didn't look at Sage when she spoke.

"I should have had them already," she said quietly.

"Your powers, you mean?" Sage asked.

"Yes. Most elves know their powers at an early age, but some are a little older. I should know by now," Anila said blankly. "I am horrible with plants, and even Terran can't help but laugh when I try to do anything with forest animals."

"I'm sorry," Sage said consolingly. "That must be very frustrating."

"It is frustrating, but that's not bothering me as much as … Well, you know I told you about my sister, Delaney? The one who makes clothing? She's pregnant with her first child. She and her husband are thinking of leaving," Anila said, sorrow filling her words.

"Oh, no wonder you're upset," Sage sighed. "So … you weren't really upset about your powers?"

"I haven't even told Terran yet," she replied, turning to look at Sage. She paused for a moment, holding Sage's eyes. "If I don't get my powers soon, I may be going with her." For some time, she and Sage sat silently looking out over the lake. Sage didn't know how to respond to what she heard or how to comfort her friend. Finally, Anila turned toward Sage again. "You won't say anything—to Terran, I mean?"

"No, I won't say anything," she responded quietly.

The four boys began to pop out of the water and dry off. The sun had long since moved into the western sky, and Sage figured it was time to head toward home for dinner. Lamar said his goodbyes and jumped back in the lake, laughing impishly.

"Have a nice walk, everyone!" he said. Then he dove down into the darkness of the lake, and the others started for the trail.

"Everything okay, Anila?" Douglas asked, noticing her mood.

"Fine! I'm just a little tired, I guess. We didn't get much sleep last night," she said, giving Sage a significant look. The group approached the split in the trail.

"See you tomorrow?" Terran asked.

"Yeah, let's meet at the lake," Douglas suggested.

They waved goodbye, and Douglas and Sage began heading for the cabin.

"I wish you could go down there with me," said Douglas.

"It sounds really wonderful—and a lot different than Ashtyn. I can't go with you, but you could come to Ashtyn with us when you're done exploring Layton," she said.

They walked a little farther, Douglas telling her more about the underwater village.

"I don't know how it works yet. The bubble has skylights of some sort, and it magnifies the light that comes down from the surface. There are these tubes and magic and—" He was still talking, but Sage had stopped listening to him and begun paying attention to her own senses. She hadn't discerned what the feelings were yet, just that they were growing stronger as they approached the cabin.

"Are you listening? Hello? What's wrong?" Douglas was asking, trying to get her attention.

"It's Mom," she said. She was finally close enough to tell what she was feeling. "I don't know.... Something's wrong."

They both rushed the rest of the way to the cabin. Their mother was lying on the couch, turned on her side while clutching a pillow in her arms. She was staring blankly into the room, her eyes quite bloodshot from crying and her face blotchy red. Douglas and Sage looked at each other without really knowing what to do. They slowly walked into the living room area and took seats in the armchairs opposite their mother.

"Mom?" Douglas began.

"I don't want to talk right now," she said softly, wiping her nose with a tissue.

"What happened at the meeting with the lawyer?" Douglas continued, undeterred by her request not to discuss the matter.

"Douglas!" Sage scolded between clenched teeth.

"I'm going to go lie down until dinner," Adel said through the beginnings of more tears. She rose from the couch and made her way to the bedroom on tired, dragging feet.

"What was that all about?" Douglas asked Sage.

"I know as much as you do!" she barked at him.

Their father came down the hallway from the bathroom, stopping to close the bedroom door behind their mother.

"The meeting with the lawyer was really difficult on your mother today," he said, once in the living room. He took a seat on the couch across from them and shuffled some papers from their meeting around on the coffee table. "We went through your grandfather's will and his accounts and investments. It was tiring and frankly a bit overwhelming. I felt as if I was losing him all over again, so I'm sure it was the same for your mother. It's the finality of it that has been the hardest. Reading the will means that he is really gone, and she hasn't been ready to accept that yet."

Avery stacked the pile of papers and sank back against the couch. Now that Sage could study his face, dark circles under his eyes accentuated his weary appearance. He was feeling not only fatigued but nearly as depressed as their mother. He glanced toward the kitchen and took a deep breath, preparing to force himself out of the comfort of the couch.

"Wait, Dad. Why don't you let Douglas and me cook dinner tonight? You can go lie down with Mom until it's done," Sage volunteered.

"Are you sure? I am just feeling so tired," Avery said appreciatively.

"Sure, Dad. It's no big deal," Douglas added. Avery gave a weary smile before he headed down the hall to the bedroom.

"She's seemed fine since the funeral," Douglas said to his sister after the bedroom door closed.

"She hasn't done any grieving yet. Haven't you noticed? She busied herself with packing for the trip after she found out. And since we've been here, she has cleaned every inch of the cabin at least twice! She's been avoiding this, just like Dad said, not wanting to accept it," Sage responded. "It's probably going to be tough around here for a few days."

With a sigh, they made their way to the kitchen.

"So much for my news about Layton," Douglas complained as he opened the refrigerator to check the dinner options. "Spaghetti?"

"Spaghetti."

Avery was up before the rest of his family the next morning; he needed to go to Ashtyn for a meeting. Sage chose to stay home to take care of her mother and things around the cabin while Douglas headed to the lake by himself. Adel slept for a good portion of the day, worn out from crying and overcome with all the painful emotions she had been avoiding since her father's death. Between heat-ing cups of tea and a bowl of soup for her mother's lunch, Sage busied herself with household chores. She emptied all the dirty clothes from her duffle bag to begin a few loads of laundry.

Oh, I almost forgot about you, she thought as she uncovered the book her grandfather had sent to her for her birthday. She set the book aside and walked through the rest of the house in search of more dirty clothes. Bathroom towels, a few things in her parent's room, the sheets she had been using on the couch and then … the loft.

"Good grief!" she muttered.

Clothes were piled or strewn or tossed throughout the space. White sport socks, blackened on the bottoms from Douglas walking outside with no shoes, were balled up and dotting the carpet. Douglas's sheets were no longer fully attached to the bed, having slipped off the top corners. And there was a smell. Sage crinkled her nose in disgust. She followed the foul odor until she found a pile of wet beach towels with swim trunks bunched inside.

"Yuck!" she grumbled, shaking her head. She picked up the clothes and sheets—choosing to hold some of them at arm's length—and put them into a laundry basket to take back downstairs. With the first load of clothes in the washer, the floors swept, dishes put away, and her mother resting again, Sage decided to sit down and look through her book. Her hand brushed over the cream leather surface. It was smooth and soft, as if untold numbers of hands had done just as she was doing now. She opened the cover and gasped at the first image. This was not the first time she had seen the picture, but what had once looked like a beautiful painting of some fictitious place was real to her now.

"Ashtyn," she whispered, in awe of the picture.

"How's your mom doing?" her father asked.

Sage jumped with surprise, not having heard or felt him enter the cabin. The book slipped from her lap and landed with a thump on the floor.

"I'm sorry," he laughed. "I certainly didn't mean to startle you. You must be really into that book!"

"Yeah … I guess," she said, gathering the book from the floor and placing it back in her duffle bag. "She's been sleeping a lot. Mom, I mean."

"Well, she probably needs it." He stopped, hearing the washer and dryer running. "You're doing laundry? Even Douglas's?" he asked, and she responded with a nod. "Brave girl!"

Sage chuckled, knowing Douglas couldn't wait to share his exciting news with his parents. As soon as dinner was dished onto everyone's plates and they began to eat, he dropped a huge hint to start the conversation.

"Layton sure is beautiful, don't you think?" he said, bringing his fork to his lips. Sage smiled.

"I have never been there, but I have heard …" Avery began to agree, then stopped. "What do you mean 'Layton is beautiful'?"

"You went to Layton?" Adel asked with a twinkle in her tired eyes. "You do have that power! Grandpa was right again."

"Yesterday. I went yesterday! I didn't have any problem getting in and saw the serpents up close and everything!" Douglas all but shouted.

Everyone ate and listened as he shared the rest of his story and answered questions from his parents. Avery and Adel were certainly a bit surprised but very proud as well.

"Well, well. I guess that officially makes you both elves—the only two who have ever had an elf and a human as parents," Avery told them almost sadly.

"Is something wrong, Dad?" Sage asked, reacting to his change of mood.

"No, no. I just wish I had told you sooner. You would know what others your age have already learned. I haven't ever shared the history of our people or how we are meant to use our powers. So much … so much I could have, should have told you already," he replied, shaking his head, disgusted with himself.

"You can't beat yourself up about it, Avery," their mother soothed. "We didn't think it was possible. No one did."

She rose from the table and bent to kiss her husband on the forehead before beginning to clear the dinner plates from the table.

"We'll get this, honey," Avery said. He stopped his wife and took the plates from her hands. "You get some rest. Maybe go sit on the porch?"

Adel nodded her thanks and walked to the front door to relax on the porch in the cooling evening air.

"Douglas, could you run some errands in town in the morning? I think I'll stay with your mom tomorrow," Avery said after she had closed the door behind her.

"Sure, no problem," replied Douglas.

"Could I go, too?" Sage asked them. "I would like to go to the library to e-mail Wendy. I haven't done that yet this summer, and we've been here almost a month already."

"Fine with me," Douglas said, looking at his dad. "Oh, Sage. I forgot to tell you that Terran and Anila said they would meet you at your usual spot after lunch—if you are able to go."

"I will be home tomorrow, and I'll watch your mom. It would be good for you to go out with your friends," their father told them.

Sage and Douglas hadn't been into town since the Fourth of July celebration. They often came into town with their grandfather for breakfast or groceries when they were on vacation at the cabin. This year, however, they had only been in town for the memorial service and the celebration. Sage sighed, thinking how everything was different this summer and, because their grandfather was gone, how things could never again be the same.

Douglas dropped Sage at the library before starting his errands. The cabin had phone service, but their grandfather had not yet decided whether he wanted a computer or internet service in his home. That meant the library was the closest place to get online. She read the e-mails from her friends. The e-mails from Wendy showed she was obviously irritated that Sage had not responded to earlier messages. Sage did her best to explain about not being able to get to a computer and that time had gotten away from her, hoping her excuses would be accepted. But Sage knew that was all they were: excuses. In fact, she wasn't missing her friends back home and hadn't given much thought to contacting them yet that summer. She closed her e-mail and saw she had a few minutes left before Douglas was expected back. Simply out of curiosity sparked by Douglas's birthday present from their grandfather, Sage decided to search for the meanings of their friends' names.

"Baby names," she typed into the search bar. Several possible sites came up on the computer.

"Names and Meanings"

That will work, she thought.

"Lamar," she typed.

"From the sea" appeared as the name's meaning.

Hmmm. Interesting.

"Terran," she entered next.

"Of the earth" popped up on the screen.

Very interesting. Sage's heart was already pounding in her chest in anticipation.

"Anila," she punched in, predicting the meaning of her name.

Oh, my! she thought, and she hurried from the library to meet her brother.

CHAPTER 8

The Tornado

The ride back to the cabin was excruciatingly slow. Sage stared out her window, tapped her fingers, and willed the car to move faster.

"What's your problem?" Douglas grumbled at her constant fidgeting.

"Sorry. I'm just a little, uh, antsy, I guess," she apologized. "Are you even going the speed limit?"

"Give me a break! We're only two minutes from the cabin. What are you in such a hurry about?" he snapped.

"You're right. Maybe I got a little stir crazy yesterday and need some fresh air, a walk in the forest," she said. Sage forced herself to relax. She didn't want to provoke questions that she wasn't ready to answer yet.

Douglas took his eyes off the road and raised an eyebrow at her. He turned away again and shook his head. She knew that look. It was the look he gave her when he thought she was acting even more strangely than usual or when he suspected she was up to something. She smiled innocently and looked back out the window until they reached the driveway. It was lunchtime now, and she knew that Terran and Anila would be waiting for them after they ate. Fighting the desire to leap from the still-parking car, Sage waited for Douglas to take the key out of the ignition and casually opened the door to get out. Again, she looked at Douglas with an innocent smile on her lips. He squinted his eyes at her as if he was now certain she was up to something.

It was quiet inside the cabin. Their father was setting all of the fixings for deli sandwiches out on the kitchen counter.

Good! This will be quick, she thought with relief. That is, unless Douglas has to have seconds. She rolled her eyes.

"How's Mom?" Douglas asked after checking around the room for her.

"Still pretty down but better than yesterday," Avery replied.

"Has she been up yet?" Sage asked.

71

"A few times. She came out for some coffee earlier and sat on the porch for a while. She's just finished a shower, and that will help her feel a bit better too. She'll be out in a minute," he informed them.

Sage felt a little bad about not asking how her mother was feeling. She was so caught up in her own thoughts and getting to where she wanted to be that the events of the previous days seemed to have disappeared from her mind altogether. The pain in the house had subsided to a quiet ache. Sage could no longer feel the intense sorrow from her parents, but somehow that didn't make her feel any less guilty for not being more considerate of her mother.

"Hi, Mom," Douglas and Sage said nearly together when she entered the room.

"Hi, guys," she responded with a weak smile. "Hope you haven't been waiting too long for lunch."

"No, we just got back from town," Douglas told her.

"Go ahead and make your own sandwiches up," Avery told Sage and Douglas. "I'll get one for you, honey," he said to Adel.

"Hey, I have to go up to Ambara in a couple weeks. Would you two like to come along?" Avery asked after everyone sat at the round kitchen table.

"Ambara? Where's that?" Douglas asked. He had a mouthful of his huge, everything-on-it sandwich. Sage was certain there would be no need for him to have seconds.

"It's at the highest point on the highest mountain. That's where I grew up. Well, until I was a teenager," he explained.

"You are from the sky realm?" Sage asked with surprise.

"Yes," he said. "I serve as a representative on their Council. Most of the Council work I do centers around Ambara. I travel to other sky communities around the country and report back to the full Council at our yearly meeting."

"That was what was going on when I saw you, right?" Sage asked.

"Yes again. As you may have already been told, we have a yearly gathering in Ashtyn. Elves come from all over—or used to—for a week around the Fourth of July. It doesn't attract as much attention to have lots of people coming to the national park at a peak camping and vacation time. Anyway, all the Council members from the three realms gather to discuss important issues. Our numbers were really down this year. Only about half as many people came compared to the last few years," he said, shaking his head with great disappointment.

"Is that what you and Frayne were meeting about yesterday?" she inquired, remembering that Frayne had been leaving to meet with Evron to go over results from the gathering.

"That, and other things, too. He asked if I would be willing to travel a little bit more to some of the other, farther communities. On one hand it is difficult to conduct effective meetings without people there to listen and vote, and on the other hand, it's difficult to get people to come when they know about the strange things that have been happening." Avery had rambled on without realizing what he was saying until it was too late.

"What kind of strange things?" Douglas asked. He set his napkin down on his empty plate, smiled, and gave his full attention to their father.

"Well," Avery began, clearly choosing his words carefully, "unusual things. Things like animals acting strangely toward the elves, serpents traveling up the river instead of staying in the lake, or whole patches of healthy crops shriveling up overnight—that's what." He spoke with concern and agitation in his voice. "Anyway, it makes people stay away, even if there hasn't been anything big or dangerous happening."

Sage helped to clean up the kitchen when everyone had finished eating and went into the living room to sit with her mother on the couch. She wrapped her arms around her mother's neck but said nothing. When she saw that Douglas was ready to go, she gave her mom a light kiss on the cheek and a quick squeeze before following him out the door.

Now that they were outside and on their way, Sage's previous anxiousness began to creep back. Once again, she was having difficulty looking relaxed and walking leisurely down the trail with Douglas. She saw Terran and Anila as she and Douglas approached the split and wanted more than anything to run wildly to where they stood waiting. Anila took a deep breath, squared her shoulders, and smiled brightly. Sage tried to calm the pounding in her own chest. She didn't know how much longer she could keep from blurting out what she had learned at the library.

"Hi," Terran called out.

"No Jason today?" Douglas asked as they began along the trail to the lake.

"Not today. He wanted to hang around Ashtyn," answered Terran.

"I think Lamar is going to meet us, too. You're going swimming, aren't you?" he asked Terran.

"Yeah. Is that all right with you two? I don't want you to feel left out," Terran said to Sage and Anila. He was obviously concerned about Anila's unusually glum mood.

"You go ahead. I wanted to talk to Anila anyway. Maybe we could all do something when you are done with your swim," Sage answered. She smiled her best innocent smile, trying to cover for answering a little too quickly.

Things were moving just too slowly for Sage. She wanted to shove the boys faster along the trail as she and Anila walked behind them. It even felt as if the boys were moving in slow motion, removing their shirts and shoes. Sage fidgeted anxiously again, though Douglas, lost in conversation, did not seem to notice this time. Finally, Douglas and Terran jumped from the rocks and were far enough away for Sage to talk to Anila without them hearing.

"Anila!" she exclaimed so excitedly that Anila almost slipped on the rock she was balancing on. Sage reached out her hands to help steady her friend before she fell backward into the water. She pulled Anila down and sat facing her. "I have been waiting to talk to you! I went to the library this morning to send messages to some friends back home. You know how Terran said the meaning of Douglas's name was quite fitting? Well, while I was at the library, I was curious, so I looked up some more names on the computer. Douglas's name, meaning 'dark water,' may not be quite the coincidence we all thought."

"Okay," Anila said slowly.

"I looked up your name, Anila! I know what it means, and I think I know why you haven't shown any sign of having powers!"

Sage was still holding Anila's hands and was instantly aware that her words did not have a comforting effect on her. The fear of never having any powers was obvious in her clenching muscles and lowered head.

"No, Anila! It's going to be all right," Sage assured her. She smiled at her friend. "What do you know about your name?"

"My name? I ... I don't really know, Sage," she replied, her voice trembling. "I've never thought about it or asked. Why? What did you find?"

Still holding Anila's hands, Sage softened her tone to help ease her friend's worry. "Because your name, it means 'child of the wind'!" Sage saw the confusion in Anila's eyes yet could feel Anila's pulse quicken with anticipation all the same. "Don't you see?" Sage continued. "You won't have the same powers as your family because, if I'm right, you will have the power of the wind!"

Sage watched a complex evolution of expressions cross Anila's face. Anila pulled her hands from Sage's and looked away, shaking her head. There was doubt in her furrowed brow, but Sage could also see there was hope this could be true.

"I don't have anyone in my family who has the power of wind. Powers are usually passed through family members," Anila mumbled to herself. She turned to Sage with a glimmer of excitement and expectation in her eyes that had been missing for days. "I've never had any thoughts of powers outside of those of my family. Actually, I've never even heard of it happening." She took Sage's hands and giggled. "How do we find out?"

"Oh …" Sage hadn't thought about that. She paused for a moment, looking at what there was around them to work with. "I don't know. You should start small—something light. Let's go down there," Sage said, pointing to the small stretch of dirt between the rocky shore and the trees. "Maybe you can blow some of that dirt around?" The two girls scurried off the rocks to the clearing at the head of the trail.

"Blow it around?" Anila's eyes were wide and unblinking.

"I'm the wrong person to ask, Anila! What have you seen other people do?"

"Nothing really," Anila sighed. "Powers are almost gone, and it's not like people from Ambara are down here all the time just blowing things around!"

"You can do this! Concentrate, Anila!" she encouraged her friend. "Imagine a bit of wind swirling the dirt there."

After too long of a wait for Sage's mounting anticipation, Anila nodded her head once and adjusted her feet, anchoring them shoulder width apart. Anila pointed the palms of her shaking hands downward toward the dirt. She closed her eyes then took one more buoying breath.

Sage tried to just remember to breathe at all. She dared not move and risk distracting her friend. Her heart pounded wildly with nervousness, wanting more than anything to see just a tiny puff of dust rise from the soil. Several seconds went by before Sage's joyous squeal seemed to startle her and break her concentration. Sage could feel something inside her friend change. Waken. Unable to contain her delight, Sage jumped up and down, clapping her hands before running to stand beside Anila.

"Whatever you did, do it again, Anila!" Sage shouted. "Do it again! And don't close your eyes!"

With more confidence showing in her eyes and her stance, Anila again aimed her hands to the ground. Sage didn't know what Anila had pictured but what resulted was a small tornado of twisting dust and fallen leaves dancing a few inches above the earth. Anila gasped and slowly lowered her hands. Tears filled her eyes and she collapsed to her knees, lowering her head into her hands.

"Oh, Anila! What's wrong? Isn't this what you've been wanting, what you've been hoping for?" Sage knelt in front of her friend, trying to unravel the tangle of intense emotions coming from her.

"What happened?" Douglas shouted from the direction of the lake.

Sage turned her eyes from Anila and up to see all three boys gripping the rocks tightly, staring down at them. Their serious faces revealed their worry, and they were gasping to catch their breath. Sage realized they must have heard her cry out at Anila's success and, thinking something was terribly wrong, swum back to the rocks as fast as they could.

"I think I upset her. I didn't mean to," Sage tried nervously to explain. The three winded boys jumped off the rocks and rushed to the girls. "I was just trying to help."

Terran knelt down beside Anila, gently lifting her chin. "Anila! What's hap—"

"I have my power!" Anila interrupted. She was still crying but smiling and laughing at the same time. "I have my power!" Then Terran smiled, too, showing he understood the importance of what she was saying. Reaching out a hand, he helped Anila rise off the ground.

"Didn't you already have them?" Douglas asked in confusion.

"No!" she told him. "And I don't have the powers of the forest. I should— but I don't! I thought I was never going to have any elvish powers. Now I know! Watch!"

Showing considerably more self-assurance, she focused on the ground centered between the friends and turned her palms to the earth. Once again, a tornado, even stronger than the two before, arose from the dirt and hovered over the ground.

"Wow! Anila, that is awesome!" cheered Lamar as he watched the tornado swirl near his feet.

"Sweet!" Douglas said. He started clapping for Anila.

Anila lowered her hands and watched the dirt settle back on the ground before turning back to her friends. There was no mistaking how Anila felt now, smiling broadly with tears Sage now knew were of joy still pooled in her eyes.

"Sage figured it out. She found out what my name means. It means 'child of the wind.' She thought I should try before—" Anila inhaled sharply. "I won't have to leave!" she interrupted herself happily.

A pained shadow crossed Terran's face, but he said nothing.

"It's good to see you smiling again," Lamar told Anila. He paused for a moment, thoughtful. "I've never heard of anyone having powers outside of their family line. That's really crazy—especially about your name." He turned to Sage with a twinkle in his eyes. "Out of curiosity, I don't suppose you looked up what my name means," he said.

"Yes, as a matter of fact," she said, chuckling. "It means 'from the sea,'" Sage informed her friend. "And I know yours, too," she said, turning with a smile to Terran. "Terran means 'of the earth.'"

Both boys smiled and seemed pleased—proud, even—at the meanings of their names. They all chattered about the chances of their names meaning what they did, except Anila. Soon everyone's attention turned back to her, standing silently with an odd expression on her face. She was lost in her own thoughts, and her eyes were focused at some point in the sky above Sage's head. One by one each of the friends turned to see what Anila had spotted. It was the same barely visible mountaintop Anila had been staring at before. Whatever she saw was pictured in her own mind.

"That strange lady in town was right," Anila said slowly, lowering her gaze. "She told me that I feared the decision I had to make. That was about leaving for the human world." She looked at Terran, who, by the expression on his face, was hearing her speak her fear for the first time. "She said that a friend would find the solution," she said, turning to Sage, "and you did."

"She told Sage that her discoveries would ..." Douglas thought for a moment, trying to remember the exact words. "... lessen the burdens of others," he said, connecting the woman's comments with the odd coincidences that were presenting themselves. "After Sage found out about my dad and the elves, he told her that her discovery had taken a terrible burden off of him from keeping it a secret." Douglas raised his eyebrows. "Very weird."

"What strange lady are you all talking about?" Lamar asked, being the only one who didn't follow what was going on.

"We went to a shop in town during the Fourth of July celebration. We thought it would be fun to go see this woman who was claiming to be a psychic, a fortuneteller. She told each of us something—something that must only have meaning to the one she told." Anila looked at the faces of Terran, Sage and Douglas and felt sure they knew what she meant. "Then she pretty much said we would all be facing challenges and making discoveries over the next few summers. I felt really uneasy when I walked out of there. I don't think I expected her to say anything that was true or that I could relate to."

"She's a Seer," Lamar said. His statement was very matter-of-fact and rang of the truth.

"A what?!" Terran asked. "You mean, you think she's real?"

"Sure. My parents said Seers used to be very well respected. Every community had one, sometimes two if the gift was handed down to the next generation as well. They couldn't tell someone their exact future or anything, but they could see images or hear things—bits and pieces of things that would eventually happen. They usually wrote them down for people to use as a guide later. Sometimes, many Seers spread over time saw different pieces that eventually fit together like a puzzle. There aren't any left that I know of," he explained. "I suppose there could be humans who have that power, too."

"I don't think I have ever heard of them," Terran said. "My parents might not know, but my grandfather certainly would. He's always talking about the history of our people. I wonder why he never mentioned that."

"Well, this has been an interesting day. The strange lady in town apparently knows what she's talking about, and our names seem to have some connection to the type of powers we hold or where we're from," Lamar recounted in his most scholarly voice. "I am afraid I can't stick around for any more of the excitement, though. One of the serpents went kind of crazy last night and knocked out a few of the light tubes. A whole section of the town had to have their lights on all day. I told my dad that I would come down to help if they needed it, so I guess I'll see you guys later." Lamar gave Anila a bear hug. "Hey! Congratulations, Anila!"

"Can I go with you?" asked Douglas.

"Well, we still haven't found out if you can make it to the bottom. That could be another interesting addition to the day," he said, waving Douglas to come along.

Both boys jumped into the water and waved goodbye before disappearing in the lake. Sage was thinking that the light tubes getting damaged by a serpent must be another unusual event. She was glad that it was only the light tubes and not a person—and was sure her father would want to hear about it.

Terran was frowning at Anila. That one look showed how disappointed and a little bitter he was about her keeping the possibility of leaving from him. Anila may have been practicing another tornado but was clearly trying to avoid Terran's eyes. Standing with them in the clearing became uncomfortable for Sage. She felt as if she was in their way, so she rose from the rock she was resting against and was just getting ready to say goodbye when Terran spoke.

"Why didn't you tell me you were thinking about leaving?" he asked in a controlled tone.

Anila turned and took a deep breath. She looked at him for a moment, obviously choosing her words carefully. "I didn't want to leave and was trying to convince myself that something would turn up, something would work out. You're my best friend, and I knew you would worry—or try to solve my problem for me." Her tone was sincere, and Terran softened a little with the truth of her words.

"You wouldn't have had to leave, Anila," he said tenderly.

"I couldn't stay here—not without powers. I would have been looked down on, and then just think what Evron would have said. I grew up here, so most would not have cared if I had been allowed to stay, but he would have been furious! Terran, you know how he feels about humans, and that's all I would have been to him." She stopped there, shivering a little. Sage knew the feeling. Evron. "And yet it may have been worse if I'd left."

"Yes, he would have overreacted in either case," Terran agreed, "but I wouldn't have told him about your powers. I've been worried about you, Anila. You shouldn't have kept this secret."

"I'm sorry, Terran," Anila said hugging him. "I guess we won't have to worry about it anyway. And," she smiled playfully, "Evron won't have to get all worked up or end the engagement he keeps planning for us." Terran and Anila both started laughing.

"Ahem," Sage grunted, getting their attention. They had been so engrossed in their conversation that they hadn't noticed Sage trying to skirt around the edges of the small clearing. She had been tiptoeing back and forth in an attempt to find a way back to the trail without walking right between them. "I didn't mean to listen in. I was going to sneak away when Terran started talking, but there's really no easy way to get by you without interrupting."

"Oh, we weren't arguing or anything," Terran tried to assure her. "We've just had this rule, Anila and I, since we were children. We promised each other that we wouldn't keep secrets." He sighed. "Yet this summer has already been full of them."

"I'm sorry, Sage. We certainly didn't want you to feel uncomfortable," Anila said.

She really did have a way of making people feel at ease. It was her smile on the first day they met that had made Sage so comfortable, and it was her sincerity and kindness now that made Sage feel less like the odd man out.

"Terran is right. I should have told him. We always try to help each other with our problems." She faced Sage and took her hands. "You are a good friend, and I hope I—" She stopped and smiled at Terran. "I mean we can be there to help you if you ever need it."

"Come on, Sage," Terran said, putting an arm around each girl's shoulders, "Anila and I will walk you home."

"Are you two really engaged?" Sage asked after a few steps.

"No!" Terran and Anila answered together as they began laughing again.

CHAPTER 9

The Book

Sage was glad to have her friends walking back to the cabin with her. The conversation Terran and Anila had at the lake made her think of some things she had been wanting to ask, but the timing had never seemed right. Now, she not only felt comfortable asking, she was fairly certain no one would be offended.

"Anila, what did you mean when you were talking about Evron and said 'you know how he feels about humans'?" Sage glanced at Terran to make sure she had not touched on a sore topic.

"He just doesn't like them," Anila said flatly with a shrug of her shoulders. "He won't get near them if he can help it, which means he almost never goes into town. He even hates that he can see them on the beach across the lake. He'd prefer they weren't allowed into the park at all. We were surprised he went to your grandfather's memorial service, because it was in town and there were *humans* there." She laughed a little, but it was clear that she found no humor in Evron's viewpoint.

"Why, though?" Sage wanted to know. "What happened to make him dislike them so strongly?"

"My dad said it was something that had to do with a girl … way back when he was a teenager," said Terran. "He doesn't really know any more than that, just that it had something to do with a girl."

"But that was what, fifty years ago?!" Sage exclaimed.

"Just about," Terran answered. "Like I said before, he is just grumpy and unpleasant. It's how he has always been. I used to be disappointed that he never really wanted to do family things with us. Now I'm just glad I didn't have to grow up in the same house with him, like my father did." The friends had reached the cabin and waved at Adel, who was sitting on the porch loveseat reading a book.

"Hello," Adel said. She was smiling a little and looked as if she were feeling much better.

"Hi, Mom," Sage said. "Is Dad around?"

"He's inside, getting ready for a meeting," her mother replied.

Sage turned to Terran and Anila. "Do you have a second? I would like to ask my dad something." With no objections, she ran into the house. Avery was sitting on the living room couch, with papers spread before him on the coffee table. He was dressed in the traditional clothing Sage had once thought so unusual but had already begun to grow accustomed to.

"Dad?" She spoke softly, trying not to startle him from his thoughts. He looked up at her and smiled. "You know how you said we could go to Ambara with you in a couple of weeks? Could Terran and Anila come, too?"

"Sure. They've both been there before and would be great company for you and Douglas. Oh, and we will be staying overnight—long trip—so they would need to talk to their parents about it, okay?" Avery told her distractedly and then returned to his work.

"Thanks, Dad," she said as she was shutting the cabin door.

Terran, Anila, and Adel paused their conversation, obviously waiting for Sage's attention.

"Anila was just telling me about her newfound powers," Adel said, beaming at Sage. "She said you had a little something to do with their discovery."

"Everything to do with it, actually," Anila jumped in enthusiastically.

"It was an accident, really," Sage stammered. "She liked Douglas's necklace, so I thought it would be fun to look up everyone's name. That's how I found out."

"Well, I think it is wonderful, no matter how you found out!" Anila exclaimed.

"Thanks." Sage smiled at her friend. "Hey, my dad has to take a trip to Ambara sometime in the next couple weeks, and I asked if you two could come with us. He said that it was fine with him if you want to come, but you'll have to talk to your parents because we're going to have to stay overnight."

"Should be fine with my parents. I'll ask tonight," Terran told her.

"I was just a little girl that last time we went there," Anila said. "It would be fun. I'll talk to my parents, but it will really depend on Delaney. The baby is due right about then, but she could have it anytime now."

"Well, we can just play it by ear, then," Sage said understandingly.

"We better get heading back now," Terran said. "See you tomorrow?"

She nodded and told her friends goodbye.

"It was nice talking to you, Adel," Anila called out as they walked toward the trail.

"Congratulations again, Anila!" Adel replied.

Sage sat beside her mother on the loveseat. Her mother did look much better today, although Sage knew it would always be hard on her to have her father gone.

"You certainly made her day," Adel told her daughter. "Next time you're at the library, look up your father's name, and I'll get him a necklace like Douglas's. He would like that, I think."

As if on cue, Avery came out on the porch, briefcase in hand. "Sorry I have to miss dinner tonight," he said sounding a bit exasperated. "Evron is determined to get an early start on the agendas for the year. I should be back before dark … I hope."

"It's all right, Avery. I'll be fine. I'm feeling much better today, thanks to my wonderful family," Adel said appreciatively.

"Where's Douglas?" he asked, finally realizing he wasn't with them.

"Oh," Sage said. She struck the palm of her hand to her forehead. "I forgot to tell you. He went to Layton to see if he could help fix some of the light tubes. Lamar said a serpent knocked out some of them."

"Knocked out some of them? That's odd," Avery mused. "They have never disabled one before." Even without knowing that the serpents were normally docile creatures, Sage figured this wasn't their usual behavior.

"He actually said it went a little crazy," Sage elaborated.

"I'll tell the rest of the Council in case they don't know already. See you later," he said. With a wave goodbye, he was heading down the steps and into the forest.

Douglas returned later that afternoon and shared his somewhat dramatized story with his mother and sister. The serpent that had damaged the tubes had also injured itself in the process. A crew of people trapped and checked the creature to make certain the injuries were not serious or life threatening. Luckily, the serpent had only sustained minor cuts and bruising and was able to be released without them causing it any further distress. The tubes, on the other hand, needed a great deal of time and effort to fix. In fact, more than one had to be removed entirely for reconstruction. Douglas told them that some of the inhabitants of Layton were still able to hold their breath for long periods of time. They were the ones who remained out of the city bubble as the main crew of workers, returning only for brief rests and fresh air. Others, who could only hold their air for shorter lengths of time, assisted in shifts. It took several hours to repair the light tubes and treat the serpent that caused the damage, but eventually both were as good as new.

"How did you help?" Sage asked her brother.

"I helped with the serpent. That's where Lamar and his mother were working. I didn't get to do anything with the light tubes because I didn't know how long I could go without heading back into the town for air. That's all they needed to worry about, me running out of air while they were trying to work and having another rescue on their hands." He laughed.

"I'm surprised you haven't tried to find out. I mean you really should know how long you can last, and who knows, maybe you can breathe under water or something," Sage said, chuckling.

"No, I just haven't tried to see yet. And ... Lamar has never heard of any elves that can actually breathe underwater. Maybe I'll do a little bit of experimenting," he said adventurously until he looked at his mother. "Of course," he continued in his most sincere-sounding voice, "I'll be sure we are in very shallow water and that Lamar is with me ... ummm ... in the very unlikely event things don't go well."

"Well, you better make sure he is with you! And be careful!" Adel waved a finger at him.

"I will. Sooo ... would it be all right for me to go back for a while after dinner?" he asked with a sly smile. "Lamar wants me to meet the rest of his family."

"And I wanted to go out to the forest to read for a while, if that would be okay," Sage added.

"I suppose that would be fine as long as you are both home before dark," their mother said with a shrug of her shoulders.

After dinner, Douglas grabbed his towel, Sage her book, and together they walked until the split in the trail.

"Where are you heading?" Douglas asked.

"Right in here. I have a spot where I like to sit and read," she said without telling him exactly where. She chuckled a little at his confusion about her choice of reading locations.

"Okay. See you later, then," he said, shaking his head a bit and turning down the trail.

Sage walked back along the trail, retracing her steps a little way toward the cabin until she spotted the deep green area of moss she and her grandfather shared as their special place. It had nearly disappeared under the fully grown vegetation surrounding the site. Holding back the long red thorny stem of a wild raspberry, she stepped off the well-worn trail. The knee-high plants swiped against her bare legs, pricking her skin and giving her cause to reach down to scratch them. The carpet of moss had been reduced to a space barely large enough for her to sit comfortably without the plants rubbing against her. She adjusted herself so her back could recline against a tree and looked up into the leaves above. She smiled. She was just happy to be there, alone in the forest.

She lowered her head and took a long, deep breath, her hand gliding across the smooth surface of the leather book. She opened the book to the first picture, the one she had recognized as the village of Ashtyn. Even in the fading light and shadows of the forest, glints of burnished gold reflected from the illustration. She wondered what secrets this beautiful book was going to share as her fingers found the top edge of the picture, lifted, and slowly turned the page. Again, there was a picture that she had remembered seeing when she had opened the book for the first time on her birthday over a half year ago. This picture, too, held a different meaning for her. It was the bridge with the carvings, the river, and the strong, old ash trees. But on the opposite page, once blank, were now words, penned in a delicate, flowing script. She took in a sharp breath at the magic that had been revealed to her and began to read.

**A tree grows strong and tall and fair. She sends
her boughs to touch the sky, caress the wind,
to bower birds and shelter forest friends.**

**The lake nearby reflects the sky, the sun,
the tree but touches none. He laps at roots.
He wants the tree and he to be as one.**

The lake now sees, beneath the tree, the roots
that sink in earth. With cool, rich soil, earth gives
the tree her life, an anchor for her shoots.

The lake, it howls, sends water to the sky
to rain his anger down upon the tree.
When lightning strikes, roots torn from earth now cry.

The sky is clear, the rain and thunder gone.
The tree that fell has lost her forest home.
The earth and one frail shoot are all alone.

Sage re-read the page, trying to grasp the meaning of the verse. She flipped through the rest of the book, examining the pictures and quickly scanning through the words on each page. *Is it just an Elvish book of poetry?* she wondered. Her grandfather loved poetry and often read it to her when they sat together on that very spot. Now she wondered if he knew the words were in the book all along and if they had revealed themselves to him. She heard steps scuffing on the path ahead of her. It was Douglas on his way back to the cabin, and he didn't see her hidden there. She sat there, amused, waiting to see how long it would take him to notice her. But Douglas was rubbing his towel over his wet hair and continued to walk right past the spot where she sat. She didn't say anything, deciding not to give her secret place away, and watched until he was out of sight around a bend in the trail.

Knowing it was time to leave, she closed the book. *It would be difficult to continue reading in the dark anyway*, she thought. She placed her hands on the ground on either side of her, preparing to stand, when she once again heard steps coming toward her. The voices of two men, barely louder than a whisper, caught her attention. Although they spoke quietly, she could tell they were engaged in an intense discussion. The coming darkness made it nearly impossible to see the men before they had reached the split in the trail, but she already knew one of the men was Evron. Her stomach churned a bit as they continued to approach. The man walking with Evron was her father, returning from his meeting in Ashtyn. She considered announcing herself to the men, not wanting to be dis-covered overhearing their obviously private conversation. Once again she began to stand but lowered herself back into a squatting position when Evron raised his voice to her father.

"I knew one, once—a very long time ago. I read it for myself when I was with her. You must know the time is near, Avery," Evron said.

Then her father suddenly stopped directly in front of where Sage sat hidden in the foliage and turned to face Evron. He looked tired—tired of trying to be polite and tactful. There was no hiding his exasperation.

"I don't know what it is you read. I don't know why these things are happening. And I *don't* know what time is near. I do know that we need to keep what remains of our people safe, find out why things are happening, and make sure that these *incidents* don't get worse. Someone could get *hurt*, Evron."

"It has all been foreseen," Evron continued. "These incidents, as you call them, will continue until the three realms unite ..."

"... and then our people and our power will return," Avery interrupted. "I have listened, Evron. I have heard all that you have said. What is it you want from me?"

"Your word. Your commitment. That is what I want from you," Evron urged Avery, his voice smooth and persuasive. "It is clear that the strongest from each realm will be needed to fulfill the foretelling."

"I want what is best for our people, so I will consider your *offer*, Evron. But let me be clear: I will make no alliances that diverge from the objectives of the Council," Avery said, firmly squaring his shoulders.

"Of course, of course. The Council has accomplished a great deal in the last few years, especially since you have been representing Ambara and the other sky communities," he said with syrupy flattery. "The time is near, and there is more to learn. I will need an answer soon."

"I said I would *consider* your offer. That is all." He spoke slowly and deliberately, making certain his meaning was clearly received. "My family is expecting me. Goodnight, Evron," her father said with a finality that Evron could no longer ignore.

She could feel Evron boil with irritation and impatience, but he managed to keep his expression a pleasant mask, hiding his true feelings from Avery. Without another word, Evron bowed his head respectfully, turned sharply, and began retracing his steps on the trail toward Ashtyn, his cloak snapping behind him.

Avery watched him walk for a moment. Then he relaxed a little, letting out a heavy huff of air before continuing on his way. Sage sat very still for several minutes before she stood up and walked toward the trail, carefully feeling in the dark for the thorny raspberry stems. Her mind raced as she walked. She knew they were talking about the prophecies of a Seer, just like Lamar had told them about. *But what does Evron know, and what does he want with my father?* she wondered. *Maybe Dad doesn't know how dark and angry Evron is*, she could only imagine. She contemplated telling her father that she had heard some of the conversation between him and Evron, revealing to him that Evron was infuriated when her father wouldn't give him the answer he wanted. She wanted to warn him about the kind of person she believed Evron to be, but she knew her father had spent much of his childhood at Evron's house. *Maybe he already knows*, she thought as she reached the cabin.

"You're running a bit late," her father said with the slight hint of a reprimand. The porch light was on, and he stood leaning against the railing, a silhouette waiting for her to return home.

"I guess I didn't realize how quickly it was getting dark," she said apologetically as she joined him. "I didn't mean to make you worry. Following the trail is a bit more challenging at night, even for me. I'll pay closer attention next time."

"Being able to stay on the trail is only one of the reasons we want you home before dark," he said, looking seriously at his daughter. "You know there are other things happening that make it unsafe for you to be out after dark—especially by yourself."

"I guess I should have stayed with Douglas. I just wanted some time to myself."

"It's okay to want time for yourself. Just be smart about where and when." He raised his eyebrows at her and waited for her to agree. When she did, he turned back toward the forest, watching the last glow of sunset fall behind the trees. "I just came back a few minutes before you," he said more cheerfully. "Did you pass Evron on your way?"

She didn't want her father to know everything she had overheard in the forest. Still, she knew this was her opportunity to tell him what she had been sensing from Evron since their first meeting.

"No. I didn't pass him, and that's just fine with me," she said enticingly, pausing for her father to take the bait.

"You don't like Evron?" Avery asked with mock surprise. "I didn't realize you have had many chances to associate with him. It seems a bit unfair to judge him before you get to know him."

"It's just how I ... um, *feel* ... when he is anywhere near me. I am very ill at ease when he is close," she said, and then she added under her breath, "*Literally.*" She turned to face her father more directly. "Do you know if he is angry with someone in the family?" she asked, hoping to lead her father further into the discussion.

"Angry? With someone in our family?" he contemplated out loud. "No. Not that I know of. Why?"

"That is the only feeling—emotion—I ever sense from him, and it's really intense." She paused for a moment. "I wasn't joking. It really makes me ill. Nauseated, actually."

"He has a lot on his plate right now. Maybe you are feeling his stress or frustration about something else. It probably has nothing to do with you—or us—at all," he said, placing a reassuring hand on her shoulder. "I've known Evron for many years, and he comes across a little ... well, strong and often quite cool. It takes a while to get to know him and for him to get to know others. He's pretty careful about who he gets close to. It could be what you are sensing from him are his own reservations about you."

"Maybe," she said humoring her father, "but I think the less we have to do with him the better."

CHAPTER 10
The Legends

Sage was up and out of the cabin bright and early one morning several days later, wanting to read more in the book of poetry before meeting up with Anila and Terran. After nestling into her quiet hideaway, now filled with white, flickering sunlight, she opened the book. Sage flipped to the page she had read that evening close to a week before, the last time she had been alone. She re-read the poem a number of times but was still unsure of its meaning. Sage figured there must be more to learn about the elves and their history before she could understand the writer's view. Terran and Anila would know important events or stories, she decided, and her father would probably be excited to teach her as well.

Painted on the following page was the large Council building in Ashtyn. Ivy and flowers climbed the sides of the building and draped over the arched windows and doorways just as it looked this summer. The painting showed what appeared to be the Council holding session with all of the stone seats inside the building filled and more people overflowing into the town center. Blankets were spread under the shade of the trees within easy listening of the meeting being held inside. Bright flags and streaming ribbons decorated the tops of buildings and the entrances of homes. Children ran and played with balls in the open center of town. It really was very festive, and Sage imagined this was what the town looked like before the elves had begun to leave. After she examined the picture, she turned her attention to the writing that had appeared on the opposite page. It was written in completely different handwriting from the first page Sage had read.

**Led by Wisdom and guided by Nature herself, the Chosen
will unite the three realms against those who falsely seek to rule.
Their successful union will return order and
purpose to our communities and power to our people.**

Oh my, she thought, *this is what Evron was talking about that night*. This page was not at all in the same style as the previous verse. The first page was a poem, sad and full of metaphor. *This*, she thought, *this is a foretelling*.

"Hey!" called a familiar voice. Terran had spied her as he walked along the trail, apparently heading for the cabin.

"Hey, Terran!" She smiled as he came off the trail to join her.

"You really like this spot, don't you? A bit smaller than the first time I met you, eh?" he said. Sage slid over, giving him room to sit beside her.

"Yeah, this was where my grandfather and I used to come to spend time together," she replied. "Mostly we read poetry and stories."

"It's a great place—one of my favorites, too. Well, where you saw me that day … over there," he said pointing just a short distance down the trail. "I like the quiet. And there are some animals that I tend to here."

"Tend to?" she asked with interest.

"Feed, play with, talk to … that's all," he said, shrugging his shoulders.

"A regular Doctor Doolittle!" she said jokingly.

"Doctor who?" he asked.

"Oh, never mind. It's … um … cool, I guess," she said. Sage lowered her head and felt suddenly embarrassed for forgetting he might not know about Doctor Doolittle. She squirmed uneasily, wishing for something to say that wouldn't sound completely awkward. Still at a loss for words, Sage looked up, hoping Terran wasn't offended. She squinted at him, curious about his expression. Just one corner of his mouth had curled into a smile, and his eyes flashed his amusement. He had been teasing her and seemed to be waiting for her to figure that out. Sage's stomach fluttered.

"Keelin, Anila's father, has a huge library, and I like to read," he said. "It was one of my favorite books when I was young."

"Mine, too," she smiled. "Where is Anila today?"

"Her sister finally had the baby last night," Terran informed her, "so she stayed in Oakley today."

"We're leaving for Ambara tomorrow. Maybe we can see her on our way through," she suggested.

"She's still planning on going and said we could just meet her at her house. Her parents thought she would really enjoy the trip up there, especially now that she knows her powers," he told Sage, bumping her playfully to acknowledge her role in helping Anila. "Besides, there are lots of people around to help Delaney until she gets back."

He took the book from her lap and opened it to the first page, the painting of Ashtyn. His eyes grew large, and light reflecting off the page streaked his face.

"This is Ashtyn!" he cried in disbelief. "Where did you get this?" He began to turn through the pages, scanning the images.

"My grandfather sent it to me for my birthday. I think it's a book of elvish poetry or something," she said. "I was kind of hoping that you and Anila could help me figure some of it out. I don't know much about the elves or their history."

"It's your history, too," he said sincerely. She smiled, blushing slightly. "I don't know if I can help you much on the poetry, but I can answer questions about our history."

Terran closed the book and stood up. He stretched a hand out to Sage.

"Come on. Your secret spot is a little small," he teased as he helped pull her up from the ground. He walked back to the trail with her following closely behind.

"Where are we going?" Sage asked. They had started down the trail toward Ashtyn.

"You'll see," he said slyly as he glanced back to her, continuing to lead the way.

She blushed at the look he had given her, her heart beating more quickly. She dropped her head, hoping he wouldn't see the redness in her cheeks. They had not gone far from the split in the trail before Terran turned in the direction of the river. The roar of the river was getting louder. He looked back and smiled at Sage, who was now bursting with curiosity.

"Almost there now," he called over the sound of the rapids.

She could see the river now and the fast-moving current crashing over and into the rocks in its way. Terran followed the river up to where the waters were calmer ahead of the rapids. Again, he reached out his hand to her, smiling mischievously. She cocked her head, examining his expression, regarding him a moment longer before she lifted her hand to his. He grasped it, instantly sending a flash of excitement through her along with a mix of other feelings she hadn't really recognized in herself before. He took a sharp turn directly toward the river. Sage should have pulled back fearfully as they approached the edge of the rocks that would drop them straight off into the water below.

"It's all right. Stay right with me," he said, looking in her eyes reassuringly— but there was no need. With her hand in his, she was safe, protected. He turned back around and continued walking closer to the edge, Sage following, clasping his hand more tightly. Terran slowed his pace, cautiously watching his footing on the rocky ledge above the river. The rocks seemed to descend like stairs toward the river. They were jagged and, where they were wet, a bit slippery. Sage could tell Terran knew his footing well, and after a few more careful steps she saw it, a cave set into the rocks just feet above the rushing water. He stepped into the opening, crouching down to avoid hitting his head, and pulled Sage forward until she too was ducking her head slightly inside the cave. Terran slowly let go of her hand, backing away to sit on the rock floor, setting the book down beside him. Sage's heart began to settle.

There was enough room inside for just two or three people to sit comfortably. The top of the cave was slanted so that the opening was taller than the back or the sides. Sage moved about, touching the cool, gray rock above her head as she followed its slope down to a sliver of light at the rear of the cave. A foot-long, narrow slit in the rocks faced the trail at a little below what would be knee level of anyone walking along it. Sage moved to the front of the cave again and sat across from Terran.

"How did you find this place?" she asked.

"By accident. When I was about ten, I was canoeing down to the lake like I had done dozens of times before and happened to glance up here. It took me awhile to find it by foot. You can't really see it from the trail. I've been coming here ever since. And you," he said grandly, "are my first guest."

"I am the first one to your secret place? I am honored, Terran, and I won't say a word to anyone else." She moved her hand across her lips as if zipping them closed.

He smiled at her. This was the first time they had really been alone since their first meeting. Sage was suddenly aware of how blue eyes his eyes were and how his habit of brushing loose curls out of them made her smile. The warmth of a blush filled her cheeks yet again. Something in his smile and the feeling of the moment brought her back to the first day they met. She had thought him very handsome then, and the truth was, she still did. But there had been an instant connection between them that day that had nothing to do with his good looks and easy manner. Terran shared something with her, something she had shared only with her grandfather before: her love of the forest. So far, Sage had found Terran to be such a genuine person she rarely had to guess or try to sense what he was feeling, but right this moment, with his eyes upon her, she felt uncertain. Curious, she tried to focus on him, tried to feel what he was feeling right then, tried to learn whether he was …

"So, I thought we should start with the legends," he said interrupting her thoughts. "The history you wanted to know about. I thought we'd start with the legends," he repeated.

"Oh … yeah. That would be great," she said, regaining her focus.

"I'm sure they are written down somewhere, but I learned them from my father, so I'll tell you the way I heard them. I'm going to start with the legends of Oakley and Ashtyn."

In the distant past, when the forest was new, there was a boy who played among the young trees, and there was a girl, too. One day the boy and girl met and were together every day thereafter in the woods near the river. They grew as the years went by, and so, too, did the forest around them. One day, at the edge of the river's embankment, the boy and the girl found a young tree that had been struck by lightning in the storm the night before and was split in half down its trunk. Feeling the pain of the tree, the girl set to work bandaging it back together with cloth strips as the boy held the two halves closed for her. For many days the two checked on the tree and watered it to keep it strong.

Terran drew his hands together as if he were the young boy holding that very tree.

One day, the boy returned to the tree, but the girl was not with him. It was clear to the tree that this saddened the boy. "She had to leave," he told the still-healing tree. He sat at its base and did not play. The years passed and the boy became a man and the forest continued to grow. Every day the man came to the tree near the river, sat beneath its now strong branches and ate bread and cheese.

As he sat eating one afternoon, he saw a great bear watching him at a distance. The man was not scared, and when it was time for him to leave, he left some bread and cheese for the animal. The days passed in

95

the same manner; the man sat beneath the tree, he ate his meal with the bear watching, and he left him a piece of cheese and some bread.

One day, the bear approached and sat before the man, but still the man was not afraid.

"Nature herself gave me the task of caring for the animals of the forest. The forest has grown, and the animals have prospered here. There are too many for me to protect and manage now," the bear said. "I have watched you grow and know your love of the forest and its creatures. If it pleases you, I would welcome your assistance, and Nature, who sent me to you, would gift you powers to ease your task."

The man did love the forest and accepted the offer presented to him. He followed the bear a long way to a grove of trees older than the rest of the forest the man knew. They were oak trees, the largest the man had ever seen, growing tall and broad above him.

Sage was drawn into Terran's story, the excitement of his voice, the way he moved, reaching with his arms to show the breadth of the trees, his eyes meeting hers with such intensity she sucked in a deep breath.

"Here is where you will build your home and care for the animals," the bear said to the man.

So the man built a fine home and tended to the needs of his forest friends.

Some months passed, maybe a year, and the bear saw a beautiful woman with auburn hair enter the forest. She walked to the river and searched the trees, stopping at the base of a tall, expansive tree with shredded remnants of cloth clinging to the jagged edges of bark high above her. The woman smiled and laid her hands on the trunk of the tree she had mended many years before. The tree quivered at her touch and spoke her name, but she was not frightened.

"You have returned," the tree greeted the woman, "and I am grateful for the kind and healing care you gave me when you were but a child. My branches are strong, and my roots grow deep because of you."

The bear had approached silently and sat behind the woman as she listened to the tree. The bear spoke and his voice startled the woman, yet she did not run from him.

"Nature herself gave me the task of caring for the animals of the forest. The forest has grown, and the animals have prospered here. My time is spent caring for the animals, but the plants, too, are in need of care and protection," the bear said. "I know your love of the forest. If it pleases you, I would welcome your assistance, and Nature, who sent me to you, would gift you powers to ease your task."

The tree told the woman to consider the offer and asked her to walk with the bear while she thought. The bear walked along the river to a fallen tree that spanned the rushing water like a bridge. He crossed to the other side, and the woman followed. The bear climbed stair-like stones that rose high above the river to a clearing surrounded by trees, and still the woman followed.

"Here," the bear said, "is where you would make your home and tend to the needs of the plants and trees of the forest."

The woman was pleased and accepted the bear's offer. She made her home and did as the bear said.

Days passed quietly in the forest, and the bear came again to the man. The man enjoyed his work, but he was lonely. The bear asked the man to follow him, and they walked for some time along the river until the man could see a clearing in the trees that he did not remember from before. The bear walked into the clearing and approached a small home built with stones from the river. Hearing the bear approach, the woman stepped from her home and saw that the bear was not alone.

The man and the woman knew each other and smiled. From then on, they were together and were soon married in the forest.

The bear came to them and said, "Your children will grow here and share the strength of both your powers. They will raise their families here as well, and they, too, will have powers to tend the needs of the plants and the animals of our forest. Your kind will know magic and have powers to manage and command the elements around you. They will grow to realize powers beyond our forest: the wind, the waters and the creatures found there. Magic and your kind are known throughout this world in forests, at the highest peaks, and in the water's depths. You are the first of the elves in this new world. Beginning with you, the elves will thrive here and increase in numbers and power."

The bear returned often to visit with his friends and watched as their children grew in the protection of the forest. Each child left the forest. Some found their happiness outside of the forest but held a deep respect and appreciation for the land around them. Others returned in their own time, as the bear had said, bringing their families back to the place they loved, helping their parents, teaching their children about the forest and learning their powers.

"That," Terran finished, "is the legend of how Oakley and Ashtyn came to be."

Sage clapped her hands and smiled while Terran took a seated bow.

"That was wonderful, Terran. You're a really great storyteller." She put her hands on the ground behind her and leaned back on them, stretching her legs out in front. "You said that was a legend. Do you think any of it was real? True?"

"I don't know, but I would like to think so," he shrugged. "We'll never really know for sure, right? I'll tell you the other two about Ambara and Layton when we're up there. Your dad will be in meetings, so we should have plenty of time."

"My dad thought that Anila could get a flying lesson while we're up there. I bet that would be fun." Though a little afraid of heights herself, she smiled at the thought of soaring high above the trees.

"Yeah, it looks like it would be a lot of fun. Too bad the power is leaving us. All the elves used to be able to do that—at least a little, anyway." One corner of his mouth hooked down in disappointment.

Sage sat up hurriedly, a thought crossing her mind. "Do you think—" She looked directly at Terran. "With all of the things that are happening, do you think nature is upset with the elves? Maybe they—I mean *we*—have forgotten why we have our powers in the first place ... or have done something wrong? Maybe nature is taking the power from the elves until we fix whatever it is we need to fix."

Terran wrinkled his brows and pursed his lips, considering the idea. Sage smiled at his expression. Without Douglas or their other friends here, she was noticing things about him in a different way and was enjoying their time together.

"Never really thought of it like that. And what are you smiling at?" he asked with laughter in his voice.

She shook her head, not answering but smiling still. They looked at each other for a long moment before Sage shyly lowered her eyes. It was quiet for what seemed too long.

"Well, I know it's not really getting late or anything, but I'm getting hungry and still have some packing to do," Terran said breaking the silence. He offered his hand to Sage. "So … I guess we'd better go."

They pulled each other from the rocky floor of the cave and found themselves face to face, still holding hands. Sage could feel his his heart pounding, his hand turning cool and damp in hers. It was the first time she could feel his emotions—just a little now. It was the same odd mixture of feelings she herself had felt before. Yet Anila was her friend, and Sage knew it was wrong to even consider these new feelings that were making her stomach jump. She tried to turn away, but her gaze stayed fixed to his.

"Thank you," she said softly, finally letting her hand drop down. Sage turned to retrieve the book lying on the ground near where Terran had been sitting. Terran peeked out through the slit in the rocks, checking for anyone passing by.

"Looks clear. Will you be okay on the rocks?" he asked.

"I'll be fine," Sage said, wondering if he was avoiding taking her hand again.

They climbed the uneven steps to the top in silence and continued until they were on the trail once more. Feeling awkward, Sage held the book tightly against her chest.

"Well," Terran squirmed, "I guess I'll see you tomorrow. My house?"

Sage nodded, and he turned to head toward Ashtyn. She watched him for a moment and then turned the opposite direction for the cabin.

"Sage?" Terran had stopped, and she turned back to face him again. "I had a nice time today … with you."

"Me too, Terran."

He grinned at her, taking a few steps backward before turning in the direction of home. She watched him walk away, allowing the corners of her mouth to rise and the rush of color to fill her cheeks.

CHAPTER 11

To Ambara

Sage's mind wandered back to her time with Terran. She smiled, thinking of the legend he had told her and how captivating he was as a storyteller. That wasn't all she thought of, though, and she shook her head as if it would help shake the feeling of his touch from her memory. Sage tucked the last of her clothes into her backpack for the trip and picked up the book, debating on whether she had any room to take it with her. Her dad told her she would probably need to pack a sweatshirt because of the cooler air and stronger breeze, and it had taken much of the room she had left in her bag.

"It's a long hike," her father said as he entered the room and saw her looking between the bag and the book cradled in her arm. "That backpack is going to feel pretty heavy by the time we reach Ambara. You may want to consider saving your reading for when we get back."

He gave her a wink, and she reluctantly placed the book back into her large duffle bag. Her father had been whistling as he moved from room to room, seeming to be in very upbeat spirits. He grabbed some papers from the kitchen table and all but skipped back to the bedroom. Douglas had peeked over the edge of the loft as their father walked past. He threw his backpack to the floor below and came down the stairs.

"He's excited. Mom said he never thought he would be able to take his own children to see where he grew up. That's what all the whistling's about." He skipped in place, imitating their father.

"I can't believe we have less than two weeks left here," Sage sighed. "This summer just flew by."

Sage had never been disappointed about summer ending or the start of a new school year before. She loved school, being with her friends, and leaving the boredom the end of summer usually brought. It hadn't been the same this summer; it certainly hadn't been boring, anyway. And though she missed a few of her friends at home, she thought leaving her new friends for an entire school year would be much more difficult.

"Yeah, I'm going to miss it here, too," Douglas agreed.

Douglas had been excited about entering his senior year of high school. He was sure to be the captain of the basketball team and was a straight-A student. Even though he was so successful and popular in school, Sage could tell by the tone in his voice that they felt the same about the cabin and their new friends. Douglas grabbed Sage's backpack with his own and set them by the door for their trip to Ambara the next morning.

"Maybe we could come visit at winter break, or maybe Lamar, Terran, and Anila could come to our house," he suggested.

She smiled. "I wonder how they would like the city."

"See you for dinner tomorrow?" Adel asked Avery early the next day.

"Yeah, if we get a good start after lunch, we should be back in time for dinner." He kissed his wife and threw his pack over his shoulder, stepping out of the way for Sage and Douglas to say their goodbyes. Adel waved to her family until they were out of sight in the shadow of the forest.

Sage was excited about the trip to Oakley and Ambara. She was also looking forward to spending more time with Terran. Her smile at the thought of him faded. She would never want to hurt Anila. The end of summer would take her away from Terran and her newfound feelings for him. That, at least, would be the one good thing about going back to school, she thought.

Sage was jolted to an abrupt stop as she walked into Douglas's backpack. She had been walking, unconsciously following the others on the trail while her mind continued to wander to thoughts of Terran.

"Ouch," she moaned.

"Well, watch where you're going," Douglas laughed as Sage rubbed her sore nose. "This ... is ... cool."

Sage had forgotten that Douglas had not yet been to Ashtyn or seen the bridge that he was now admiring. He stepped onto the bridge and ran his hand over the carvings on the handrail, stopping in the center to watch the river flowing below.

Sage looked up at the ash tree standing tall on the edge of the embankment. She smiled, thinking about the legend Terran had told her. Maybe this is the very tree from the story, she imagined as she spread her hands on its trunk. The tree trembled at her touch. Sage leapt back in alarm. Her heart pounded in her chest, and the air seemed to be sucked from her lungs, leaving her staring up at the tree and gasping for breath.

"Are you okay?"

Her dad ran off the bridge to her. He followed her eyes up the tree.

"What did you see?"

"I'm fine, I'm fine," she said still wide-eyed. "I just thought … It's nothing. I'm fine."

She ran to the middle of the bridge with Douglas, and the three continued to the stone steps leading to Ashtyn. As she reached the top stair, Sage glanced back to the tree. She paused there a moment, wondering, before stepping through the curtain of ivy into the clearing.

"The village square is up ahead. Like Layton, that's where most of the daily activity happens … *used* to happen," Avery explained.

Their dad was already pointing out the sights to Douglas and describing what used to be. Sage was glad she didn't have to talk; she was still a bit shaken. *It must have been my imagination*, she thought.

"… the Council building. That's where Sage saw me …"

She wanted to see Terran and tell him what had just happened. She wondered what he would say, if he would even believe her. *Maybe I'll just wait to tell him when no one else is around*, she decided as they stepped into the garden outside Terran's house. Linaeve opened the door and greeted Avery.

"Welcome back, Sage," she smiled. She grasped Sage's hand warmly before reaching for Douglas. "You must be Douglas. Terran is very fond of you and truly values your friendship. Please come in," she said, opening her arm to the house. "Terran just went to grab his bag."

A thud hit Sage's stomach as Jason came to the door with Frayne. *Oh my gosh! We didn't think of inviting Jason to come along*, Sage thought. She was instantly disappointed in herself for not thinking of inviting him.

"Are they here?" Jason asked.

Sage could feel he was excited, making her feel even worse. Maybe Dad invited him, she thought hopefully.

"No, Jason. They will be here shortly. though." Frayne grinned at his nephew, patting him on his shoulder. "Jason's parents are coming to visit for a few days. He hasn't seen them in months, so he's pretty excited. We all are," Frayne explained. Sage was instantly relieved. "You sure this is no trouble, Avery?"

"Not at all," Avery replied. "All the kids get along really well, and they don't have a lot of time left together before Sage and Douglas head back to school."

Terran had come down the stairs while Frayne and Avery talked. He set his eyes on Sage first before turning his attention to Douglas, flashing him a friendly smile. Terran returned his eyes to Sage just as Avery asked if everyone was ready to head out. She was grateful for the interruption. It made it easier to break eye contact with him.

Everyone waved back to Jason and Terran's parents as they walked farther into the village, farther than Sage had gone on her previous visits. The main path from the village continued to wind between houses and tall ash trees. To Sage's relief, Douglas had joined up to walk with Terran. She walked with her dad, letting him point out landmarks and share his memories. They passed a large grassy area spotted with cows and sheep, and a small bakery that smelled strongly of yeasty breads. Sage could hear the river again. Her dad told her they were going to follow the trail along the river as it wound through the woods and up to Oakley. The trail climbed at a steady but easy pace, and the woods were becoming thick along the path again. Shadows sheltered them from the already hot morning sun. Only the river was out of the cover of trees, and the water sparkled in the light. Sage could see a building, larger than a house and unlike the other buildings of Ashtyn. As they got closer, she saw a wheel turning slowly with the power of the river. It was a mill.

"It remains empty and unused for much of the year anymore," he explained. "We still take our grain harvest there every fall for processing. Our crop is much smaller now than it was when I was your age."

They had been walking for about ten minutes when Sage began noticing changes in the forest around her. The trees were a mix of ash and oak now and spaced farther apart, making room for the broad, leafy oaks. They were tall with massive trunks, verifying what Sage had already suspected: They were entering an older part of the forest. The smells, the undergrowth, the overall feel were very different from the forest she had grown so familiar with. Soon the trees were almost entirely oak. The sun found it harder to penetrate the canopy, and

Sage's eyes had to adjust to the new level of darkness. Squirrels darted in front of them and up a nearby tree. Birds chattered and flitted between branches.

It may be darker and shadowy here, she thought, smiling, *but it is certainly not gloomy.*

These woods were very much alive. They were vibrant and electric, stimulating her senses. Sage didn't know if it was the newness of the place or the energy she sensed, but she felt refreshed, stronger. She closed her eyes for a moment and took a long deep breath, drinking in the smells. When she opened her eyes again, the boys were still lost in conversation ahead of her. Her connection to this place was hers alone ... and in a way, it spoke to her.

Terran and Douglas had talked the entire way, barely paying attention to the forest that surrounded them. Terran, she supposed, had walked the trail to Anila's too many times to count and was no longer surprised or impressed by the changes around him. He glanced back at her now and again, as if checking to make sure she and her father were still there. Sage had tried to appear as if she wasn't noticing, glancing past him into the forest or on the trail ahead. More than once she found she was not fast enough to avoid his eyes, and they would smile at each other and she would blush, making her thankful for the dim light of the forest. Anila would be with them soon, and that, Sage knew, would make it easier for her to keep her mind off Terran.

She began to hear voices ahead and knew they were very close to Oakley. There were people near the river and children splashing in its calm water. A friendly-looking older couple, dressed in the airy traditional clothing of the elves, walked toward them on the trail, smiling and nodding in greeting. Avery stopped to visit with them, telling the others he would be along shortly. Terran and Douglas continued to walk, with Sage a few steps behind.

This must be it, Sage thought. A short distance ahead of them, two enormous oak trees stood on each side of the trail, their branches woven intricately together, making a grand arch. There were people on the other side of the entrance, maybe even more than in Ashtyn, walking in an expansive open area that Sage assumed was the village square. A single, colossal oak tree, rising tall above the others, stood in the center, its limbs extended out in all directions, nearly covering the space. Long, brightly colored triangular flags dangled below its branches, waving gently in the breeze. Sage looked for more signs of the village—houses, a Council building—but saw nothing more.

"Sweet!"

Sage turned at her brother's exclamation to see Terran pointing into the trees. She gasped. Houses. Houses built high in the oaks circling the town center. Each one was different, as different as the tree that held it. Cheerfully painted rope bridges connected tree to tree, resembling swags of streamers at a birthday party. On the occasional tree, stairs spiraled from its base to large, railed platforms where the rope bridges joined. People were sitting on smaller platforms outside their homes, their children sitting along the railed edges, swinging their feet.

"What do you think?"

Sage jumped and gave a high shriek. She was so engrossed in what she was seeing she hadn't even noticed her father coming up alongside her. He put his arm around her shoulder to help calm her but couldn't help laughing out loud.

"It seems I have been doing that to you a lot lately," he said apologetically. "You must have been lost in thought again. Different than Ashtyn, eh?"

"Yes. Very," she said, still with her hand over her pounding heart. "It's wonderful. Do they have roofs?"

"Do they have roofs? You're funny," he chuckled, shaking his head. "We should get to Anila's house. The boys are already heading up there."

Sure enough, she saw the two of them as they disappeared behind the backside of the spiral staircase, reappearing moments later as it circled to the front. She and her father walked to the same staircase and climbed to the platform. Terran and Douglas were leaning against the railing, waiting for them. Sage's eyes widened. Now that she had reached the top of the stairs, she could see beyond the trees that lay on the edge of the open, rectangular village square. Rope pathways led farther back into the forest, deeper than she could see an end to. Every few trees, a home had been built. She could see them much better now, the way they looked, their sizes and shapes. Shake siding seemed most common, looking like and blending with the bark of the tree that held them. Some homes were very earthy looking, with brown moss and ivy covering the exteriors. But all of the homes were tall, climbing into the highest reaches of the boughs.

She was mesmerized with the beauty, the smells, and the fantasy of the place. It was a place she could never have dreamed existed, even knowing what she now knew about the elves. As she took in every little detail, she caught Terran smiling at her.

"What?" she said.

"Oh, nothing," he replied. "I just think you like it here."

"It's beautiful," she said dreamily, still looking around her in every direction.

"It's nothing new to me," he continued. He moved a few steps closer to her and leaned against the railing. "I've always spent a lot of time here. It is a beautiful place, though. You should see it at night. It's even better."

Sage joined him at the railing, looking out to the tree in the middle of the town.

"I suppose you think I'm silly being so taken by it all … but it is all new to me," she said.

"I don't think you're silly," he told her. "It reminds me—watching you—of the first time my aunt and uncle took me to the city where they live. All those buildings, the lights, noise, everything—and that would be nothing new to you. Come on. We need to get a move on if we're going to catch the lift."

"Lift?" she asked, following him off the platform and onto a rope bridge leading into the forest. They landed at more platforms and crossed more bridges until she had lost her sense of which direction they had entered the village. She saw her father and brother standing inside the doorway of a home with gray-brown shake siding and window boxes overflowing in colorful flowers. She and Terran crossed a final short bridge to join them at the front entrance. Anila ran out and threw her arms around Terran, nearly knocking him off balance.

"You have to see her! She's beautiful," she exclaimed, looking between Terran and Sage. "She's here with Delaney right now—sleeping of course. Come in, come in!"

She was so excited she seemed to be bouncing into the house, turning to the first room on her left. The room was narrow and already crowded with Anila's family. Anila ran right up to a bassinet standing in the center of the room. It was rocking slowly side to side. She beamed as she looked down at the sleeping baby dressed in a pale lavender sleeping gown.

"Her name is Parisa," she proudly announced.

"A-hem." A man Sage assumed was Anila's father raised an eyebrow at her.

"Oh, right. Sorry," she grimaced. "Sage. Douglas. This is my father, Keelin; my mother, Hannah; and my sister, Delaney."

"Very nice to finally meet you both," her father said warmly, extending his hand. "You have given Anila a great gift," he told Sage. "She knows her true powers now, and we have our happy, light-hearted daughter back. Thank you."

Sage smiled in embarrassment. Then she and Douglas took turns shakings hands with the rest of the members of Anila's family. Conversations filled the room. Sage felt very comfortable with Anila's family, laughing easily at the stories Delaney told about Anila.

"The clothes you make are beautiful," Sage complimented Delaney.

"Thank you." Delaney nodded her appreciation. "It is a passion of mine, and Anila is a wonderful model," she said stroking Anila's long black hair.

All the talk and laughter in the room started the baby crying, signaling to the group that the visit was over.

"Time to head out," Avery said in a hushed voice. "If everything goes as scheduled, we should be taking the midday lift back tomorrow."

Anila kissed the baby now resting in Delaney's arms and waved to her parents as the group slid out the door. They followed Avery across the maze of bridges and back down to the ground, walking beyond the town center to the trail running along the river's edge.

Sage figured the trip would seem a lot quicker with someone to talk to. She would be able to devote her attention to Anila and not to her thoughts about Terran. It crossed her mind just then how she would never be able to describe to her friends at home what it was like talking with Anila. *No*, she thought, *a conversation with Anila is something that has to be experienced*. She smiled because, just then, Anila was talking even faster than normal, telling everyone about the baby. Sage marveled at the way she kept speaking without pausing to take a breath. *Maybe the power of the wind makes it easier to go on and on like that*, Sage thought, chuckling to herself. She watched Anila's hands fly around wildly while she continued to talk. She was fun to watch, so animated and happy. Sage believed she must be the life of every gathering here, and if she went to her school, she could be the most popular girl there. She was beautiful, too. Even now she made shorts and a plain t-shirt stylish, her long, shiny black hair tied neatly back at the nape of her neck for the hike. *Yes*, Sage thought, *she would be the most beautiful, most popular girl in school and, because of the kind of person she is, she would never understand what all the fuss was about.*

The walk was becoming increasingly steep. Any other trail in the park with the same rise would be recommended only for experienced hikers, but the broad, deep steps carved into the trail took much of the work out of the hike. Still, the way was long and tiring. Sage found herself watching the trail closely for footing, all the while trying not to miss any of the changes in the landscape around her. A mountain rose sharply on the opposite side of the now gently flowing stream that would become a strong river as it approached Oakley, enclosing it on that side. Small brooks running from the forest crossed the path of the trail. Run-off waterfalls cascaded from the rock face and splashed into the stream. She could smell the distinct, fresh scent of pines encroaching on the oak forest. It was becoming lighter up ahead, and Sage knew the forest would soon become all pine, offering less shade from the nearly midday sun.

"Just a little farther," her father announced, pointing to the approaching curve the trail and stream took to the left.

They rounded the curve and found themselves face to face with the side of the rocky mountain. It felt as if they had been walking for hours, and Sage's heart sank, thinking they still had to climb the monstrosity in front of them.

"Did we miss it?" Terran asked Avery.

"No. It's still a little early, maybe ten minutes or so," he replied.

"Miss what?" Sage asked, dropping her backpack to the ground and sitting gently on the brown pine needles next to the trail.

"The lift," Terran said. He had his hand over his eyes like a visor, looking up to the top of the mountain. "It used to run all day and into the evening but only runs a few times a day now. Oh, look! It's on its way down."

Everyone scanned the mountain to see what Terran had spotted, shielding their eyes from the glare of the sun. A tiny brown square was descending from the top of the mountain almost directly above them. It moved slowly and gave everyone a chance to rest while waiting. Backpacks came off tired shoulders and everyone searched for a cool bottle of water. Her father had been right. Sage was glad that she had decided not to bring her book. She shrugged her shoulders, trying to loosen their tightness. After a few minutes, everyone turned their eyes upward to check the progress of their approaching ride.

Sage could see the lift well now. It was a large open box with railings, which didn't please her. It reminded her of the glass elevators at a fancy hotel they had stayed in when she was younger. Douglas loved the height and the speed of that elevator, delighting in making Sage look at things far below them. Sage had never had a problem with heights before that elevator but had never before been as high as it had gone. For that reason, she wasn't looking forward to the slow rise to the top of the mountain. She glanced up again, seeing the people aboard looking down and waving. Finally, the lift box reached the ground, and the passengers opened the railing gate to exit. Avery greeted the departing passengers as they exchanged places on the lift and closed the gate.

CHAPTER 12

Soaring

The ride to the top of the mountain was slow and steady. By the looks of it, Sage had expected the lift to be rickety and creaky, but just the opposite was true. Even so, she stood toward the back, closest to the mountain and away from the three open edges. Her family and friends leaned unafraid against the wooden rail as they continued to climb skyward, pointing to notable aspects of the landscape. Sage's nervousness began to disappear as the lift climbed above the trees and showed the group a spectacular view. Below them, green treetops flowed in gentle hills. The mountains rose around them in staggered elevations yet still never blocked the shimmer of the lake far off in the distance. She turned her head upward, seeing that they had nearly reached the top of the mountain, and prepared to exit the lift.

Anila, as if readying for a special event, had taken her brush from her backpack, removed her hair band, and brushed her long black hair smooth again. Sage could see that besides her father, Anila was the most excited of the group to be visiting Ambara. This would be the first time since her childhood that she had made the trip to the sky village and, more importantly, the first time since discovering her true powers. Sage could feel the anticipation building inside of Anila, could almost feel Anila's heartbeat quicken. Everyone turned to face the mountain, watching as the lift cleared the top.

Avery opened the gate to a rocky plateau dotted with large pine trees and patches of bright green grass where mountain goats grazed. It was flanked on the right side by a higher section of the mountain. Sage could see to the other open edges of the plateau. It was as if this great expanse was created simply as a platform for viewing the forests below. One by one the group stepped from the lift, continuing to look at the surrounding view. Just as Anila left the lift, a strong wind, seemingly from nowhere, blew a forceful welcome. Anila's hair flew wildly back behind her, and she closed her eyes against it. It was obvious that the feel of the powerful, cool air on her face gave her great pleasure. She smiled and took in a deep breath of the fresh air. The wind died away, and she opened her eyes, her cheeks flushed pink. Sage thought Anila looked even more radiant than ever before.

The group followed Avery across the plateau, approaching a modest gathering of people forming a semi-circle around something Sage could not yet see. Many of their eyes were aimed skyward. Sage scanned the sky along with them until she spotted a huge bird circling, diving, and gliding above. Drawing closer still, she realized that it was actually not a bird at all, but a young girl wearing stiff, feathered wings on her arms. She was on a harness suspended from a long arm attached to the bordering mountain. A tethering rope was affixed to the girl and held by a tall, slightly built woman standing in the center of the crowd. The crowd applauded the girl, who had begun her descent, landing swiftly in the circle. She was quickly released from the harness and aided in the removal of her winged arms. Avery continued walking through the now dispersing crowd until he reached the woman and young girl.

"Hello, Avery," the woman said warmly. "Jake will be along shortly."

"Thanks, Aderyn," he replied, turning his attention to the young girl. "That was some very fine flying, Sora."

"Thank you, sir," she panted, the thrill of her flight showing on her bright cheeks.

Avery stepped aside so the group could see the woman and girl more clearly. She and her daughter held a close resemblance, large brown eyes, tanned skin, and dark hair cut short to frame their slender faces. Sage couldn't help but think they perfectly matched her image of a fairy, delicate in features and graceful in movement.

"I would like you all to meet Aderyn," he said gesturing to the woman, "and her daughter, Sora," indicating the young girl. "Aderyn and her husband, Jake, have been my friends for a great number of years. They have been kind enough to invite us to stay in their home tonight." He turned a little, addressing the woman and girl. "Aderyn. Sora. I would like to introduce you to a few people. Of course, you both know Terran." Terran bowed his head respectfully. "These are my children, Douglas and Sage."

"So wonderful to finally meet you both," Aderyn said excitedly and warmheartedly. "We have been waiting for this day for a *very* long time. Your father has told us so much about you. Well, my husband and I feel like we know you both already." She grabbed Douglas's hand in both of hers and turned to give Sage an unexpected hug.

"Aderyn. This is Anila," he announced, stepping aside to allow the woman to better see Anila.

"It is nice to officially meet you, Anila," Aderyn said. "I have seen you many times before as you were growing up in Oakley … and also, I'm sure, at the Yearly Gathering. Your parents have been friends of mine and my husband for many years, though distance has kept us from knowing you better."

"Yes, ma'am," Anila replied. "I have heard about you and Sora from Jake and recognized you right away."

Aderyn's eyes narrowed as she studied Anila, looking at her from head to toe and back again as if checking to see if she were acceptable. Anila fidgeted uncomfortably under Aderyn's gaze. Finally, the woman smiled and turned to Avery.

"Yes, I think she is more than strong enough," she told him.

Avery nodded, seeming to understand what she was talking about, but everyone else exchanged looks of confusion.

"I'll tell you what she means after we eat some lunch," Avery laughed. "I'm starving!"

Aderyn, still smiling, excused Sora and herself with a nod. Avery led the group to a nearby cluster of pine trees and pulled a bag of sandwiches and apples from his duffle bag. The group sat in the grassy shade of the pines to eat and rest. Only a few minutes had passed when Sage saw a man crossing to them. She recognized him from the Council meeting that she had interrupted in Ashtyn. That seemed so long ago to her now. This was the man her father had let take over for him then and whom he waited for now. He looked very pleasant with bright cheery eyes and a broad, easy smile. He was a darker skinned man, olive in complexion and weathered from the summer sun and winds. His straight, shoulder-length black hair was pulled neatly back away from his face and shined like Anila's hair did when in the sunlight. He laid a hand on Avery's shoulder and beamed at the rest of the group sitting on the ground.

"Well, isn't this a fine-looking group!" he exclaimed.

Avery stood now and clasped his friend's hand. As he proceeded to introduce everyone, each rose from the ground to shake the man's hand.

"This is my dearest friend, Jake," Avery said fondly.

Sage could feel the genuine love her father had for his friend and that he was truly excited to finally introduce his own children to Jake.

After the introductions, Jake clapped his hands together loudly and smiled. "Now then, who would like a tour of our fine village of Ambara?" Expecting no objections and without waiting for one, he turned swiftly and began walking toward the place they had first met Aderyn and Sora. When the group reached the center of the plateau, the place where the harness was suspended from the mountain, Jake stopped and turned to them.

"This is where our young elves practice flying techniques. They use the wind to support and elevate themselves when they have flying wings on. Once they learn how to successfully manipulate the air around them, they are allowed to practice without the security of the safety harness. It is still useful to learn this skill, even though we don't have the need of the wings as in times past. With the lift and fine trails leading down from the mountain, we rarely have a need to use the wings for transportation." He smiled again, looking directly at Anila. "This area also serves as our main gathering place, as there is no other spot large enough. I'll show you why," he said waving his hand for everyone to follow him again.

They walked through the practice circle and toward the opposite edge of the plateau, a peninsula of sorts, with only one of its sides bordered by the mountain. Sage had no idea she would be able to see so far—miles and miles. She was certain she could see the town of Grace on the outskirts of the park and several large rivers that she figured fed the lakes. They walked right up to the farthest edge visible from the lift. Jake stopped with his toes extended over the edge, waiting for the others to come up as well. He was looking down, and soon everyone else was there doing the same, except for Sage, who stood back behind her father, still too close to the edge for her taste. Anila gasped at the sight below her. Douglas called out his usual, "Sweet." Sage inched a bit closer to see what they were so excited about. Terran looked behind and saw Sage trying to peek over the edge.

"Here, Sage. This is a great spot."

Sage sighed and moved near him, trying not to show her fear of the high elevation. She wanted to grab his arm and hold on to him while she looked but forced a weak, trembling smile instead and took a step forward. After a deep breath, she tilted her head over the edge. It went straight down, no gradual descent, no trees to break her fall. Her head felt light and her balance unsteady. Sage took a little step backward, certain the blood had drained from her face.

"Did you see it?" Douglas asked her.

"What?" It had been more of a peek than a good look and she had seen nothing but the long drop she would take to the bottom of the mountain if she lingered over the edge any longer.

"The town! Didn't you see it? Look again, Sage."

She slowly slid one foot so her toes were even with the edge and then slid the other up to meet it. Cautiously she leaned forward, dropping her head. There below her were canopies, awnings like you might see above the entrance of a shop. Unrailed walkways carved into the mountain ran under the canopies, with people walking fearlessly along them. That was enough for her, and she took another step backward, nodding recognition to Douglas.

"The village is built into the side of the mountain. The awnings you see cover the entrances to our homes," Jake explained. "Come this way," he motioned to his left, following the edge of the cliff. They could see more canopies on the opposite side of an enormous V-shaped fissure in the mountain. Three, sometimes four, rows of homes, stacked like the stories of an apartment building, stretched across the facing side of the mountain. Douglas, unafraid of heights, walked right to the edge and looked down along this side of the cliff.

"Cool. They are on this side, too." He pointed down past his feet.

"Yes," Avery nodded. "The homes are on these three faces of the mountain, and Jake lives right over ... there." He moved his hand through the air to the point of the V shape where the two cliff faces met. "On the second level down ... the one with the blue awning. Do you see it?"

Everyone followed his finger, counting down the levels until they had spotted the entrance to Jake's home.

"You will be our welcome guests for the night," Jake said happily.

"How do we get down there?" Douglas asked, ready to go exploring.

Jake walked back a few steps in the direction of the peninsula and stepped right off the edge. Sage shrieked, throwing her hands up to shield her eyes. Everyone was laughing. She peeked through her fingers to see Jake standing in what appeared to be midair about a foot below the cliff's edge. Steps. He was standing on the first step of a staircase that could not be seen until you were looking straight down at it. Sage's heart was beating hard, thumping in her ears. So far, she wasn't sure she really cared very much for Ambara.

"That wasn't funny!" she scolded. It took time for Sage to recover her breath, almost as much time as it took the others to stop laughing.

"Well," Jake continued as things quieted down. "I guess there is only one more thing to take care of before we turn you young people loose on Ambara."

With that he clapped his hands and began walking once more. Avery and Jake moved briskly, the others close behind. They came to a stop in the center of the plateau, greeted with a warm smile from Aderyn. Avery, Jake and Aderyn exchanged eager, knowing glances. The four friends looked at them curiously, like parents might look upon a child they know is trying to keep a secret.

"Aderyn has graciously offered to help me with something," Avery announced, unable to contain his excitement. "She is going to be giving Anila her first flying lesson."

Everyone turned to look at Anila, clapping and cheering. Anila stood with one hand over her mouth, looking at Avery. No one, except for Sage, knew the intensity of what Anila was feeling at that moment. It seemed a very long time before Anila lowered her hand and, with watery eyes, she bowed her head to Avery and the couple.

"Thank you." Her voice wavered with a mix of emotion and exhilaration. She clasped her hands together in front of her face and bounced on her toes joyfully. Avery and Jake waved goodbye, saying they would meet up with everyone at dinner.

"Come on, Anila." Aderyn motioned for her to enter the circle. "Let's get you into the harness. I have taught dozens and dozens of beginners. The most common belief is that the wind will just come to you and support you in flight. This is the first thing you have to realize; you will have to use your powers to control the wind, manipulate it. Unlike birds that can use their wings to lift and propel themselves, you won't be able to flap your wings, and you will not rise or soar without the wind at your disposal," Aderyn began as she finished hooking Anila snuggly into the harness. Anila listened, absorbing every detail of Aderyn's directions. "It is common for beginners to only make it up with the help of the instructor holding the harness, and they don't stay up for very long the first few times. When you have finished your lesson, you will find yourself feeling greatly taxed, both physically and … magically. It will be important for you to be aware of how you are feeling, so you do not overextend yourself. Understand?"

Anila nodded, anxious to begin. Aderyn smiled and continued with more instructions. That wasn't what Anila wanted to hear. Sage chuckled to herself at Anila's disappointment in having to wait longer, but finally Aderyn moved away from Anila and took the rope to support her.

"Now, let's get down to business. We are going to practice a bit here on the ground to go through the basics of what you will be doing when you are fifty feet in the air. Put your arms out to your sides, hands stretched out and palms down. Okay, close your eyes and imagine a great breeze coming from below you. Your job is to resist it—to fight against it and keep it from blowing your arms and hands straight above your head."

Anila listened intently and closely followed Aderyn's directions. Her hair began to move gently, her shirt rippling. Quickly, the air circling around Anila could be felt by Sage and the two boys. Sage found herself squinting her eyes against dust that had blown up from the ground. She struggled to focus on Anila again, finding her hovering several inches above the ground, apparently unaware.

"Excellent, Anila!" Aderyn praised. "Now keep your thoughts and open your eyes."

Anila did what she was told, but when she realized she was no longer standing firmly on the ground, her eyes widened and her concentration broke. She seemed to lose her balance in midair and toppled to the ground, landing hard on her rear end. Douglas jogged over and helped her stand. She smoothed her clothes and rubbed her bruised bottom. A few people from the town had come to watch. They clapped for her small accomplishment.

"Oooowwww," she moaned.

"It seems you are already ready for your wings," Aderyn said holding two long, feathered arm extensions.

She slid them onto Anila's arms and tightened the adjustable straps. Two longer straps went across her chest and across her back, connecting the two arms. They were stiff, and Anila was unable to bend her elbows. All in all, Sage thought they looked rather uncomfortable, but sliding them on had given Anila a thrill. She glowed, flushed from the wind and new anticipation.

"Remember what you did a moment ago. In order to control your speed and direction, you have to be able to visualize how the wind must move around you to get you where you intend to go. I will be holding the rope to the harness as a spotter, so you will be perfectly safe to experiment a little." Aderyn's expression grew more serious. "Anila," she said to gain her complete attention. "Don't expect too much this first time. It takes a lot of practice, and I don't want you to feel disappointed. You have already done more on the ground then some of my students do the first three or four sessions."

Anila nodded again and took in a slow deep breath. Aderyn gathered the rope, pulling it taut and wrapping it several times around her gloved hands. She braced her slender frame, anchoring herself to the spot. Then, smiling at Anila, she said, "All right, have fun."

Anila closed her eyes, arms out as before. She raised her head to the sky, the sun full on her face. Again, the wind began to circulate around Anila, lifting her into the air. She opened her eyes, which were narrowed with focus. Instantly she ascended straight up into the sky. News had carried about the session, and more people had come from their homes to watch. Everyone clapped for her. Her legs went behind her, and with great speed she circled to the farthest reaches of the harness. She was graceful and powerful. *She belongs here*, Sage thought. Anila, with her naturally joyful personality, was happier than Sage had ever sensed. Her eyes were closed again, feeling the cold wind on her pink cheeks. The growing group below cheered and applauded for what Anila had been able to accomplish in her first session. Then, with startled gasps from those watching, including Aderyn, Anila stopped in midair, her long hair flying around her. She had lowered her winged arms to her side, yet she hovered there in the sky with the air swirling around her in a whirlwind, unsupported by the safety rope. She was in her own little world, like a trance, oblivious to the astonished people below her. Sage and Douglas knew from the crowd's reaction that she had done something amazing, but having little experience in the elf world, they didn't know what it was. Anila lingered there a moment longer before opening her eyes and calmly raising her arms to the sides. She spiraled slowly and gracefully to the ground. With roaring cheers from the now sizable crowd, she landed, full of energy and breathing normally, as if she had exerted no effort at all.

The people crowded in on Anila before Aderyn could even release her hold on the safety rope. Sage, Terran, and Douglas were pushed back by the encroaching crowd. They watched as Aderyn squeezed her way to the center of the throng, unfastening the harness straps and the straps holding the wings securely to Anila's arms. People were still closing around them, asking Anila questions and congratulating her. Sage could feel Anila becoming anxious and uncomfortable.

She turned with concern to Douglas. "All those people ... Anila's getting really upset!"

In an instant, Douglas was weaving through the crowd to where Anila and Aderyn were standing. With help from Aderyn, he guided Anila back to where Terran and Sage stood waiting, his arm circled protectively around her shoulder. The excited and well-intentioned crowd followed at their heels. Aderyn, in a voice larger than her size would suggest, spoke to them with her hands up in front of her to keep them from pressing in more closely.

"My friends, as you all know, this was our guest's first flying session. I realize you are all very excited about what you have seen and want to speak with her, but ..." she lowered her hands, "right now she needs rest and water. There will be opportunity for you to talk with her later."

She waited without moving until the disappointed but apparently understanding group slowly began to disperse. They left toward the village, turning and pointing back at Anila as they walked. Douglas had grabbed Anila's bag and gotten her water bottle for her. She thanked him, taking a long drink.

Aderyn turned to Anila, who was sitting in the grass, shaken. Sage couldn't quite discern the flow of emotions from Aderyn. She seemed nervous yet excited. Fearful, too. Aderyn collected her thoughts and smiled unconvincingly before speaking.

"You were wonderful," she said quietly but encouragingly. She took a spot sitting across from Anila. "You say you just discovered your power this summer?"

Anila nodded. "Yes. Sage figured it out. I never thought—Well, with my parents and sister being so good with plants— Did I do something wrong?" Tears welled in her eyes but did not fall.

"No, oh no," Aderyn assured her, placing a hand on her cheek. "It's just that no one—that I have ever heard of—could do what you just did after a lifetime of flying. The people who saw you do that were reminded of stories handed down from generation to generation—old legends." She stared at Anila with amazement. "You don't even look tired."

"What did she do, exactly?" Douglas asked.

"I don't think anyone has ever just stopped like that—in the air. That's when everyone got so quiet for a minute before they started cheering. Is that what it was?" Terran asked Aderyn.

She nodded thoughtfully.

"You have a control of your powers that I have never seen before—that *they've* never seen before. If you're up to it, let's try again tonight after dinner. We can experiment a little more." She looked at Anila's beautiful face, still distressed from being trapped within the crowd. "People are going to want to talk to you whenever they see you. They are going to be happy for you, but some might also be a little … frightened," she said with concern in her voice. She stood up and gathered the harness and wings. "You may want to stay close to your friends while you're here—and don't spread the news about meeting again tonight. It will spread fast enough on its own."

"Yes, ma'am," Anila spoke, her voice trembling.

They all watched Aderyn head back toward the village.

Sage looked at Terran. "I think it's time you told us the legend of Ambara."

CHAPTER 13

The Legend of Ambara

Terran explained to Douglas and Anila that Sage had mentioned wanting to learn more about the history of the elves and that he had begun by telling her the legend of Ashtyn and Oakley. He promised Douglas he would tell him the full legend soon, but for now he just needed to know that a man who loved the animals of the forest and a woman who loved the plants were gifted powers by Nature herself and that they were the first of the elves in this land. "They married, and from them, their family grew to fill what are now the villages of Ashtyn and Oakley." He cleared his throat.

For many years, the plants and animals of the forest were cared for and protected by the descendants of the man and woman of Ashtyn and Oakley. A beautiful girl from Oakley loved the forest but was unsatisfied and had a desire to know what lay beyond. She was always asking questions of everyone. "How high are the mountains?" "How deep is the lake?" "What is on the other side of the mountains?"

She also wanted to know where the river came from. Her parents told her, "From the mountains" and that was all they could say. She asked other elves in her village, elves considered to be wise, "Where does the river come from? Where does it begin?" They would all answer the same way, pointing to the mountaintops and saying, "From the mountains."

One day, the girl decided she would go alone to find the beginning of the river. She followed the river, watching it grow smaller as the land became steeper and steeper. The trees changed; the smells changed. She jumped over small streams that joined together to make the river. The girl marveled at the water flowing down the rocks to the stream and danced in the cool waterfalls splashing into the stream from the rocks above. She continued to follow the diminishing water until she found herself looking up at the sheer face of the mountain. She was awed by the size of the mountain. The girl touched the rocks of the mountain, feeling their coolness. The cry of an animal, one she did not recognize, drew her attention. The sound of this animal did not frighten her. Instead, it filled her with more curiosity. She listened closely, waiting for the sound to come again. When it did, her eyes lifted to search the skies. Instantly she spotted it, a great bird soaring in circles above the tallest peak of the mountain. It was graceful, and watching it left the girl breathless with a longing she had never felt before.

Terran's eyes were lifted to the sky with his arm stretched high, circling. Sage had been mesmerized watching Terran tell the legend of Ashtyn and Oakley. It was no different now, except that Douglas and Anila, too, had also been drawn in by his storytelling. Anila smiled, picturing the story in her head, sitting with her arms around her drawn-up knees. Douglas looked perfectly relaxed, reclining back on his elbows, his long legs stretched in front of him, crossed at the ankles.

The girl searched the mountain for a way to climb to its top. There was no easy passage; she would have to climb the rock face. Slowly the girl climbed, finding rocks that jutted out from the mountain enough for her to secure her feet and grip with her hands. She had stopped looking upward, as it had been daunting to see how little she had conquered and how much was left to go. Even so, the girl's determination to reach the top did not wane. She forced her weary body to continue up and up. The bird circled, moving closer to the girl and shrieking. The winds were cold and felt refreshing on her hot, overworked body. She reached above, feeling for a handhold, but felt the flat top of the mountain instead. Quickly she pulled herself over the edge and lay down on her belly on the cool, dusty ground to catch her breath and rest her cramping, blistered hands.

Another screech from the bird roused her. She pushed herself up and sat back on her knees to look around. The top of the mountain was flat, with a larger mountain face to one side. She surveyed the plateau to all sides, still too tired to stand. Quietly she watched the bird circle above. It was an eagle, she realized, though she had never before seen one. She was sure it was crying out to her. Still shaky and stiff from the climb, she rose to her feet. A great, cold wind gusted its greeting. The girl loved the feel of the breath of the wind on her face and the feel of it dancing through—

Terran stopped abruptly and looked across to Anila. She met his gaze with understanding and lowered her eyes to the ground in thought.

"What?!" Douglas looked back and forth between the two.

It hadn't occurred to Sage until now that Anila would already have heard these legends as she was growing up. But now, something in Terran's retelling had taken them both by surprise. Anila lifted her head to look directly at Douglas.

"The girl loved the feel of the breath of the wind on her face and the sensation of it dancing through her long, raven hair," she said.

Douglas raised his eyebrows. "That's … interesting," Douglas said slowly. "Probably just a coincidence, don't you think?" He smiled at her.

"Yeah, probably," Terran said. He tried to sound convincing, but Sage knew that everyone was picturing Anila with the wind blowing around her as she stepped from the lift only hours before.

"It's a story, Anila. And Douglas is right, it's just a coincidence—the description, I mean." Sage laid a hand on Anila's knee.

"Oh, I know that," she replied. "I just don't want people to be frightened of me. I'm sure Aderyn knows the story and is already worried, what with all the similarities."

"There are more, then? Similarities, I mean. In the story?" Sage was asking Terran more than Anila. "Keep going, Terran."

The girl breathed in the cold air, her closed eyes lifted to the sky. Again, the bird shrieked down at the girl. She opened her eyes and followed its large, dark shape against the blue sky. It was beautiful, and her heart beat faster to see such power and grace moving so close to her.

Sage tried to hide the shiver that ran down her neck. Those were the same words she thought of as she watched Anila soaring through the sky: *powerful* and *graceful*.

She raised her hands out to the sides, trying to imagine the joy the bird must feel when it soared through the sky, the power it felt when it flapped its great wings, lifting higher into the air. She turned in place, angling her arms this way and that, the wind whirling about her. All through her early years and now as a young woman, she felt as if she did not fit with other elves close to her age. She was far more curious and adventurous than they and much less content to remain in the forest. At the first sight of the beautiful bird, she had been struck by a desire stronger than any she had felt before, and now she wanted to soar with the wind encircling her.

Now, the bird had been watching the girl. He admired her courage to climb a cliff that was so steep. He wondered if there had been any other before her who had dared to try. Then he saw her face, flushed from the cold wind. She was the one he had been looking for, the one he had been waiting so long to find. One last time he circled the spinning girl before landing on the plateau near her. She was beautiful, strong, and her green eyes were bright with curiosity for all things new.

"I have been waiting for you," he said to her. "The forest has been well cared for by your people. Now is the time for the elves to harness the strength of the wind to extend their reach to the farthest edges of this land and beyond. Your people will spread to wherever Nature needs them. You are the first to long for and seek out what lies beyond. You are the one I have been waiting for. You are ..."

Terran paused for a moment and swallowed hard. He looked at Anila once again, and together they finished, "the Child of the Wind."

"Whoooaaa," Douglas sighed almost too quietly too be heard.

Someone whistled loudly and broke the friends' silence. Avery and Jake stood waving for them to come along.

"It must be close to dinnertime now," Sage guessed, speaking solemnly.

Between the flying lesson and the legend, they had all lost track of the time. They each stood and grabbed their bags to head toward Jake and Aderyn's home, too overcome to speak.

"You four must really have been involved in your conversation," Avery said. "We had tried calling out to you but had to resort to the whistle to get your attention. Everything all right?" He had noticed the serious expressions on their faces and the looks the friends had been exchanging.

"Yes, sir. We were just talking and lost track of time," Anila replied quickly, letting her friends know she wanted to keep their discussion between them for now.

"How did your flying lesson go?" Jake asked with interest.

"Great. It was great. Thank you," she said, trying to sound more like herself.

"Wonderful! I hope you are all hungry. Aderyn is a fabulous cook. Lucky for us, it is one of her favorite hobbies," Jake said clapping his hands together again and walking briskly to the steps.

Jake and Avery bounded down the steps first, still talking about Council business. Douglas followed closely behind Anila, taking Aderyn's warning of sticking close to friends seriously. Terran gestured for Sage to go ahead of him on the steps. She hadn't given the steps much thought since Jake had scared her on the tour earlier that afternoon, but now Sage gulped and hesitantly took the first step down from the edge of the cliff. She couldn't help looking down, and the fear gripped her. The steps were steep, there were no railings, and it was a very long way down the fissure to the forest below. Frantically she turned and scrambled back to the mountaintop. She crashed hard into Terran, knocking them both to the ground and landing on top of him.

Great, she thought, *and just when I thought I couldn't get any more embarrassed.*

"You really don't like these heights, do you?" Terran said sympathetically. He helped her up and held out her backpack. "Power of Protection," he stated.

Sage gave Terran a puzzled expression. "Power of Protection? From whom?" Terran chuckled.

"No," he said dusting himself off. "The Power of Protection doesn't just act as a shield from humans. It protects us in our own environment, too. Watch."

He stepped onto the top step and tried to push his foot off the edges of it. With effort, he was able to move his foot a few inches beyond the boundary of the step. In all directions, other than the way down the stairs, he was held by some invisible wall, a force keeping him safely inside the edge.

"The Power of Protection," he repeated, holding out his hand for her to take.

She clasped his hand nervously. Calm was all she felt when touching him. With no reservations, she stepped. Terran kept her on his left side, close to the mountain, as they slowly made their way down the stairs and along the walkway to the entrance of Jake and Aderyn's home. His hold on her was appreciated and comforting. Before they entered, Sage silently thanked Terran with a squeeze of his hand. He smiled, giving her hand one last squeeze before letting it go and opening the door. Everyone inside was lost in conversation and didn't even seem to notice their delayed arrival.

Sage didn't really know what to expect the home to look like on the inside and was surprised. The entrance opened to the living room, which was large and well lit. Two comfortable-looking couches and an old rocking chair draped with a soft purple throw welcomed guests to sit and chat. Sora told Sage and Anila they would be staying in her room for the night and invited them down to drop their bags off. The long hallway led deeper into the mountain and to all of the rooms in the home. Sora's room, painted in pastel colors, was at the very end of the hall. Sora was about ten years old, Sage guessed. She was cheerful, polite, and very excited to be having guests sleeping over. In fact, she had already gone through the trouble of making up beds, with blankets and pillows spread on her light blue rug.

"Oh, Sora!" Anila beamed, knowing Sora had been holding her breath, hoping they would be impressed. "This is a lovely room! And look, Sage! She has our beds ready for us!"

That was exactly what Sora was waiting to hear, and Sage felt the little jolt of happiness the words had given her. For the next several minutes, Sora gave her visitors a tour of her room, including her small but well-loved collection of dolls, the traditional elvish dress she was going to be wearing to the End-of-Summer Celebration in Oakley, and her framed eagle feather.

"There hasn't been an eagle around here since my dad was my age," she explained. "This was one he found when he was a little boy."

Just then, Jake called from down the hall. Dinner was ready, and everyone else had already gathered in the kitchen. The large eating area was well suited for guests. Aderyn had set the table festively in blues and reds and had certainly proven her love of cooking, with platters of foods presented in an artistic and gourmet fashion. Fresh herbs garnished the platters, and sauce had been poured in a perfect spiral atop homemade pasta. With wide eyes and eager stomachs, everyone sat, ate, and talked over her delicious meal. Avery and Jake were still talking about Council business when Aderyn cleared her throat in an obvious attempt to interrupt them.

"So," she began when she had their attention. "Anila is going to go up again this evening. Do you have much more to do tonight, or could you break free long enough to come watch?"

"Don't you think that would be pushing it a little?" Jake asked, knowing the effort involved, especially for a beginner. "She said she did great—but twice in the same day?"

"Great?" Aderyn repeated. She gave Anila a sideways glance. "Is that what she said? Hmmm." Anila pushed some sweet corn kernels around her plate and did not look up. "She did better than great, Jake. You should see her. She's a natural, and she has people talking already."

"She stood still in the air, Daddy!" Sora blurted out.

Jake looked at his wife to clarify what Sora meant. Aderyn nodded slowly.

"She can do ... things. I can't explain it. You two will have to see for your-self." With that, she stood and began clearing the table, with everyone joining in to help.

Terran walked closely behind Sage on the way up to the plateau. Even though Sage was not as petrified of the walkway as she had been the first time, she felt grateful he was there, ready to help her if needed. She was so focused on not looking down or looking scared that she hadn't noticed the large numbers of people staring out their windows and doors at their group as they walked along the path to the stairs. It wasn't until a strong mix of their emotions distracted her that Sage began to pay attention. She braved a glance behind her to see that people had indeed spread the word about Anila and were going to come out in the chill of the evening to see if the rumors were true.

Before turning off at the small Council building, Avery and Jake assured Aderyn they would be along as soon as they were finished. It was only moments before Anila was strapped into the wings and harness. A crowd continued to gather outside the practice circle. Anticipation and excitement had filled Anila earlier that day, but now she was very nervous. Sage worried that her friend would lack the concentration to be successful tonight. The buzz of the crowd hushed when Anila took her last instructions from Aderyn and received a nod to go ahead. Just as she had done that afternoon, Anila closed her eyes and ascended straight into the air. There had been no need for Sage to worry. She sensed Anila's confidence rushing back with the pleasure of the first blast of cold wind on her skin. The audience below chattered, and a few people even applauded.

Sage knew Aderyn had instructed Anila to have fun but also experiment more with stopping in the air. For now, though, Anila was circling, climbing, gliding, diving, and enjoying herself. Then, with the restlessness out of her system, she slowed to a stop as before, looking relaxed and peaceful. She hovered in a standing position above the crowd with her eyes closed and arms at her sides. The crowd's reaction was varied. Those seeing Anila for the first time were gasping, while those who had seen her earlier were cheering. Anila began to increase the air circling around her until she was engulfed in a whirling tornado drawing up loose dust from the ground below. People held their hats, and children covered their ears against the roar of the wind. Sage could feel fear rising in the crowd. Anila lifted her arms to the sky, and the tornado rose with them. She released the whirlwind to the darkening sky, and people began to cheer again.

Avery and Jake had been drawn out of the Council building by the noise of the crowd. They were stunned, and their faces showed it. Together they watched as Anila hung perfectly motionless in the air, her arms still stretched above her. Sage noticed Anila's hair beginning to fly around her face again, and then she heard the growing howl of wind. She searched the darkening sky anxiously even as Anila remained calm.

The tornado! Sage thought. *Where did it go?*

Her concern was clearly shared by everyone. The nervous crowd became silent—watching, waiting. The dust began to fly. Children were drawn in close to their parents. Then the first shrieks of fear were heard as the twister was spotted. As if by her command, it returned to Anila's outstretched hands. She held it there for the briefest moment before closing her hands in around the air, molding the whirling mass until it became smaller and smaller. Applause and cheers for this young magician replaced the cries and gasps as the amazed crowd forgot their fear. Now the excitement was there again while watching this beautiful newcomer play with a dusty ball of spinning air.

Jake had walked to Aderyn's side as she pointlessly held the safety rope. He was shaking his head in disbelief. Sage scanned the crowd for her father. He was still watching but now from the other side of the crowd. Anila let the ball dissipate and began flying through the air once more. Everyone watched as she slowed, gliding gracefully through the air, preparing to end this practice session.

Avery smiled up at Anila and cheered along with the crowd. He stood in awe for a moment longer before heading away toward the steps. Sage wanted to talk to him alone about the legend and everything that had happened during the day, so she slipped through the crowd, running to catch up with him before he reached the stairs.

"Dad!" she yelled when he was within earshot. Avery turned around, stopped, and waited for Sage to catch up with him. "Are you done with your meeting?" she asked hopefully.

"Yes. The rest of what we need to cover can wait until morning," he answered. "That was really amazing," he said, pointing toward Anila.

"Yeah ... about that. Could I talk to you for a minute?"

"Sure. Something wrong?"

"No, nothing's wrong," she began. "It's just that ... Well, everything is so new to me, and I have questions."

"Of course. Shoot." There were loud cheers as Anila set down on the ground with a flourish. "Terran has been telling me the legends of how the elves began here. He had just finished telling us the legend of Ambara when you and Jake called us for dinner."

"Oh," he said. "That explains a lot."

"Are the legends real? True, I mean?" she asked.

"I think all legends are partly true or begin in truth. Over time, the stories change or get added to until they are very different from what they were originally. Why do you ask?"

"Is Anila a family name? Or maybe a traditional elf name?" she continued without answering him.

"She is the first Anila I have ever met or heard of, so I don't think so. Why? And what does that have to do with the legend?" he asked with more interest.

"In the story, the eagle calls the girl the Child of the Wind, and that is exactly what Anila's name means. She has black hair like the girl in the story, and green eyes, too. Aderyn has never seen anyone fly like her before and said that people were a little frightened by what they saw. I know it's true, I can feel it in them," her voice rose in intensity with every fact she presented. "And some people think that something big is getting ready to happen—something that has already been foreseen. Maybe Anila has something to do with having power return to the elves." Maybe she had gone too far with the last idea. Her father still didn't know she had overheard his conversation with Evron in the forest.

"Where did you hear that?" he asked, laughing it off just a little too loudly.

"I don't know. Just bits of things I've heard people talking about, that's all." She gripped the seams of her shorts tightly to keep from fidgeting and drawing suspicion.

"Don't go reading more into this than there is," he warned her. "I'm sure Anila does have people talking. Her ability is beyond what has been seen in many years. But there is no need for you to search for a logical solution, a reason for her power. It is a good thing for our people to see, Sage—especially right now. Listen to me. People are often afraid of change. Seeing what she is able to do is definitely a change, and people may appear frightened of her because of it. But I can assure you there are—and will be—many more to whom she brings hope, hope for the future of our people," he said placing a hand reassuringly on her shoulder.

"But Dad," she continued determinedly. "What about the other names? Lamar? Douglas?"

"More coincidence," he chuckled, shaking his head at his daughter's need to have everything make sense. "Douglas was named after your grandfather, Spencer Douglas Baker. And you got your name because your mother and I liked a song that had a line in it ..." He hummed a little, and she screwed up her face at him. "Well, we just thought it was a simple, beautiful name. Don't worry. Everyone in Ambara is going to love Anila." He smiled reassuringly, then turned to head down the stairs. The discussion with her father had left Sage unsatisfied and unconvinced. Where he saw coincidences, she saw pieces of a puzzle.

"Douglas is going to walk Anila back when the crowd clears a little. I saw you run this way. Are you okay?" Terran asked as he approached her. Sage had seen him waiting just outside of the crowd, not wanting to interrupt her conversation with her dad.

"Yeah, I'm fine. My dad thinks that everything with the legend and Anila is just a coincidence. I know we all said the same this afternoon, but it can't all be coincidental." Sage frowned. "You don't think so either, do you?"

"No." He shook his head. "I think it's downright weird!"

A change she couldn't describe and didn't quite understand drew Sage's attention toward the crowd. They were leaving the practice area, heading back to their homes. As they approached, Sage began to discern a mix of emotions from them; the older the person, the more unease they felt over what they had just witnessed. The closer they came, the more clearly she could pick out the strongest reactions of fear or joy or excitement. The curiosity held her interest until, finally, Anila, Douglas, Jake, Aderyn, and Sora were heading toward them. The last stragglers of the crowd, who had been hanging close to Anila, started down the stairs as she and Douglas joined Terran and Sage. Jake, Aderyn, and Sora waved and followed the crowd down. For the first time since that afternoon, it seemed quiet.

"You were amazing, Anila," Sage congratulated her.

"Thanks. I'm tired. And thirsty." She had no sooner said the words than Douglas was handing her a bottle of water.

"Thank you." She smiled, then took a long drink before they all made their way back to Jake and Aderyn's home.

CHAPTER 14
The Legend of Layton

The next morning, no one was in a rush to get out of bed. They had all stayed up late the night before, talking together in the living room. Sage enjoyed Jake's positive outlook and energy and Aderyn's sharp and clever wit. She wished now that she had been raised knowing what she had only found out this summer. It was impossible to go back or change things and pointless to hold it against her father for doing what he thought was his only choice. Yes, she had forgiven him, and it had been easy to do. Still, these people could have been a part of her and Douglas's lives growing up. *At least*, she thought as she lay on the small bed Sora had made up for her, *we will see them at the celebration in Oakley before we head back home.*

Finally, the household was roused by the smell of Aderyn's cooking. Jake and Avery were already finishing their morning meeting when everyone met in the bright kitchen for breakfast. The remainder of the morning went by quickly. Too soon they were grabbing their bags and backpacks and saying goodbye to Aderyn and Sora. Jake walked with the group to see them off at the lift. People were again peeking out their doors and windows as Anila passed. Many waved, and some greeted Avery and Jake with respectful nods.

A smile spread across Anila's face as they reached the training circle. The strength of her emotions gave them clarity. Happiness, freedom and a complete sense of belonging flooded over her as she remembered flying the day before. Sage smiled, too, happy that Anila had finally found her true power. Anila let the wind blow her hair across her face as they walked, hiding her smile but not her newly found strength and confidence. She stopped suddenly, looking up to the sky. It took a moment for the rest of the group to notice. They all came to a halt, waiting for her.

"What?" Jake started.

"An eagle!" Sage exclaimed, pointing at the large bird circling overhead.

"There hasn't been an eagle roosting in this area since …" Avery thought a moment as he watched the bird. "… since we were boys, Jake!"

"Well, how about that!" Jake clapped his hands together in delight.

Douglas, Sage, and Terran looked from one to another, saying nothing. Anila brushed the hair from her face and walked up to where the others stood waiting. One by one, they all turned their eyes from the bird and started toward the lift again. They had to wait for only a few minutes before the lift rose to the top of the mountain, ready for the passengers. The boys shook hands with Jake, and he hugged both girls goodbye.

"Thank you for having us all at your home, Jake," Avery told his friend. "I'll be getting right to work on those issues we talked about."

The gate shut, and as the first jerky motion of the lift began to lower them, the great bird shrieked so loudly that all eyes, including those of the Ambarans standing on the plateau, turned to the sky. Sage raised her eyebrows and smiled smugly at her father. He shook his head with the same you're-reading-too-much-into-this look on his face, but Sage knew he had no explanation for what had just happened.

There were people on the ground below, waiting for the lift. Before she could make out their faces, Sage knew that Evron was one of them. It wasn't long until he knew she was there, too, and a wave of his usual disgust reached her. She was keenly aware of his dislike for her, even if she didn't know the reason. It took all of her concentration to hide the queasiness caused by the intensity of his emotion and the descent. He stood with both of his hands resting on the top of his walking stick, looking up at them. The expression on his face was blank, unreadable—neither smiling nor unpleasant—just as it was the first time Sage and Douglas had met him. Evron approached the lift when it reached the bottom and opened the gate for the passengers. He nodded briefly to Avery, Terran, and Anila but ignored Sage and Douglas.

"Evron. How are you today?" Avery asked with a long nod of respect.

"Very well, Avery," Evron replied unemotionally. "Your meeting with Jake was productive, I hope?"

"Yes. I think we have a plan of action for the park situation," Avery said, nodding, "but we are going to meet again this fall to work on the safety issue and yearly meeting data."

"Very good. I have some business with Jake myself, but I will be back this evening if you have anything you would like to go over," Evron said, still not acknowledging Douglas and Sage's presence.

"Your aunt and uncle have arrived for a visit," he said, turning to Terran. "I believe they have changed their plans and intend to stay through the End-of-Summer Celebration. I'm sure they will be glad to see you."

"Yes, Grandfather," Terran responded.

It was strange for Sage to see such coolness between a grandfather and his grandson. Terran obviously held Evron in high esteem, but she could feel no exchange of tenderness in their voices and nothing of Terran's feelings.

Evron greeted Anila as she stepped from the lift and the circling eagle shrieked again, drawing all eyes skyward.

"It's an eagle, Evron!" Anila told him proudly.

"Yesss …," he said slowly, drawing out the word. "Isn't that *wonderful*, Avery? An interesting time for such a creature to return to these parts, don't you think?"

He stepped onto the lift with the other three passengers without looking at Avery or even waiting for his response. Avery shut and latched the gate, and the lift started its climb back to the top. Though Sage didn't believe Douglas had noticed, she understood Evron was making a point not to acknowledge them. That suited her just fine; a direct address may have caused more than just a bit of nausea.

Sage joined the rest of the group putting their packs over their shoulders to begin their long walk back to Oakley. Only now was the group beginning to feel the heat of the day. The air was still, thick, and moist, so very different than the relative cool of the Ambaran elevation. As they progressed along the trail, streams merged, and the water falling from cracks in the mountain poured into them, increasing the flow of water that would grow to become the river. Sage took out her water bottle and refilled it with the fresh, cold water spilling out of the rock face. Everyone agreed it was a great idea and followed her lead. After splashing the icy water at each other, Douglas and Terran dripped with more water than they had managed to get into their bottles. Laughing and shaking his head, Avery started ahead of the group on the trail, leaving the four friends to follow behind.

"Hey," Douglas said to Terran. "There are legends about how the other villages got started. Is there a legend of Layton, too?"

"Yup."

"Well, it's a long walk," he said punching Terran in the arm.

"Okay, maybe talking about the lake will help cool us down even if we aren't actually in it," Terran said hopefully.

In a day gone by, there was a small boy. From the first time his mother dipped his toes into the lake, he loved the water. Before he could walk, he could swim. As he grew, his strength in the water grew. He explored every corner of the lake: its rocks, its streams, its plants and creatures. All day he would swim, and in the evening he would rest on the warm, smooth rocks to feed breadcrumbs to the fish that gathered near him when he was there.

Every year he dove as deep as his strength would take him. Swimming into the depths as a young man, he discovered a cave cut into the wall of a mountain deep below the water's surface. He dove, trying to reach its entrance, to no avail. He didn't know what he would discover when he entered the dark opening, but he was certain there was something there he was meant to find. The young man went to the lake every day through the summer, and every day he dove until his body was weak from exertion. Still, his determination did not waiver.

Soon, though the days were still warm, the evenings held the chill of autumn. He knew his opportunity to reach the cave was nearing an end. He woke with the first light of morning to start his dive fresh. "This," he thought, "will be my day." He swam close to the mountain, directly above the cave opening. Filling his lungs with one great breath, he dove below the surface. The young man kicked skillfully with his feet and pulled with his cupped hands through the water to the cave entrance. No light from the surface penetrated the water-filled cavern. His air was nearly depleted. He knew he must soon turn around and head back to the surface but felt drawn farther in. He continued until he had no breath remaining. The darkness confused him, and he lost all sense of direction. When he tried to turn to swim from the cave the way he had come, there was only the dark and cold.

There was no panic clouding his thoughts, no fear gripping his heart. He felt comforted by the water around him even as the last trace of breath left him. Death was certain, and his last thoughts were of his love and respect for the power of the depths.

Sage turned to Terran with a horrified look on her face.

"It can't be like that!" she snapped, coming to a complete stop facing Terran. "How can there be a legend if the hero dies?"

"Well," he said, restraining himself from laughter, "I wasn't actually finished."

"Oh. Sorry," she fumbled, fidgeting from another bout of embarrassment.

"You should have seen her when she heard the story of Beauty and the Beast for the first time," Douglas said. He placed his hands on his hips and set his face to look as bossy and snooty as he could.

"You're reading that all wrong. The Beast can't die. Don't you know how a story is supposed to go?" He mimicked the voice and mannerisms of a little girl so well that the only person not laughing was Sage.

"I was four years old!" she snapped. "How many times are you going to tell that story?"

Realizing her current posture, she slowly removed her hands from their station on her hips and began to stalk ahead of them all. Terran caught up with her, matching her stride and watching her purposefully indifferent face. She felt him staring at her, and he nudged her shoulder with his own. He nudged again, and the corners of her mouth began to turn up into a smile.

"Would you like to know what happens next?" he asked.

"Only if nothing bad happens," she said, returning a bump with her shoulder. He smiled at her, waited for the others to catch up, and continued.

Nature knew this young man. She was drawn to him when he was but a boy. She wasn't surprised when he sought the cave with such determination and daring. Having already foreseen his current predicament, she called a strong rip current to suck him from the cave. There was little time left for the young man, but the great lake, who also admired the young man, moved quickly, spitting him onto the rocks with such a force that the water was heaved from his drowning lungs. Breath returned to him in great, deep gasps. He lay tired, pained, and disappointed on a long, cool rock just above the surface of the dark water.

When he had recovered enough strength, he turned on his side, looking out over the lake. The fish had seen the young man there and moved about hopefully at the surface. The morning sun had risen full over the edge of the mountain now, and its rays warmed him but could not take away his sadness. He had made it into the cave and, though he knew he had almost lost his life because of it, he felt broken still. For the first time in many years, the young man cried. Tears flowed down his cheeks and into the water below.

At first unnoticed by him, the waters had begun to gently churn. Dark beasts slithered in the water beneath him, splashing their great tails on the surface of the water before disappearing into the depths. The young man pushed himself back from the water in alarm. When the disturbance calmed, he moved closer again and peered over the edge. The beasts had returned to the surface and waited there just as the friendly fish wanting his breadcrumbs. One of the creatures raised its head from the water and spoke.

"Nature herself has watched you these years of your youth. There are those who have been chosen to care for the creatures of the forests, the plants of the forests, and the winds and winged creatures of the mountaintops. Now she has need of another to care for the great waters and all that live in their depths. She has chosen you." The serpent paused. "You respect and need the water. You have the will and determination to build a fine community that will someday protect and care for the waters around the world."

The young man looked at the strange creatures with disbelief but with no fear of them. "I failed," he stated sadly. "I am not strong enough for what you say she asks of me."

"You will not be alone the next time, and all the powers you will need have been given to you already. The very tears that fell from your eyes created these creatures you now look upon. The serpents will forever serve and guard the water community you will begin. You are not alone. Come, there is much to see in the dark water."

The serpents circled back from the rock so the young man would have space to re-enter the lake. This is where he had always belonged, and he felt the excitement of a beginning adventure. He slid off the rock without looking back and followed the diving serpents to his future in the darkness below.

They were well into the comfort of the shade of the oak forest. The temperature was cooler here. Along the trail, the rush of the water was louder and the river nearly its full size. The return trip down the steep incline took much less time than the trip up to the lift, and Sage figured they were almost to Oakley now. She could hear the others talking but became lost in her own thoughts about the different legends. *Too many coincidences*, she thought.

"You tell it just like I remember from when we were kids," Anila told Terran happily.

"I'd like to hear you tell the one I missed sometime," Douglas added.

"Sure."

Sage stopped along the trail and looked out into the forest while her friends continued ahead. Terran walked back to check on her.

"You're not still mad, are you?" he asked her.

She didn't know what he was talking about at first.

"What? Oh … no," she answered without looking at him.

"What are you looking at?" he finally asked.

"Something is wrong," she said. She concentrated, trying to figure out what was bothering her.

While Terran had been telling the legend, she had begun to feel like she should be looking over her shoulder, like someone was watching her. The sensation had grown stronger, sending chills down her spine. Light flared before her eyes, and she jerked her head away, throwing up her hands to shield herself.

"Are you all right?" Terran exclaimed. He grabbed her arm and turned her to face him. There was concern in his eyes, and she could almost sense a strong desire to protect within him.

"Yes. Did you see that?" she cried, her face full of fear.

"What? What did you see?" he demanded.

"You two okay?" Douglas yelled back to them.

"Sage said something is wrong," Terran said urgently.

Douglas yelled ahead to his father, and they all started back to where Sage and Terran stood. Sage looked out again. This time her eyes had focused on a spot on the forest floor several yards away. Terran saw it too. The underbrush was moving in a path toward them. Douglas and Anila had almost reached them when the movement in the undergrowth suddenly increased in speed. Terran stepped in front of Sage and pushed her out of the way so forcefully she stumbled to regain her balance. Something snakelike coiled around his right ankle, yanking his feet out from underneath him. Terran was on his back, being dragged into the forest, scraping and knocking against trees and catching thorny stems on his arms and face. He reached out, trying to grab at plants and saplings, but they only slipped through his hands. Sage started running after him, followed closely by the others.

"NO! STOP!" Sage screamed out.

Instantly, the thing pulling Terran stopped, and so did he, but the angst and sense of danger did not abate for Sage. There was something more. She continued to scan the forest as she ran. Avery, Sage, Douglas, and Anila wove in and out of the trees until they reached Terran. He was struggling to sit up, and Sage could already see that his t-shirt was dirty and bloody. A cold, cruel laugh echoed through the forest, and all heads turned in the direction of the sound in time to see a dark figure running deeper into the woods.

"Wait here!" Avery ordered. He dropped his bag and took off running in the same direction as the man.

The others crouched around Terran. He had cuts and the beginnings of bruises on his arms, legs, and face. Sage hadn't seen his back yet but figured it was much worse than what they were already seeing. He was sitting now and working on his ankle.

"I think it's a sprain," he said, unwrapping what Sage could now see was a thick, woody vine.

Douglas cut the vine the rest of the way off Terran's ankle with a pocketknife from his backpack. He felt around the bones in the tender area.

"It doesn't seem to be broken," Douglas said. Then he reached into his backpack again and took out a t-shirt. Douglas cut the t-shirt and ripped it into strips. As he wrapped the swelling ankle, Sage pulled her water bottle out and began cleaning the deeper cuts on Terran's face.

"Oh … Your *back*, Terran," Anila said. She was already crying freely.

Terran winced as Sage tried to lift his shirt. Douglas reached up and slit the front of Terran's shirt open so they were able to peel it off without having to pull it over his head. Anila grabbed Terran's water bottle and gave him a drink while Sage continued to clean the cuts on his arms and back.

By the time Avery had returned to them, Terran's ankle was wrapped and most of the dirt had been cleaned from his open wounds. Avery knelt down to look at the bandaged ankle.

"Is it broken?" he asked Douglas.

"No, I don't think so. But it's a bad sprain at the least," he answered. And then he asked what everyone had been too busy tending to Terran to ask. "Dad, who was that man? And why did that vine go after Terran?"

"I don't know who it was. He seems to have just disappeared. And I don't know why he made that vine do that."

Douglas shook his head, not understanding what his father meant.

"Plants—especially plants—can't behave like that without being told to," Anila explained to Douglas. "That person told the vine to attack Terran."

"Not Terran. Me," Sage said. "It was trying to get *me*. If Terran hadn't pushed me out of the way, he wouldn't have gotten hurt."

Her eyes burned with tears. She covered her face with her hands and began to cry.

"No, no." Still sniffling herself, Anila scooted closer to where Sage sat and draped an arm over her shoulder, her head resting against Sage's. "You don't know that. It could have been any of us."

Sage continued to sob, unable to speak. Terran reached up and took one of her hands, lowering it away from her face.

"What did you see?" he asked her. He was in a great deal of pain and spoke through gritted teeth. "What did you see before ... when you asked me if I had seen it?"

Sage had seen Terran wince and pull back a bit with the sting of water on his wounds while they had been treating him, but he hadn't said a word. This was the first he had spoken since he'd started to free his foot from the vine.

"It happened so fast. It was someone's foot. I guess it was your ankle with that vine wrapped around it," she answered. She looked over to her father. "It was like a picture right in front of my eyes: a really bright flash, then it disappeared. I didn't know what it was. It's never happened before. Maybe if I had known …"

"We'll figure it out later," Avery interrupted her gently. "Right now, we have to get Terran someplace where he can rest and be treated." His eyes continued to scan the forest. "Somewhere safe."

While the girls gathered all the bags, Douglas and Avery carefully helped Terran to his feet. With his arms over each of their shoulders, he was able to put light pressure on his foot, cringing with each step. The fifteen minutes remaining of their walk to Oakley stretched to nearly forty-five. Avery continued to search the shadows of the forest for any sign of the person they had seen, but Sage no longer had the feeling they were being watched.

Finally, they reached the edge of town and were quickly met by several townspeople ready to help. Together, they gently carried Terran up to Anila's home. Sage could already make out the murmurs of questions as they passed from platform to platform. "How did this happen?" "Is he okay?" "Was he attacked?" The questions did not surprise her. The clarity of the anxiety behind the questions did.

"He is going to be just fine," Avery assured everyone, brushing off their concerns. "Thank you so much for your help. Terran is in good hands now and needs to rest," he told everyone politely. But he did not answer their questions.

Once safely inside Anila's home, with the worried crowd still chattering on the other side of the closed door, Avery pulled Keelin aside. While they spoke in hushed tones, everyone else worked quickly to make Terran comfortable. Sage sat nearby but out of the way as Douglas gently unwrapped his swollen ankle. Through everything, Terran made no sound. His tightly clenched jaw and deeply creased forehead dripping with perspiration were the only signs of his discomfort. Anila, Delaney, and Hannah busily combined an assortment of herbs, roots, and other plants into two bowls. The contents of one bowl were coarsely chopped, then steeped in a steaming mug of water for a tea they were told would ease Terran's pain. The more finely ground ingredients were mixed with small amounts of water, creating an ointment for his open wounds.

"It's time we get going so we can let his parents know what happened," Avery began. "Terran can rest until they can get here. It's lucky that his aunt and uncle are visiting. They'll be able to do wonders on that ankle."

"I don't suppose we'll be seeing you for a couple of days," Douglas said to Terran.

"I'm so sorry," Sage said, trying to keep her chin from quivering. "Maybe we can come visit you tomorrow."

"We'll have to see about that," Avery told her gently. "It may be better for you two to stay away for a day or so."

Terran had taken the tea Hannah had prepared for him. Between its effects and just being worn out, his eyes were drooping when the three of them said their goodbyes. Avery, Douglas, and Sage walked in silence, following the river as it flowed down to Ashtyn.

"Ophelia and Hugh are visiting with friends," Frayne said, reaching over to hold his wife's hand after Avery had shared their story. "I'll go get them while Linaeve gathers some of Terran's clothes. He may have to stay in Oakley for a day or so."

"Thank you for taking such good care of him." Linaeve gave Sage and Douglas a tender smile, instantly bringing fresh tears to Sage's eyes. "You are very good friends."

Thoughts and images of the last two days were racing through Sage's head as they left Ashtyn on their way back to the cabin. She glanced over at Douglas. His cheeks were flushed from the heat, and he was lost in his own thoughts. Everything about him, from his posture to his stride, appeared tired. She was tired too, both physically and emotionally drained. She wanted to talk to her dad about everything that had happened, just not now. Sage didn't need facts or advice; she needed comforting. Whenever she felt this down, there was only one person she turned to, and she was waiting for the three of them at the cabin.

CHAPTER 15
A Mystery Revealed

A blast of cool from the air-conditioned cabin greeted them when Douglas opened the door. Compared to the outside, it was cold—almost too cold against their damp skin. Dinner was waiting for them in the kitchen, and the smell of fresh bread and roasted vegetables filled their noses. All three sighed, welcoming the safety of home and the change from the sticky heat still holding into the evening.

"I was expecting you home a little sooner," Adel called out from the kitchen. She was drying her hands on a kitchen towel when she rounded the corner. As soon as she saw her dirty, sweaty, and weary family, she stopped abruptly, the smile on her face fading. "What in the world!" she exclaimed. Already her eyes were examining the red smears and muddy spots on their clothing and arms.

"Everyone is fine, Adel," Avery said at once after reading the alarm on her face. "I'll explain everything, I promise, but right now the kids are dehydrated and exhausted. Let's give them some time to rest."

This did very little to ease Adel's worries. She stood facing them, frozen with a mixed expression of shock and fear on her face. Sage took a few steps toward her mother, and although she was trying to control her emotions, her bottom lip began to tremble and her eyes once again burned with tears.

Adel wrapped her arms around Sage. After a few moments of her mother's comforting, Sage regained composure. Fatigue and stress had always made it hard for her to contain her emotions. The more tired she was, the more likely she would lose control. Her mother held her at arm's length, examining every red scrape and smudge of dirt.

"Is that *blood* all over your clothes?" she asked with increased concern. She swung her gaze between Douglas and Sage.

"Let them rest a moment," Avery repeated, more firmly this time.

Adel reluctantly released Sage and stepped back to allow them through to the kitchen. She poured cold lemonade into tall, ice-filled glasses and began serving her family. Sage and Douglas sat silently, sipping their lemonade and picking at their dinners, as their father told Adel everything that had happened on their walk home. Sage registered her mother's concern and horror but tried not to let the emotions add to her own. When he was finished, Avery took a long drink from his glass and waited for his wife's response. Adel had been sitting straight—rigid even—while he was speaking, and she hadn't eaten a bite. Now she fell back against her chair but could only shake her head, unable to say anything.

"You should be very proud of how they handled things, Adel," he continued. "I'm sure they will feel a lot better after a hot shower and a change of clothes."

Sage heard whispers. She was still not quite awake and couldn't tell if the softly spoken words were real or just part of an unfinished dream. She struggled to open her eyes.

"Go back to sleep, Sage," her mother whispered. "I'm just going into town for some groceries. Douglas is still asleep, too."

"I want to go with you," Sage mumbled, managing to push herself into a sitting position. She was still wearing her robe over her pajamas and figured she must have fallen asleep before thinking to take it off. In fact, she didn't even remember lying down after her shower the night before.

"You need more rest. You can go another time," her mother assured her.

"Dad said he wanted us to stay out of the forest today. I don't want to sit around all day. I need to check my e-mail, anyway. And there are some other things I want to look up," Sage told her mother. She rubbed the sleep from her eyes and tried to get them to focus on her mother.

"Are you sure? You had a really rough day yesterday."

"Yeah. Just give me a few minutes to clean up," Sage said. With a yawn and a stretch, she headed to the bathroom. A few minutes later, Sage and her mother were on their way into town.

"I have to go to the post office and the grocery store. I won't be an hour. Will that give you enough time at the library?" Adel asked.

"That should be plenty of time. I'm certain Wendy thinks I have forgotten about her this summer. There are probably fifty messages waiting for me. And I was also going to look up Dad's name, like you asked. That shouldn't take very long," Sage said. Her mother pulled the car up along the curb in front of the library. "I'll meet you at the grocery store when I'm done."

She stepped out of the car and shut the door. It was going to be hot again today and uncomfortably humid. She was glad she would be in air conditioning most of the day but worried about Terran and his comfort in this heat. The library was quiet, and she was the only person at the computers. As expected, Sage's e-mail was filled with messages from her friend Wendy. She suddenly felt guilty, even though Wendy had already known she wouldn't be able to write every day. After reading and replying to her messages, Sage grabbed a pencil and paper from the tray in front of her and wrote her father's name as she waited for the names website to load.

"Avery," she typed into the meaning search.

Well, no surprise there, she thought, writing the meaning next to his name.

Avery—"Elf ruler"

With plenty of time left before she had to meet her mother, Sage decided she would look up a few other names to surprise her.

Adel—"Noble and kind"

Sage thought that meaning was a perfect match for her mother.

Spencer—"Butler, steward"

"Huh," Sage said out loud. She thought back to her grandfather's funeral. That was what the forest ranger had called him: steward.

Nayana—"Eye"

Sage shot a glance up to the clock on the wall. About forty minutes left. She jumped from her chair, starting for the door before rushing back to clear the web page and grab her paper. In another moment, Sage was sprinting down the street, passing the grocery store, and crossing the road, heading to her left. The grocery, post office, hardware, and library were located one block behind the main street of town. When she reached it, the main street and its small artsy and touristy shops were already busy with tourists browsing in an attempt to escape the continuing heat wave. Sage stopped in front of a small storefront with a large window. The CLOSED sign hanging on the window of the entrance door surprised her. There were no posted hours, so she tried to peek through the covered windows for any movement inside. Sage tested the handle. It turned, and she hesitated. After taking a deep breath, she opened the door slowly. She was quiet as she stepped inside. As she closed the door behind her, the tiny bells hanging from the inside handle began tinkling.

"I'm sorry," a voice called out to her. It came from a room down a hallway opposite that of the doorway. "I am closed now but will be opening just after …" The woman had moved into the doorway and froze in surprise upon seeing Sage. "I will be open again after the lunch hour."

She turned her head, shielding her face in one of the ends of the sheer scarves secured at her forehead. Sage recalled her impression of the woman at their first meeting. She had been guarding more than her face at the Fourth of July Celebration—she had been hiding her feelings. So far, she was not being as successful on this visit. Sage sensed the anxiety welling in the woman, who was obviously caught off guard by her visitor. Other emotions coming from the woman were jumbled, making them difficult for Sage to distinguish. Excitement, fear, delight, sadness …

"Is there something I can do for you? As I said, I am closed," the woman said again, this time with more assertiveness.

"Ummm … yes," Sage began. It had only just occurred to Sage that she hadn't thought of what she would do or say when she saw the woman. She took another step through the doorway and closed the door, still holding the handle. "I … Well, my brother, some friends, and I had a reading with you earlier in the summer."

"Yes, I remember."

"You said some things. Interesting things. You said I would make discoveries—and I have. You said my discoveries would help others with their challenges. That has been true, so far, as well," Sage said. She was gaining the courage to say what she had come to say. The woman knew what was coming, too. One corner of her mouth turned up, and her eyes softened on Sage.

"Your name isn't just Ana, is it?" Sage asked slowly. "It's Nayana."

Sage was no longer hesitant. She stepped fully into the room. In truth, there was no other way to ask such a question. She didn't have time left before meeting her mother to tiptoe around the topic, and even if she'd had the time, she would have taken the direct route anyway.

"You are my grandmother."

Sage didn't know what she had expected, maybe the woman laughing at such an absurd idea or arguing with her or maybe even kicking her out of the building. But instead, the woman smiled in a satisfied way and turned to face Sage directly again.

"This is true," Nayana said. She brushed the scarves away from her face and slid the rest of the headdress away, backward and off. For the first time, Sage saw her entire face unhidden. Her once fair skin was now freckled and weathered by the sun. She'd once had auburn hair, just like Sage's. The color was still there, though it was now dominated by gray. Sage studied the woman—her grandmother—studied her features, her coloring, her shape.

Nayana spoke with great pride. "Your grandfather said you were very clever."

"He ... he thought you were dead," Sage responded hesitantly. "You mean ... he knew? He knew you were alive and didn't tell us?" Sage asked in disbelief.

Nayana smiled calmly and gestured for Sage to sit on the couch. Sage moved behind the table and sat, her grandmother taking a seat beside her. Sage's mind was racing with questions, but Nayana spoke first.

"He did think I was dead, and I ... Well, I didn't know what had become of him. We were very fortunate to have reunited early this spring."

"Why? I mean, how could he not know you were alive? You were *married*!" Sage said, confused. "He said you died after my mother was born."

"It is a long story—one your grandfather and I planned on sharing with your mother and the rest of you when you came for your vacation this spring. When he died ... Well, it changed things." She paused sadly. "I never expected you and Douglas to walk into my shop, but once you did, well, I knew I would be seeing you again."

"Why did you leave in the first place? Didn't you ever wonder about him— or my mother? How could you let them think you were dead all these years? You didn't want them—*us*? And why didn't you come see us after Grandpa died?" Anger rose in Sage's voice.

Nayana smiled broadly, only irritating Sage more. She started to rise from the couch when Nayana grabbed her wrist, pulling her back down and speaking gently to her.

"Of course you will have many questions, but as I told you, it is a long story, one that hurt everyone involved. I didn't mean to offend you. I only smile because you are so much like Spencer described. *Please*. Sit down," Nayana said.

Sage sat back on the couch, crossing her arms tightly across her chest, and waited for Nayana to explain.

"One summer, I met Spencer—your grandfather—at the lake. His parents had bought the cabin as a summer home, and he loved being in the forest and at the lake. In fact, he spent most of his time there. I had seen him every summer from the time we were children, but we didn't speak to each other for the first time until we were both teenagers. We were instant friends. He was charming, smart, funny—and not allowed in our community."

"You mean because he wasn't an elf," Sage interjected.

"Yes, but I didn't know if you knew about all of that yet," Nayana said with relief. "That will make this story a little easier to explain—and, hopefully, to understand. You see, before I met your grandfather, I was promised to another. Betrothals were made to strengthen the magic in and between families. My parents thought his powers were a good match for mine, that our status in the communities would be higher if we married. I had known him all of my life, and we liked each other well enough. Well, the friendship between Spencer and me made the man I was betrothed to very jealous. I started seeing more glimpses of the anger I had always sensed in him, anger that had stayed just below the surface. After a few summers, it was clear that my heart belonged to your grandfather, and I broke things off with the young man. He seemed to take it well enough and wished us the best. Your grandfather and I were married that next spring. We were very happy together, but since we were not accepted into the elf community, we moved to the city, where Spencer had gone to college and wanted to begin his own business. It was hard for me to be away from my family, my friends, and the forest. When I found out I was pregnant, I begged your grandfather to move me to the cabin so I could be close to my parents when the baby came. It was wonderful to be home again, even if I wasn't actually in the forest. Your grandfather was happy there, too." Nayana sighed and lowered her eyes for just a moment, fiddling with one of the many bangle bracelets around her wrists.

"When your mother was born, Spencer was so excited! A little girl. He insisted that your mother have a pink outfit right away and that I deserved a special gift. So, he left me at the cabin in the care of my parents while he drove into town for groceries and presents. While he was gone, the man I was supposed to have married showed up at the cabin. He brought flowers and *ooh*ed and *aah*ed over your mother sleeping in the bassinet. He was really quite charming. Then he heated some water and brewed some tea from herbs grown in his own garden for us. I can remember drinking the tea...." She lifted her eyes to meet Sage's.

"He drugged you?" Sage asked with astonishment.

Nayana nodded slowly, her eyes distant and unfocused. Sage did not interrupt the thoughts of the woman she now knew to be her grandmother. She simply waited, silently watching until Nayana was ready to continue.

"Your grandfather and I thought we finally had it all figured out just before he died," she continued, turning to look directly at Sage. "I know this is a lot to take in, and I have wanted to go to the cabin so many times to be with the family I never was given the chance to know. There is much more to the story." She glanced down at her watch. "Good heavens!" she cried, springing up from the couch. She grabbed her scarves and set them properly over her forehead, adjusting them to drape over her hair.

Sage's heart leapt into her throat. She was late to meet her mother. How would she explain this?

"I have an appointment coming any moment!" Nayana exclaimed. "We'll have to stop for now. Will you come back?" She reached out and took both of Sage's hands in her own. Sage could feel the warmth of her and hear the sincerity and urgency in her voice. "Please," she continued, "I want you to know everything—at least everything that I know."

Sage couldn't think of anything to say, with all of the thoughts that were racing through her head. She needed to get to the grocery store. This woman was the grandmother she never had. What else had happened to keep her away for so long? The words spilled from her mouth before she had thought them through. "I'll come back tomorrow morning. I'll bring everyone," she said, surprised at the sound of her own voice.

Nayana drew her hands back from Sage as if she had been burned.

"Everyone?" Nayana cried. "Oh, no! Oh, I don't know. It's too soon. I don't know if I am ready. What will they think?"

Sage could feel panic rising in Nayana once again, her eyes growing large.

"It has to happen sometime. It might as well happen sooner than later," Sage told her, trying to sound reassuring. "My mother ... everyone can handle it. They'll want to know."

Nayana was quite petrified now and stared unblinking at Sage. Sage, however, could wait no longer to return to her mother. Running to the door, she turned the knob, then stopped abruptly with the door open.

"It was Evron," she said. "The man you were supposed to marry. It was Evron, wasn't it?"

The tiny gasp that escaped Nayana's lips was answer enough.

"Tomorrow morning, then," Sage repeated before turning and running out the door, heading to the grocery on the next block.

Thoughts of what she would say to her mother when she reached the grocery store began swirling in her head. She was almost fifteen minutes beyond their set meeting time, and her mother was sure to be getting worried. When Sage rounded the corner and crossed the street, there was her mother, standing next to the car and checking her watch. *Which excuse? Which excuse?* she thought.

"There you are! I was starting to get really worried. Where have you been? The library is the *other* way, and you weren't there," Adel said pointing down the street in the direction opposite from which her daughter had come.

"I'm sorry, Mom. I got done at the library really early and decided to take a look around town," she began. *No lies*, she instructed herself. "I ... met one of Grandpa's old friends, and we talked for a long time. I guess I just lost track of the time, listening to the stories. I really am sorry," she finished. She waited, hoping her mother would not ask too many questions.

"Who was it? One of the guys from the coffee shop?" her mother asked as she pulled the car away from the curb.

"No." Sage tried not to get flustered. "It was ... a woman. She said she knew him when he was a teenager. I think you would like her. I told her I would come back to visit and bring you, Dad, and Douglas with me."

"That's nice, but we're running out of time for you to have promised her that," her mother said. Her eyes were focused on the curvy road.

"Well, that's just the thing. I kind of said we would be back tomorrow morning." Sage squeezed her eyes shut tightly as she said the words, bracing for the worst.

"You said what? Don't you think you should have asked before you made those plans?" Adel scolded.

"We could all go to breakfast at Marge's before we see her. We haven't been there all summer," she said trying to play on the idea of a family outing. "Mom, I really want you to meet her."

"Well, we don't have any choice now, do we?" her mother retorted. She was clearly annoyed. "You kind of locked us into it already."

Sage slunk down in her seat, but she couldn't say she was sorry. Her mind told her that everything that had happened this summer was connected—and the book was part of it. Sage could feel it. And the verses she had read so far already held new meaning. Tonight she would read more in the mysterious book and prepare a list of questions for Nayana. She was excited about what this new discovery would mean for her family, but for now, the only thought that screamed in her head was *What have I done?*

CHAPTER 16

Nayana Remembers

The book her grandfather left her was large, square and thick. The pages inside were of a heavy weight and edged in gold. But not all of its pages were used. In fact, even with the many lovely paintings and sketches of the different elven communities and the various writings, there were many pages left untouched at the back of the book. Still, it took Sage most of the afternoon to make out the handwriting of what appeared to be multiple authors and decipher writing on pages that were torn, blotched, or discolored. There was some significance to the book coming into her possession when it did, she was certain. She wondered now if there was some importance in the writings that she was also meant to know.

Sage gently turned the pages back, finding a page that had caught her attention on her first reading. The handwriting and the writing style were much different, so she felt sure the author had changed from the writer of the first two poems. She scanned down to the line 'Child of the Wind' as she had the first time she had skimmed through the book. *Too many similarities*, she thought. Sage closed the book in her lap.

She rose from her usual spot in the forest and headed toward home. Sage knew she didn't actually have permission to be in the forest today and that her father would certainly not have allowed her to venture very far. Still, she needed to be in the forest. There was much to figure out, and he hadn't been home to ask when she and her mother had returned from their trip into town. How quick he had been to tell her she was reading too much into the happenings with Anila in Ambara. She hoped that he would be more willing to listen to her if she could gather more substantial proof.

No one was surprised when Avery didn't make it home for dinner. Douglas had explained that Evron had called a meeting in Ashtyn about the incident with Terran and that their father had left that morning shortly after Sage and their mother.

"Frayne, Hannah, and some other people had to be there, too," he had told them. "That is going to be one intense conversation. Evron isn't very pleasant when he's, uh, happy? He'd be downright scary when he's angry." Douglas had shuddered at the thought. That was the first time Douglas had shared his impression of Evron. Sage smiled. Until now, she had thought herself to be alone in her opinion of him. Tomorrow's meeting with Nayana would help her father to see the side of Evron she had already sensed.

The meeting with Nayana! She had been trying to occupy herself, wanting to put it out of her mind. Every time she thought about it, her heart and mind would begin to race, and her stomach would churn fiercely. *This could all end up being a huge disaster*, she thought, sighing. It was too late now. She wished she would have thought it through before rushing to set the meeting. Sage wanted time to slow down like it seemed to do when she was waiting for something she very much anticipated. To her dismay, the evening flew by. As she was preparing to go to bed, her father finally walked through the door.

"Whew! It's still hot out there." He looked exhausted but managed a weak smile. "Terran is doing much better today, a little tender yet, but up and around. He's hoping to be able to visit you two tomorrow afternoon sometime." Avery didn't seem to want to talk any more than that, and neither Douglas nor Sage thought it would be a good idea to ask how the meeting went.

Sage wasn't able to sleep most of the night and only fitfully when sleep did come. She finally decided just to get up and take a shower. The soothing heat and sound of the water offered her only temporary comfort. When she finally could find the strength to shut the shower off, she knew she would still have to face the reality of the upcoming day and the effect it would have on her family. The rest of the household still needed to rise and shower, so Sage planned to keep to herself to avoid questions she wasn't ready to answer. She worried how her father would feel about these plans she had made without his or her mother's input. She worried about what kind of comment Douglas would make when they walked into Ana's Ever-Seeing Eye again. Most of all, she worried how her mother would react when she was introduced to the mother she had always believed to be dead.

For now, Douglas was fine with getting to eat breakfast at Marge's Coffee Shop, and her mother had apparently forgiven her daughter's inconsiderate behavior. As for Avery, he was whistling when he came from the bedroom. *Always a good sign*, Sage thought.

"Everyone ready?" he asked cheerfully. "Let's get out of here before anyone comes calling for another meeting!"

The smell of fresh coffee and the shop's famous Belgian waffles filled the air when they entered the coffee shop. Most of the locals had known Spencer, and they all made it a point to greet the family when they took their seats at a large booth. They commented on how much the children had grown since the last time they had seen them and how much they missed seeing Spencer coming in for a cup of coffee.

Coming into town for breakfast had always been one of Sage and Douglas's favorite treats when they were visiting their grandfather. Douglas didn't even have to look at the menu to know what he would be ordering. Sage envied him and his iron stomach. She had to decide between something sensible for her uneasy belly or splurging on what she felt could be her last meal, her favorite Belgian waffle mounded with strawberries and rich whipped cream. Her stomach grumbled angrily again. *A bagel with cream cheese it is*, she thought.

"Are you feeling all right?" Adel asked. She was looking at the half-eaten bagel on Sage's plate.

"Um ... yeah. I guess the heat has bothered my appetite," she replied.

"It hasn't bothered mine," Douglas said matter-of-factly.

"No," Avery laughed at the empty plate in front of Douglas. "It most certainly has not!"

"So, where are we supposed to meet this mystery woman of yours?" Adel teased.

"Just in town. We can walk there." Sage squirmed uneasily.

Moisture condensed on Sage's arms when she stepped from the coolness of the coffee shop into the hot, sticky air. The skies were overcast, and though storm clouds hadn't moved in yet, thunder rumbled in the distance.

"Good," Avery sighed. "A decent storm will break this awful heat!"

They followed Sage as she took the same route she had the previous day, down the road and across to the main street. She reached the doorway of the storefront, her heart pounding with excitement and dread.

"What?" Douglas shrieked. "Here?" He looked at Sage in the most disagreeable way. His expression clearly indicated his cynicism, not that she needed to see his face to know what he was feeling.

"You'll understand in a moment." She replied so seriously that it caught Douglas off guard.

Douglas walked in first, their parents giving Sage puzzled looks as they passed through the door she held open for them. The four of them stood inside the front room for what seemed like a very long time to Sage, though it was only a few moments. Sage had once imagined that this place could be bright and cheery when filled with the morning light. This morning, however, the gray from outside seemed to mute even the most vibrant colors of the shop's décor. Douglas held his comments but made certain Sage knew he was unhappy about her bringing him to this place again. Avery and Adel looked suspiciously around the room, leaving Sage to hope Nayana would come before her parents decided to walk out.

With the softest swish of her dress on the floor, Nayana entered. Although a bit tattered, she wore the traditional dress of the elves in a pale green, with the mark of a bear embroidered on her left chest. It was evident she had taken great care in preparing herself. She wore tasteful make-up and jewelry. Her hair was brushed smooth, and part of it was pulled neatly out of her face and fastened with a gold clip. Sage could feel that Nayana was even more nervous than she was, giving her little comfort about what was to come. Avery bowed his head deeply and respectfully, bringing a slight smile to Nayana's frozen face as she returned his greeting.

"Do I *know* you?" Adel asked. Her eyes narrowed, creasing her forehead.

"Yes … and no," Nayana replied, obviously having difficulty controlling her emotions in this stressful situation. She may have shared that same trait with Sage, but her speech patterns and body movements were surprisingly similar to Adel's.

Sage was beginning to feel queasy from the strong mix of emotions coming from everyone in the room. Continuing was her only option. She didn't know how to begin but knew she should not put Nayana in the position of introducing herself. Her parents must have felt the same way, because their eyes seemed to pierce right through her as they awkwardly waited.

"Um, well … As you know, I had looked up the meanings of our friends' names," Sage began, not really knowing where to start. "I thought it would be fun after Douglas opened the crest Grandpa had given him for his birthday—the one showing the meaning of his name. Mom asked me to look up Dad's name so we could get him a necklace like Douglas's."

Everyone was staring at Sage with puzzled looks. They couldn't understand the reason for her bringing up the names now. Even Nayana, who hadn't thought to ask how Sage had managed to figure out her real name, looked at her in confusion. Sage tried to calm her nerves with a long breath before continuing.

"When I was at the library yesterday, I had a little extra time, so I looked up some other names to surprise Mom." Sage turned to look at her mother. "Spencer means 'butler or steward,'" she said, receiving a small nervous smile from her mother. "Nayana means 'eye,'" she stated. She waited, looking at the faces of her family, expecting everyone to make the connection, but Nayana was the only one who understood. She smiled, her lips still together, and nodded her head approvingly at Sage.

"Don't you see? You saw the name of this shop before we came in, didn't you?" Sage asked her family. She was even more nervous now and blinked back the tears that stung her eyes. "That's why I was late yesterday," she said turning to her mother. "I needed to know if I was right. I needed to know if the Ana of Ana's Ever-Seeing Eye—the woman Douglas and I met earlier this summer—was my grandmother!" Sage was unable to hide the feelings that had been bottled up since the previous morning any longer. Tears began to stream down her face as she silently waited for the information to sink in.

Avery and Douglas stood with their mouths gaping open, watching without being able to speak or move. Tears ran down Nayana's face, too. Sage could feel her grandmother's relief in sharing her long-held secret, the pain of all the years she had been separated from those she loved most and her fear of being rejected by her only remaining family. Adel slowly took her eyes off Sage and shifted them to Nayana. She covered her mouth at the shock, knowing what she had heard was the truth. She did know this woman and felt the bond that was forever theirs. More feelings flooded over Sage. Joy, disbelief, sadness, and shock mixed with the feelings Nayana no longer tried to shield from Sage.

A new sensation overtook Sage as time seemed to slow. She swayed, light-headed and queasy. Someone was talking to her, but it was too garbled to understand. Her legs quivered. She felt a brush of a hand just before her knees buckled beneath her.

"… Spencer suspected … empathic. How long has she known she has the power?" Sage could hear Nayana's voice, though she couldn't yet open her eyes.

"Just this summer," Adel managed to stammer in a shaky voice.

"It was too much for her, too soon. She hasn't learned how to handle all the emotions that must have been coming at her," Nayana continued.

"She could feel *everything*?" Adel asked. She gave Sage's hand a firm squeeze.

Sage felt everyone close to her. They were crouched around her as she lay on the floor.

"Here she comes," Douglas said as Sage's eyes began to flicker open. *Douglas caught me*, Sage thought as her eyes began to focus. He helped her sit up slowly and kept his arm around her shoulder for support. The emotions that had filled her and made her woozy were still present. For the moment, though, her fainting had distracted everyone enough to weaken the effects.

"Let's move her to the couch," Avery suggested. Together, he and Douglas lifted her from the floor.

"Good idea," Nayana said moving to give them a clear path to the sofa. "Why don't we all have a seat and try to calm down a bit, shall we?"

Douglas sat on one side of Sage, Adel on the other, hooking her arm through Sage's. After offering Avery the chair she usually sat in while giving readings, Nayana left the room for a moment. She returned with another chair and a box of tissues, which she set on the small table in front of the couch. Everyone had calmed down from the initial shock, even though the strangeness and inconceivability of the information had only just begun to sink in. Adel stared at Nayana, studying her just as Sage had done the day before, while Avery and Douglas shifted their eyes uncomfortably around the room, trying not to make eye contact. Feeling much better now, Sage nodded encouragingly at Nayana.

"Spencer and I met quite by accident early this past spring," she began. "He had believed me to be gone from this world and I— Well, let's just say that neither one of us ever expected to see the other one again." She turned to Adel.

"It took your father and I weeks to piece together the events of that night so many years ago. He had planned on explaining it all to you himself— but once again fate has kept me from you. And from him. I can only hope that after hearing the story you will find it in your heart to one day forgive me for my foolishness."

"Before I met Spencer ..." She began her painful retelling, twisting and bunching the tissue clasped in her hands. She continued through the story to the place she had reached with Sage the previous day. Adel was wiping her eyes with a tissue, and everyone sat silent in astonishment.

"That is where Sage and I left off yesterday morning," she told everyone. "There is a bit more to know. However, we are now entering the part of the story Spencer and I could only speculate upon. It was pieced together between the two of us. You see, the drink that had been given to me made me very sleepy. I excused myself to the bedroom to rest while the baby—you, Adel— was still asleep. When I awoke, the man who I was supposed to have married was there alone. He told me that my beautiful baby had died very suddenly while I was asleep and that my parents had taken her body to be properly buried. He said they didn't want to cause me any more pain by having to see her." Adel gasped audibly. "I was so confused by the drug he had given to me in the tea that what he said didn't seem strange. He then told me that Spencer had returned home to see me sleeping while our daughter lay dead in her bassinet. He said that Spencer was so distraught he couldn't bear remaining in the cabin, that he could never forgive me for allowing her death. This, too, made sense in a way."

Avery and Douglas watched Nayana closely now, hanging on every word of her story.

"I was told—very kindly and sympathetically, mind you—that the Council had already decided I should not be allowed to return to Oakley or any other of the communities, that I had chosen my path, and it was the human world." Nayana paused, lost for a moment in thought. "I left the cabin that night, mourning the loss of my child, my parents and ... my husband. Since then, I traveled the country, sticking close to large forested areas. I made a modest living, giving readings to those who believed or," she looked at Douglas with teasing a smile, "those who were just out for cheap entertainment." Douglas smiled at her, and for the first time since Terran's attack, Sage smiled, too. "I returned to the area late this winter," she continued. "I could not resist going to see the cabin. It had changed a great deal, so I figured after all of these years it must have new owners. I went to the door to ask if they had any knowledge of Spencer or his whereabouts and, as you can imagine, I was stunned when he was the one who opened the door. Just like that," she said snapping her fingers, "it was as if the fog that had surrounded me for all that time lifted, and the absurdity of the whole story became obvious. The same must have been true for Spencer as well because when he told me what happened to him, he shook his head and snorted at the ludicrousness of it all," she said sadly. "It was such a pained, cynical laugh—certainly not the carefree, joyful laugh that filled my memories—a laugh I had missed so very much."

Everyone smiled and nodded sympathetically, missing his laughter as well.

"What happened to my father?" Adel asked, urging Nayana to continue.

"Yes, well … Back on that same night, he had returned home to find that same person in the cabin with me and the baby. Spencer went to check on me, finding me still and not breathing. The man told him how sorry he was, told him that I had gotten very tired and gone in to rest while the baby slept. He said my parents went to wake me when Adel had begun to cry and found I had passed away in my sleep from complications of childbirth. Spencer was told that my parents had gone home to make arrangements for my funeral and that they would only be returning to retrieve my body. Spencer questioned nothing because he, too, had been offered a cup of tea to calm his nerves, making everything he heard much more convincing. The man suggested that Spencer leave immediately so he wouldn't have to watch my body being removed from the cabin. Spencer was then told he should take the baby back to the city to start their lives together and never return to the cabin again. Well, as you know, it wasn't until Adel was a teenager that Spencer chose to return and fix up the cabin, later deciding to make it his retirement home. As near as we could figure, the magic that had been used to deceive us broke when we saw the truth for ourselves. If I had just foreseen it …"

Adel was unable to speak through her tears but managed to reach her hand out across the table, offering it to Nayana for comfort. Both of the women cried and wiped their faces.

"Who was he?" Avery asked angrily. "Who was the man you were betrothed to?"

Nayana looked at Sage, suddenly afraid.

"It's Evron, Dad. Evron caused all of this to happen," Sage answered for Nayana.

"You were supposed to marry Evron?" Douglas asked. He ran his hands through his short hair just like his father did when he was frustrated or bothered.

"We have to go," Avery said sternly. "We should go now!"

"What? Why?" Adel asked, confused.

Having already anticipated the dangers of them coming to her, Nayana said calmly, "He is right, Adel."

"If Evron was capable of doing that all those years ago, he is surely capable of much more now! He cannot know she is back!" Avery had risen from his chair and moved to glance out the window. "Just our presence here puts her in danger—and maybe us, too."

"But— I just found her, Avery! My mother!" Adel pleaded, getting up from the couch.

"We will come back, Adel, but we have lingered here too long for one day," he said gently, cupping her face in his hands.

Adel nodded, reluctantly agreeing to leave. Sage rose from the couch, still a little shaky. Douglas held her elbow as they joined their parents by the door.

"Wait!" Sage said to her parents and turned to speak to Nayana. "You foresee things, right? Do you know of a book? My grandfather gave me a book—one that only reveals its pages in or near the forest."

"Yes! It was my book with writings from all the Seers in my family before me. I was the last of my family to write in those pages," she said, nodding with relief. "It is safe. Oh, thank goodness it is safe! Keep it close to you. Do not leave it at the cabin when you return home."

"Do you wish us to return it to you?" Avery asked.

"No, that is not necessary," Nayana smiled. "I believe it is where it belongs."

"Some of the poems—the ones I have been able to figure out—are happening now," Sage said slowly, looking pointedly at her father.

"Yes," Nayana said thoughtfully. "It has been long foreseen that our people will leave and our power will fade. As I recall, there are a few writings in the book about that, and Seers in other communities foretold the same end."

"Yes, that—and more," Sage replied, turning to the door.

"I am very sorry to cut your long-awaited reunion short. We will be in contact with you again soon, Nayana," Avery said clasping her hand warmly. "Until then, be safe."

Douglas and Sage each said their goodbyes awkwardly, not knowing if they were ready to give their newly found grandmother more than a handshake. Adel, however, approached her mother and warmly embraced her, whispering something that brought new tears to them both.

After one last peek out the window, the family left the small shop and walked silently back to their car. The trip home was silent as well, except for Adel's quiet sobs and the occasional rumble of thunder. When they reached the cabin, everyone walked up the steps with heavy feet. It was still early in the afternoon, but Sage was exhausted. Avery unlocked the door and let Adel and Douglas pass into the cabin. He straightened out his arm in front of the door, blocking Sage's entrance to the home.

"I need to know everything. You need to tell me *everything* you know," he said seriously.

She looked directly into his eyes and, with the conviction of someone who had proven herself, said, "I know there are no coincidences."

Chapter 17

Thunderstorm

Nothing else was said outside of the house to be certain they would not be overheard by anyone lurking in the forest. Everyone took their usual places around the kitchen table for a family meeting. Sage carefully recounted everything that had happened since the beginning of summer, from meeting Evron for the first time at their grandfather's funeral and the readings Nayana had given to the poetry in the book they now knew to be visions of what could be. Having witnessed some of the events themselves, Douglas and even Avery began to view them in a different light—and to see them as pieces of a bigger picture.

"It's just so unreal," Adel said. "These kinds of things are fantastical—made for movies. This simply cannot really be happening." She shook her head.

"I heard you talking to Evron," Sage admitted to her father. "I was sitting in the forest reading the book when you came near me, arguing, but I didn't mean to eavesdrop. He said he had 'known one once' and had 'read it himself.' He was talking about Nayana and the book, wasn't he?"

"Hmm. Yes, he must have been. It makes sense now, and it was right there in front of me all along," he said. He ran his fingers through his hair, exasperated. "We had come from a meeting about the strange things that have been happening. He said that everything had been foreseen and that the time was drawing near. I had heard of the prophecies as a child—vaguely. We all had. But I thought he was just making up what he was saying to start scaring people. If you're right," he said looking at Sage, "he doesn't remember all of the prophecies he read very clearly. He thinks he can choose who the three are and wants me to represent the Sky Realm."

"Evron would represent the Forest Realm, right?" Douglas asked his dad. "If he wants you for the Sky Realm, who do you think he would try to get from Layton? I mean, maybe we should all start spreading the word."

"No. We can't say anything yet, at least not to anyone that we don't trust with our lives." He grimaced. "We have to be sure not to let Evron suspect any change in our behavior, either. He absolutely *cannot* know about Nayana or the book." Avery set his eyes on Adel. She looked helpless and afraid. Gently, he took her hand in his own before continuing. "You need to tell Terran and Anila," he told Sage. "Anila's amazing similarities to the legend do not necessarily make her one of the foreseen, but she should know what you think, nonetheless." Avery continued, "Douglas, you need to talk to Lamar so he can keep his eyes open to anything out of the ordinary." Douglas nodded his understanding. "I will talk to Frayne, Jake, and Hannah. They have been concerned about Evron's growing influence in the communities and his desire to eliminate the representatives from the Council for several years. I can trust them to keep my confidence." Avery paused. "I will arrange for the both of you and Terran to stay with Anila and her family tomorrow night after the End-of-Summer Celebration. It will be safer if you won't have to travel back home in the dark. I'll take that time to meet with Frayne and the others." Avery looked up at the clock and out the window at the darkening sky. The storm was approaching. "Terran was hoping to see you, and it would be better to tell him today," he said. "There won't be much of an opportunity at the End-of-Summer Celebration tomorrow night." Sage could feel he was uncertain about letting them go, but she and Douglas rose from the table, preparing to leave anyway. "Stay together and make sure that you only speak about this when and where you cannot be overheard," Avery advised. "Sage," Avery called out before she and Douglas had gotten to the door, "I'm sorry I didn't listen to what you were trying to tell me. I suppose I wasn't ready to believe what was right in front of me all along. It won't happen again."

Sage couldn't help smiling as they walked along the trail. In one emotional day, she had helped reunite her grandmother with her family and her father had finally listened to and believed her. She knew there was more to figure out and that whatever was going to happen, whenever it was going to happen, would be dangerous simply because Evron was involved. Even so, she smiled to herself for remaining determined and trusting her instincts.

Thunder was growing louder, and the sky had become dark, making the forest appear as it normally did at dusk. They walked to where the path split, the place where they normally met Terran and Anila. There, reclining against his usual tree, was Terran. He smiled broadly at them and moved to where they stood on the trail. He walked with only the slightest limp, almost completely healed from what was a serious sprain only two days before. The gashes on his face were healed as well, appearing merely as faint marks.

"It's amazing," Sage said. "You look almost normal."

"Well, I wouldn't call Terran *normal*," Douglas teased as he gave Terran a friendly punch in the arm. "It's good to see you, man."

"I meant you look good...." She flushed. "You look almost healed." Terran smiled at her, making her even more flustered.

"I was really lucky that my aunt and uncle were home," he said. "I would still be on crutches and spreading goop on my cuts if they hadn't been."

"Well, we're really glad you're okay. Where's Anila?" Douglas asked.

"She's in Oakley, helping to set up for tomorrow night," Terran replied. "You guys are still planning on coming, aren't you?"

"Yeah, we're coming," said Douglas.

"Hey there!" a voice called to them from the other trail. It was Lamar, jogging up to them from the lake. He nodded a greeting to Sage and Terran.

"Where have you been hiding?" he asked Douglas.

"It's been pretty busy ... and we need to talk," Douglas told him in a much more serious tone.

"Sure. What's up?" Lamar asked, his brows knitting together.

"How about a swim?" Douglas suggested. He slung an arm around Lamar's shoulder and guided him back the direction from which he had just come.

"Whoa. He sounded serious," Terran commented as he watched them walk away.

"Yeah, he is. And I need to talk to you about the same thing," Sage told him.

Terran raised his eyebrows at her. They started to walk toward the lake when a large crack of thunder startled them both.

"Come on!" he said, grabbing Sage's hand. He moved as quickly as he could manage to the cave by the river. "We are about to get really wet."

"What about Douglas and Lamar?" she asked.

Terran laughed and said, "They're going for a swim, remember? They're probably already soaked!"

The rocks were more slippery than the last time, now that the rain had begun to coat them. Terran moved slowly and cautiously down the bank, not only because his ankle was still unstable but also to help Sage along the slick rocks. He pulled her into the cave just as the sky let loose, already bringing a refreshing coolness to the air. They sat in the dry cave as the heavy rain created a curtain across its entrance. Terran rubbed his ankle and circled it around, relaxing the stiffness. Watching him continue to stretch, point and flex his foot once again stirred up the guilty feelings Sage had been trying to fight.

"I'm really sorry about what happened," Sage said.

"You don't still think it was supposed to have been you, do you?" he asked. "It could have been any one of us."

"You won't be saying that after you hear what I have to tell you," she said, knowing it would get his full attention. "Do you remember that book I showed you?" she asked. "You know, the one with the painting of Ashtyn and the poetry?"

"The one you had the first time I brought you here? Yeah, I remember," he answered, still trying to find a comfortable position for his ankle.

"Well, I just found out today that it was my grandmother's book. It has writings from generations of her family—generations of Seers."

"Seers? Like Lamar was talking about?" he stopped fussing with his ankle and turned to her. "Wow! How'd you find that out?"

"You know that lady we saw in town, the one who gave us each a reading?" Sage didn't need to continue. She saw Terran's eyes widen with sudden understanding.

"Noooo …" he moaned. "She's your grandmother? I thought your grandmother died before you were born!"

"Yes, supposedly right after my *mother* was born, actually," she explained.

"Why didn't she say something when we were there?" he asked curiously. "I mean, why wait this long?"

"She's afraid of being found, Terran."

"Afraid?" he asked. "Afraid of what?"

"Before she met my grandfather, she was betrothed to another man—well, an elf. He was jealous of my grandfather and angry with the both of them. He did some terrible things, Terran." Sage took a deep breath before saying the hardest part. "She was supposed to have married Evron."

Terran looked at her, his face showing both understanding and confusion at the same time. It was as if he hadn't heard her correctly or just didn't want it to be true.

"My grandfather? I've never heard about …" He paused and then continued more slowly. "Oh, yes. The girl." He thought for a moment about his grandfather's general dislike of humans. "Well, that explains a lot, doesn't it?" he said sadly, shaking his head back and forth. "How did you find out? Did she just show up at the cabin and say 'Here I am'?"

"No, I found her. There's more to the story," she said as she began to tell Terran everything. He listened intently as she shared what her grandmother had told her, asking questions now and then. He lowered his head, still concentrating on her words as she explained what she had only just begun to discover in the book. When she finished talking, he sat silently for a long time in thought. Sage grew concerned at his silence, wondering how he was taking the news and even more concerned that he not tell Evron what she knew.

"I'm sorry this happened to your family," he finally said. "I have always respected my grandfather, Sage."

"He can't know about the book or Nayana, Terran! If he found out …"

"He won't!" Terran told her, grasping her wrist and looking directly into her frightened eyes. "Not from me anyway," he promised, and she knew it was the truth. He loosened his hold on her wrist and softened his voice again. "I was going to say that I have always respected Evron, but I have also always believed he was capable of doing things … dark things. I just didn't know he already had." He sighed. "So, if what you believe is true," he continued with a hint of laughter in his voice, "sometime, somehow, and in some way—none of which we have the slightest idea about—the three realms will unite, and the people and their powers will return. Right?" Sage nodded, relief replacing her previous worry. "You haven't had a chance to tell Anila yet, have you?" he asked with renewed seriousness.

"No. I haven't. I'll do it tomorrow." Sage groaned at the unpleasant task ahead of her.

"We will. We will tell her," he said. He stood up to check out the back of the cave. It was still raining, but much more softly now and the thunder was once again rumbling in the distance. He turned back to Sage.

"Someone is coming," he whispered. "I think it might be Douglas and Lamar looking for you."

"No," she whispered back. She stood to join him at the back of the cave, where a small opening allowed them to see part of the trail above. "It's Evron— and the man who was in the forest, the man who was laughing!"

Terran looked at her, bewildered. Both silently peered up at the trail. Two men walked along the trail, drawing closer to their hiding place. Although they didn't sound angry with one another, their tones were direct and stern.

"I will not tolerate any more mistakes," Evron spoke harshly.

"It was a … miscalculation," the man sneered wickedly.

"You are careless, and if another *miscalculation* occurs, I will be looking for another associate and you— Well, no one will come looking for you," said Evron coldly.

"It won't happen again," the man replied with forced deference.

Sage and Terran could not see the faces of the two men; the opening in the rocks only allowed them to see up to knee level at best. They could see, however, that the man Evron was talking to was nervous, shifting his weight from one foot to the other.

"Now," Evron's tone lightened, "there is much yet to do. In order to be prepared—when the time comes, that is—you will need to build your strength and develop new … shall we say, skills? After the event involving my grandson, no matter how slipshod your execution, you will certainly be seeing results."

"Yes." The man sounded eager. "Everyone in Oakley seems to be talking about it—him and his flying friend, that is. Hey, can't you just bring her along and not hassle with Avery?"

"No. Not yet, anyway. She has potential but also much to learn. The girl has always been a bit capricious." Evron must have noticed the man's confusion. "Flighty! She has always been a bit ditzy, you imbecile," he huffed. "No, I need Avery. He is distasteful to me in many ways, but he has assets that cannot be overlooked. It is nothing to be concerned about. I have several ways to help *motivate* him."

"Do we have the time for that, Evron? You said the time was near!"

"You must show more patience." Sage could envision a cold smirk snaking across Evron's lips. "The time is near, yes. But not immediate. After more than forty years, what is a handful more?"

Evron turned, his body no longer facing the direction of the cabin and lake.

"You said you have been hearing news in Oakley? I cannot afford to have you seen, especially tomorrow night. And whatever you do, nothing must happen to either of my grandsons," Evron warned the man. "They may be of some use to me yet. I must finish my preparations for the events." Evron turned swiftly, his cloak whipping in the air. "Do not return by the trail!"

Evron began walking away toward Ashtyn. The man stood for a moment before running into the rain-soaked woods and disappearing.

Sage and Terran stared out the small opening, watching for any sign of Evron or the man returning.

"If I hadn't believed you already ..." Terran began gravely. "How did you know it was him—I mean *them*?"

"It seems to be my gift—my power," she paused at the strangeness of the idea. "I am able to feel what other people are feeling. I felt how much your grandfather disliked me the moment we met at my grandfather's funeral. I think it's stronger toward me because I look 'remarkably like my grandmother,'" she said, making quotation marks in the air with her fingers. "I can still feel when it's him, but his anger doesn't bother me quite as much anymore. And I felt the other man in the forest before—well, before he sent the vine."

"Yeah, I remember the vine," he grimaced. "I also remember you saying that something was wrong—in the woods. I mean. You were feeling him, weren't you?"

"I could have been," she said, sounding unconvinced. "I must have been."

"So, are you able to tell what everyone is feeling?" he asked nonchalantly.

"I don't actually go around trying to tell what everyone is feeling. I seem to be more sensitive to feelings that are either very strong or very different from others."

"Well, what am I feeling right now?" he asked. Sage laughed at his obvious attempt to lighten their conversation.

"I haven't quite figured out how to read you yet," she admitted.

"Been trying, eh?" he continued teasing her. "Come on," he said after looking out the back of the cave one last time. "It's all clear."

They moved carefully, watching for any movement before stepping onto the trail. As they waited at the normal meeting place for Douglas and Lamar, Terran looked around uneasily.

"You shouldn't come into the forest alone anymore," he whispered. "You were right. That vine was meant for you."

She hadn't had time to think about not being able to be alone. The idea of losing her solitude here in the forest she had grown up loving and of others losing their sense of safety because of Evron's ambitions both angered and saddened Sage. She remained silent until Lamar and Douglas joined them. Lamar, normally cheerful and playful, stood quite solemnly next to Douglas. Sage recognized his newfound insecurity.

"Sooo," he said at a rare loss for words.

"Yeah, right?" Terran replied meaningfully. "We'll all have to be more careful—especially after what Sage and I just heard."

"What ..." Douglas began, interrupted by Sage.

"Not here, Douglas!" she shushed.

"We won't have a chance at the celebration tomorrow! There won't be a place to go that we couldn't be overheard," Lamar reminded them.

"Yeah, you're right. I'll come to the lake tomorrow morning and fill you in," Douglas arranged. "We can't breathe a word of this to *anyone*," he said to both Terran and Lamar.

They must have been gone longer than their parents expected, because Avery and Adel were waiting on the porch when they returned, concern lining their faces. Sage suggested they go inside to talk, saying that she had more news to pass along to everyone.

"So Evron has the mystery man in his service," Avery thought out loud. "It would be helpful if we knew where he's from."

"If he is still going to try to get you aboard, the man must not be from Ambara," Adel speculated.

"No," Avery agreed. "If he sent that vine, he has power over plants, like Evron. Evron may be trying to gather three strong players to do his dirty work for him. Otherwise, there would be no need for him to be working with the man from the forest. He said he only needed one elf from each of the realms. Whoever this mystery man is, though, he must be working on something with his powers." He rose from the kitchen table, raking his hands through his hair again. "That doesn't make sense, though. Anymore, there are very limited things we can do with our powers."

"You said yourself that if he was capable of doing what he did to my parents all that time ago, he would probably be capable of much more now," Adel argued.

"Well, I for one won't be taking tea with him, that's for sure," Douglas said, earning a glare from his mother. He grimaced and lowered his eyes sheepishly.

"Build strength … develop skills … event with Terran … seeing results," Avery mused aloud over the words from Sage's recounting of Evron's discussion.

"I know! I know what he was talking about!" Sage ran from the kitchen, returning moments later with her grandmother's book. She wanted to tear wildly through the pages in her excitement but forced herself to take great care with the now delicate paper. She stopped at a jotting not far from the end of the book's written pages.

"Yes, this is the one." She began to read aloud.

**Their power will be obtained
by the one responsible for their leaving.
Their return will be two-fold.**

"Their power will be two-fold," Douglas repeated. "That sounds scary."

"It is, Douglas!" Sage agreed. "Don't you see? When Terran was attacked, news spread really fast. Other than some strange activities like the serpent knocking out some light tubes, nothing has happened that was directly against a person. This was the first. There were already people considering leaving the communities before the attack happened. Some of them may now have decided it is time to go, especially if they feel it is no longer safe for them or their family. If they go, their power—actually, two-fold their power—will be given to the one who was directly responsible for them leaving—in this case, our mystery man. That's why Evron told the man he would be 'seeing results.'"

"But who knows how many years it's been since Evron has seen that book," Douglas argued. "How could he remember that you get more power when you scare people out of their homes?"

"He didn't have to remember," Avery now understood. "He lived it. Besides informing Nayana that she could no longer return to Oakley, who knows how many of the elves that have left over the years did so for reasons caused by Evron. And imagine Evron's abilities now after getting a two-fold return of the power of each of them." He traced his fingers over the words on the page. "I wish I had known about this book long ago or actually taken the time to look at it when your grandfather sent it to you." He sighed. "He knew it was meant to go to you."

CHAPTER 18
End-of-Summer Celebration

A very and Douglas met with Lamar while Sage and her mother washed laundry and began packing the things that would be going back to the city with them. Douglas had tried to convince their father he would be careful and could handle going to the lake on his own, but neither Adel nor Avery would hear of it. As much as he had protested, Sage could tell Douglas was actually relieved to have their father going with him, and they returned after about an hour without incident. For the remainder of the morning and into the afternoon, everyone worked together, completing tasks around the cabin in preparation for return home.

With chores completed, Douglas, Avery, and Sage took time to freshen up for the trip to Oakley. It wasn't until Douglas walked into the living room wearing one of Avery's silken suits that Sage realized her khaki capri pants and green t-shirt were not going to be acceptable at this traditional elven celebration. She crossed her arms, already feeling out of place.

"Don't you worry," her father told her with a reassuring smile. "I asked Delaney to make something special for you. You can change at Anila's house. Let's get going, shall we?"

"I wish you could come, too," Sage told her mother as they grabbed their backpacks.

"Oh, there are plenty of things for me to do around here," she said shrugging it off. "Besides, I would be liable to strangle Evron if I got the chance to." Adel touched her daughter's cheek and spoke more seriously. "There may be a time I will be welcome, but that time hasn't come yet. For now, I am happy that you and Douglas are able to share this part of your father's life. Have fun—and be very, very careful," Adel pleaded with her family.

"I think we can all rest easy tonight, Adel," Avery said comfortably. "For one thing, Evron is going to be right where we can see him the whole night.

Douglas and Sage deserve to have a great time. There has been far too much for us all to worry about since the summer began, so just for tonight, we should all try to relax and enjoy."

The skies were clear and the air warm. All of the energy-sapping humidity had been driven away with the storms the previous day. Sage took a deep breath and smiled. She loved the earthy smells of the forest and peaty ground, especially after a rain. Many of her friends at home would disagree with her, finding the scent too strong or dirty, but she knew Terran would agree with her—and probably Anila, too. Almost nine months would pass before she would see these woods again. Her smile drooped. *There are only a few days left*, Sage thought sadly. *Then I'll spend a whole school year longing for the scent and feel of the forest over the closed, stale air of the school and city.*

The walk went quickly, as Sage was lost in her thoughts. They were joined on the trail by several groups of people from Layton, heading in the same direction. Soon they were at the bridge to Ashtyn and standing before the stately old ash tree. *Surely what happened was my imagination because the legend was so fresh on my mind,* she supposed. The three of them passed through Ashtyn and continued on the trail toward Oakley. The numbers of people following behind them had grown, and a steady line was already moving ahead of them. As they approached the old mill along the water, Sage watched the giant wheel as it turned hypnotically with the force of the river. Soon people would be harvesting their crops, and the mill would be active with them bringing their grains for processing.

Sage found herself studying the forest again as it began to change in appearance and personality the closer they drew to Oakley. The walk was slowed because of the number of people on the trail, but before too long Sage could see as far up as the two entwined oak trees marking the entrance to the village. There were tents being set up on the edge of the village, blocking their view into the town center. The tents, Avery explained, belonged to those who had come from Layton and Ambara for the celebration and were not planning on returning home until the morning. Beyond the tents they could now see what looked like a hundred tables dressed in white linens, set up under the huge oak tree. Several people, each carrying a long, thin, glowing candle, moved between the formally laid tables. They stopped at every table, lighting the white pillar candles decorated with rings of bright, fragrant flowers.

The branches of the oak tree were still holding the colored banners Sage had admired on her first visit to Oakley. Others were placed around the town center, giving it splashes of color even in the fading sunlight. A large rectangular table raised on a platform stood alone at the edge of the other tables. It was flanked with four large flags, each bearing a different emblem. A serpent, a bear, an eagle and an ash leaf, all in gold embroidery, represented the four individual communities. A large open area lay behind it, and a long row of rectangular tables filling with food being brought by the townspeople lay beyond that.

Sage, Douglas, and Avery climbed the spiraling stairs to reach the series of platforms and bridges that would lead them to Anila's house. Sage would never have remembered the way on her own. On her first visit to Oakley, she was too curious about everything around her to have paid much attention to the complicated route, and on her second visit, Terran was her main concern.

Terran and his family had not arrived yet, and Sage decided to wait to talk to Anila until he was with her. She knew her father wouldn't be talking to Keelin and Hannah without the others being there as well. It would just have to wait for now, and that was fine for Sage. She wanted to have fun tonight, just like her father had said, and she wanted the same for her friends. There would be time to talk after the celebration, when they all returned to Anila's house for the night.

Anila took Sage to the hallway that circled the tree her house was built in. Broad stairs curved upward around the tree trunk. Near the end of the hallway—close to the top, as far as Sage could figure—was the door that led to Anila's room.

"We'll sleep in my room tonight. The boys will stay in there," she said pointing to the room at the end of the hall. "Let's put your stuff in my room, then we can get ready," Anila suggested as she opened her bedroom door.

It was a very simple room with soft green walls. It had wood floors and a large window, with branches and leaves her only view. Her bed was along the wall near the window, with a wonderfully ornate quilt Sage figured was one of Delaney's creations. A tall bookcase on the opposite wall was filled with both books and collectibles. Anila walked to her closet and lifted the garment that was hanging from the door.

"Here," she smiled. "Delaney made this for you."

Sage knew her dad had arranged something for her to wear, but she hadn't expected something so beautiful. She slipped on the embroidered tunic. It felt cool as the silky material slid over her skin and settled perfectly in place as if Delaney had taken her exact measurements. After she pulled on the flowing pants, she turned to look at herself in Anila's mirror.

"It's perfect," Anila beamed. And it was.

The girls headed back down to the main living area, finding Terran and Douglas dressed and ready. The two boys turned as they heard the girls enter the room. All of the gentlemen in the room stood respectfully, making Sage feel both flattered and self-conscious.

"Whoa." Douglas moaned long and low, watching them enter the room.

"Whoa is right!" Terran agreed.

Their reaction was no surprise to Sage. She felt beautiful with her hair twisted loosely at her neck, curly tendrils falling gently around her face. She knew she could never have managed that look on her own, but with a few maneuvers of her hands and two ornate hair sticks, Anila had worked magic. The red tones in Sage's auburn hair deepened, and the blue of her eyes intensified against the deep blue-green color of the material. The graceful cut of the suit accentuated her slimness and made her feel both feminine and elegant.

Anila was dressed in a beautiful silken suit of the palest silvery green. Her short-sleeved tunic was also very feminine and tailored differently than Sage's to complement her hourglass shape. It had a finely embroidered V-neck collar. The same embroidery decorated the bottom hem of her shirt, which hung to her knees and was split up each side to her hips. Under her top she wore cropped, wide-legged pants in the same silky material. She had on simple black ballet slippers accented with silver embroidery. As always, she was gorgeous.

Compliments were exchanged with everyone now dressed in their finest garments. Avery walked across the room to Sage and twirled his finger in the air for her to model her outfit with a spin.

"Yes," he said affectionately. "You look lovely."

He bent his head and kissed her on the cheek. Avery looked at her once more before moving back and allowing Terran to take his place before her. Terran bowed his head to Sage. She nodded slowly to him, maintaining eye contact, and blushed. Terran offered his arm. She hesitated only a moment, wondering if Anila might be uncomfortable with Terran escorting her to the celebration.

There was no need for concern, however, as Anila had already happily accepted Douglas's arm and was heading toward the door. Sage smiled at Terran and slid her hand through his bent arm. Together she and Terran followed the others outside. When they stepped from the house and onto the platform, Sage took in a sharp breath.

"I told you," Terran reminded her softly. "You should see it at night."

What seemed to be millions of soft white lights illuminated the village. Lights trimmed the bridges and platforms and even glowed from inside the houses. For as far as she could see and to the top of every tree, there were lights. High in the tallest branches, the slightest breeze moved the leaves and gave the appearance of twinkling stars or countless fireflies blinking in a grassy meadow. But this was even more beautiful. Here they surrounded her. The lights reflected on the glossy, hand-sized oak leaves above her and adorned the spiral staircases leading down to the celebration.

Joyful laughter and the smells of food filled the air. Flames flickered from the candles on the tables, casting a golden glow on the faces of those already gathered under the oak tree. The sweet smell of the fresh cut flowers was carried through the air on the warm evening breezes. Sage thought everything looked perfect and knew that, at least until they got back to Anila's house, everyone would have a wonderful night.

Anila led the way to three tables on the outer edge, close to where the long rectangular one was set up. Jason, Lamar, Lamar's younger brother, Dillon, and Sora, both who were about the same age, were already seated at one table. The friends stopped briefly at the table Lamar's parents and Jake and Aderyn sat for introductions and greetings before moving to another one nearby. It was the table where Delaney and her husband, Bryan, sat with their baby girl and two people Sage assumed were Jason's parents.

Delaney introduced Douglas and Sage to her husband, a very sharp-looking man with brown hair and soft brown eyes, and also to Hugh and Ophelia, who were indeed Jason's parents.

"Delaney, I can't thank you enough for making this for me," Sage began. "It fits me. Who I am. It's just beautiful."

"I was happy to do it. You look wonderful—all of you," she replied graciously.

Sage, Terran, Douglas, and Anila joined their friends while their parents took seats at the table at which Jake and Aderyn were already sitting. More and more people filled the tables under the giant oak until not one remained empty.

"Why do they call this the End-of-Summer Celebration?" Douglas asked. "It's only August."

"Well, it used to be in September when the harvest came in," Lamar explained. "But as people left the communities it got earlier and earlier. That way, anyone visiting for the summer months would be able to be here for the celebration and return home before the school year began."

A smattering of applause drew attention to five men, one of them being Evron, and three women walking slowly on the outside of the circle. Four of them carried the community flags that had been standing next to the raised table earlier that evening.

Terran leaned in close to Sage. "They are the elected officials of the High Council. Two from each community," he said over the increasing applause.

The clapping continued to strengthen as the officials approached the raised table and stopped in front of the stands for the flags. All the villagers rose from their seats and fell silent.

"Welcome, my friends." Evron's words carried easily to every table. "It has been a difficult year for our fine communities. But we," he opened his arms to acknowledge the other officials standing at his sides, "want to remind each of you that we have been through difficult times before. Tonight, we will celebrate our vitality."

Evron surprised Sage. *He's actually quite eloquent*, she thought, *and he's even smiling—sort of.* He wasn't looking at her, and she could feel no anger from him, just an underlying insincerity. *He really enjoys this. He loves being the center of attention—and being in charge.*

"Some of our people have had to make the difficult choice to leave, but even tonight we will be celebrating the birth of a beautiful baby girl to the community of Oakley. Some of our people have mysteriously lost their well-tended crops. But tonight we celebrate those friends who have seen the needs of others and helped replant or offered food from their own stores. Every difficulty we have seen this year has been followed by something for which to be thankful. So, my friends, tonight we, along with all of the representatives of your communities, hope you will eat well, dance until your feet are sore, and celebrate!"

Cheers and applause echoed through the forest as the four officials holding the flags set them firmly into their stands beside the head table. The eight left the platform once again, leading the gathering to the food. Sage was eating and enjoying her conversation with her friends when she felt him nearby. She had a sudden twinge of nausea, and a chill slid down her spine. Evron had finished eating and was approaching where they sat as he moved from table to table, greeting everyone.

"Shaking hands and kissing babies," Douglas whispered sarcastically into Sage's ear when he noticed whom she was watching.

"Good evening," Evron said, placing his hands on the shoulders of his two grandsons. "What a fine-looking group of young people we have here."

"Hello, grandfather," Terran said in a measured tone.

"How are you feeling today, Terran?" Evron inquired. There was no real warmth evident in his voice. Instead, he had addressed his grandson in a very businesslike manner.

"Much better today, thank you."

"Good, good. Now I know Jason will be heading back to Ashtyn with his parents tonight. I trust that the rest of you are not planning on traveling home tonight after what has happened." Evron managed to sound concerned for everyone's safety, but his genuine lack of it made Sage fume with irritation.

"No," Anila replied happily. "Terran, Douglas and Sage are staying with me tonight, sir."

"Fine. And the rest of you are planning on camping here tonight as usual?"

"Yes, sir," Lamar answered.

"Good. Well, I must continue on," Evron said, nodding sweepingly to their group. "Have an enjoyable rest of your evening."

As Evron moved to the table were her father sat, Sage exhaled and closed her eyes for a moment to calm her stomach. He had been very close again, and the strength of his anger much more concentrated, though his face had not shown it. Terran and Douglas, who sat on either side of Sage, began talking to her at the same time.

"You all right?" Douglas asked.

"Could you feel him again?" Terran asked.

"I'm fine now that he has moved on," she answered, "and yes, I could definitely feel him."

"What's going on?" Anila asked, seeing how pale Sage was looking. "Are you ill?"

"You haven't told her yet?" Lamar asked quietly. He leaned in and away from his brother and Sora, who weren't paying any attention anyway.

"Told me what?" Anila's excitement for the celebration quickly turned to anxiety.

Douglas looked over his shoulder to check where Evron had moved to. "We have to talk about something," he whispered.

"We haven't had a chance yet. But we will talk tonight," Sage told both Anila and Lamar.

Anila was still focused on their serious faces. "Did something else happen?" she asked.

"No," Sage assured her. "Everyone is fine. We just need to talk—later. After tomorrow, Douglas and I will be heading back home, so for right now, let's enjoy ourselves."

As if on cue, music started playing. Sage and Douglas stood with their friends and followed the sound, finally spotting the four musicians playing at the edge of the large clearing between the head table and the food. The music continued to play in the background, adding to the festive atmosphere. When the fiddle player of the small group started a high-spirited solo, people in the crowd began to clap and cheer. The empty clearing between the head table and the food was beginning to fill with people clapping along with the music and forming an enormous circle that filled the space.

"Come on!" Anila said, pulling Douglas out of his chair.

"Whaaaattt …" was all Sage could hear as he was dragged out to the circle.

"You too," Terran said. He grabbed Sage's hand and followed behind Douglas, who was still struggling to get his footing.

The solo fiddle had been joined by instruments that very much resembled a guitar and a flute. The flute's beautiful and high-pitched tones had little difficulty being heard over the fiddle and clapping crowd. The drummer made four loud strokes on the leather drum strapped around his shoulder, signaling the crowd. Everyone began dance steps that they all seemed to know. Sage and Douglas were completely lost on what to do and clumsy in their attempt to follow along.

"Watch us!" Anila shouted out with her usual enthusiasm.

It wasn't complicated once they took a moment to figure out the pattern. Sage joined in after only a couple of rotations of the dance steps. Douglas had to be pulled back into the circle by Anila but reluctantly proved he had caught on as well. Sage laughed out loud watching her brother. *He's not half bad,* she thought, *and he's actually having fun!*

Breathless and excited at the end of the dance, the crowd cheered their approval to the musicians. The musicians bowed and began to play what was apparently considered background music as the dance area started to clear a bit.

"You guys did great!" Anila cheered on their way back to the table. "What did you think? Wasn't that fun?"

"Yes," Sage replied, fanning herself and trying to catch her breath. "It was kind of like country western line dancing meets Irish step dancing—accompanied by folk music."

"Huh?" Anila looked at her with such a perplexed expression that both Sage and Douglas laughed themselves breathless again. Their laughter was contagious, and soon everyone at their table had joined in, even if they didn't know what had been so funny in the first place. It was exactly what Sage had needed, a good laugh and a night enjoying the company of friends.

Lamar elbowed Douglas in his side and jerked his head in the direction he wanted him to look. Sage, Terran, and Anila followed their gaze to find Avery and Evron standing together at the edge of the forest. Another chill went down Sage's spine. Evron waved his pointed finger in Avery's face. Avery shook his head and raised his hands up guardedly in front of him. Douglas only managed a few steps toward his father before both Terran and Lamar grabbed him.

"Nothing will happen here, man," Lamar hissed. "He wouldn't risk it!"

"You guys have been acting strangely all night! What is going on?" Anila demanded. She was already confused by her friends' behavior and now she was becoming a bit frightened by it, too.

Sage touched Anila's arm gently. "We'll tell you everything when we get back to your house," she promised.

They all turned back to check on Avery and Evron. Avery was walking toward them, leaving Evron standing alone with a sour expression on his face.

"It is time to leave," he announced to them. "Hannah and Keelin are walking back up with Delaney. I am going to find Jake and Aderyn at their tent. I hope they can find someone to watch Sora for a little while. I think it would be better if we all talked together. Sage should be the one to tell everything—and how she found out," Avery said seriously. "There will be a lot of questions."

"I'll go with you. Sora can stay with us until her parents get back," Lamar volunteered.

"Thank you, Lamar. That would be very helpful," Avery said gratefully. He turned to Terran. "Maybe you could find your parents and have them meet us up at Anila's house? Let's try to be up there in fifteen minutes or so."

"I'll probably see you sometime tomorrow," Lamar told Douglas. "If not, I'll come by the cabin before you leave." He and Douglas clasped hands warmly before Lamar jogged after Avery.

"Can I have a quick word, Anila?" Terran asked tenderly. He saw that Anila was near tears with frustration. He gently took her arm and walked just out of hearing range before talking.

"I hope she's all right," Sage said. "I thought she would be able to enjoy the night better if she didn't know, but it just made her feel left out. There's more bothering her than that, though. I think she's sad. Maybe about being reminded that we are leaving?" Terran and Anila embraced. Anila wiped her eyes and smiled a little at Terran.

"You can all go ahead. I'll meet you after I find my parents," Terran said when they were standing together again.

"No!" Douglas barked. "We already agreed that no one goes alone. We'll all go together."

"I'll only be a few minutes—and you know it's not me who's in danger," Terran assured him. Terran's eyes met Sage's. He said nothing. The intensity of his gaze stole her breath, and then he turned away. Sage linked her arm with Anila's, and the three of them watched Terran weave between the mostly empty tables to find his parents.

"Ready, then?" Douglas asked.

CHAPTER 19

Through Thick and Thin

"**D**id you have a good time?" Keelin began to ask when the three of them entered the home. Anila had been crying, and all of them wore their worry for Terran on their faces.

"What's wrong? Where's Terran?" he started again.

"Terran went to find his parents," Douglas answered. "My dad is bringing Jake and Aderyn, too."

Hannah rushed into the room. "Something's wrong?" she asked. "Keelin, you sound upset."

"Yes," Sage stumbled. "Well, it's just that …"

"… we have a matter of importance to discuss," Avery finished. Much to Sage's relief, her father had opened the door just steps behind her and Douglas. Jake and Aderyn followed him into the living area.

"Tonight, Avery? It's late. It's been a long night," Keelin tried to reason.

"It can't wait, can it?" Hannah interrupted.

"No, it cannot," Avery replied to Hannah. He placed a firm hand on Keelin's shoulder. "I'm sorry, Keelin. You're right; it is late. We will try to keep this as short as possible."

The door opened again. Terran entered the room, his parents with him, looking as confused as the others. Sage sighed and relaxed a little when she saw Terran, and he crossed the room to join her, Douglas, and Anila.

"What's this all about, Avery?" Jake asked. "You're being very secretive."

"Maybe we should all sit down," Linaeve suggested in her naturally smooth, soothing voice.

Everyone took a seat in the now cramped living room. Sage was nervous just looking at her father's friends. What if they didn't believe what they were going to be told? Frayne was Evron's son. Would he be angry with her or maybe with her father? How long would it be until Evron found out what she knew? The thoughts swirled in her head, her heart raced, and her mouth went dry.

"I am sorry for interrupting your plans for this evening," Avery began, "but there was no other time for us all to meet together before I leave to take my family home. Jake said I have been very secretive—and he's right. We have all been friends for—goodness, our whole lives—and I know every one of you can be trusted. What you are about to hear must remain in this room. It is truly a matter of life and death." The couples exchanged looks with their spouses and with each other, mumbling at Avery's strong and dramatic statement. "A few months ago, when the summer began, Sage and Douglas had no knowledge of our communities, of our history, or of their own powers. Since then, they have made close friends with your children and are just beginning to learn their powers. Sage has always been able to perceive what others around her were feeling, but Adel and I only believed her to be more sensitive than others, nothing more. When she came to the cabin and the forest this summer, she found those perceptions greatly enhanced. At Spencer's funeral service, she …" He paused, knowing this was not his story to tell. "Well, perhaps it would be better if she continued." Avery brought Sage forward, gave her a quick nod of encouragement to take over, and took the last available seat near Frayne.

Sage stood frozen for a moment, trying to control the thoughts of doubt that were still swimming in her head. Terran placed his hand on her shoulder and gave it a heartening squeeze. She felt bolstered by his confidence in her and by Douglas's encouragement. They both nodded for her to go on, so she began.

"At my grandfather's funeral," she started, her voice shaky. "I—Douglas and I—met Evron for the first time. I didn't know why, but the strength of his emotions overwhelmed me and made me feel ill. That was my power, my gift, but I didn't know that at the time, either. It was quite clear he disliked me. Douglas and my mother, too, but especially me. He told me that I looked remarkably like my grandmother. He knew my grandmother. She was from Oakley, and he was right, I do look like she did at my age.

"I met Terran a couple days later in the woods," she continued. She couldn't prevent the grin that spread across her face at the memory and glanced up at Terran, who still stood right beside to her. "We got to be really good friends with him, Anila, and Lamar. Lamar couldn't go with us to the Fourth of July celebration, but the rest of us went together to celebrate Douglas's birthday. We went to a new shop in town, one that was not here last summer. It's a place where the tourists can get psychic readings. We didn't think it would amount to anything more than a little fun, but the lady there told each of us something, and at least some of those things have already proven true—for each of us."

Again, there were looks and murmurs in the room. Sage could feel they were uneasy about where the story was leading. She continued through the story about Douglas's crest to where she and Douglas found they both had powers that had never before been gifted to the children of an elf and human. She explained that she knew Anila was troubled about something and that Anila had shared it with her.

"Then, I went to the library and thought it would be fun to learn the meanings of the names of our new friends. When I read Terran's name, I thought it was interesting, but when I read Anila's name, I knew I could help her, just like the woman at the shop said." Sage did her best to speak slowly and tell the events in the order in which they had occurred during the summer. She was cold, shivering from nervousness just like she always did when she had to give oral presentations at school. She told everyone about the book and that it wasn't clear what the book was at first, about overhearing her father's conversation with Evron and about their trip to Ambara. Sage smiled proudly at Anila when describing her flying and the similarities between her and the legend that Terran had retold.

Everyone remained silent, listening to her emotional retelling of the events directly before and after Terran was injured. Anila wiped her eyes again, reliving the fear. Douglas held her hand to comfort her, but whether from fatigue or emotion was rubbing his own eyes with his free hand. Sage was tired, too. She felt she had done very well up to now, but she was beginning to suffer from a room full of rising emotions. She took a slow and steadying breath.

"The next day, I wasn't allowed to go back into the forest—or to go see Terran. I went into town with my mother so I could go to the library again." Sage concentrated, trying to keep her focus on the story and not the energies in the room. "That's when I knew who she was," she said. She looked at Anila. "The woman at the shop is my grandmother."

"No," a woman's voice said.

"How could this be?" another voice overlapped.

"I went to her," Sage said unheard. "I went to her," she called above the commotion. They began to quiet again. "I went to the shop that morning. It is true. She is Nayana of Oakley, our grandmother. My parents and Douglas went with me to meet her the next morning, though they didn't know who I was taking them to see. They were just as surprised as you all are. That's when Nayana told us what happened to her."

Sage retold her grandmother's story, using as many of her grandmother's own words as she could remember. Her father's friends remained silent, apparently stunned, for several moments after Sage finished telling her grandmother's account of Evron's terrible deception. Sage was very lightheaded. She took a step back and leaned against the wall behind her.

Frayne finally found the strength to ask, "Avery, is this true?"

Avery could not bring himself to look at his friend, keeping his eyes fixed on the floor. They had been friends their whole lives, and Sage could feel the pain Avery was going through, not knowing how Frayne would take the information, truth or not.

"Yes, Frayne," he answered gently. "It is true. I am so sorry."

"My father's actions have always been a mystery to me," Frayne shook his head slowly from side to side. "But I've always known he was capable of something like this."

"You are just going to believe all of this?" Jake had almost leapt from his chair when Frayne hadn't come to Evron's defense.

"What is there not to believe?" Hannah retorted. "This should be taken to the Council immediately!"

"It happened more than forty years ago! Look what Evron has done since. Does that not count for anything?" Jake argued.

"Can the cruelty of tearing apart a family and years of deceit simply be dismissed?" Hannah snapped at Jake. It was clear to Sage that Hannah had a very dominant personality and was ready to use her position on the Council to remove Evron from his seat. Sage would normally have been encouraged by Hannah's words, knowing something would be done to punish Evron. But instead, the strength of her outrage was crippling.

"All I'm saying is that it was a long time ago, and Evron was certainly angry that the woman he was supposed to be marrying went off with someone who was …"

"Human?" Avery couldn't believe what his best friend was saying.

"You know I didn't mean it to sound like that, Avery," Jake tried to explain.

"No?" Aderyn asked her husband. "Are you saying if I had chosen to marry another man—maybe a human—and you became angry, you would have thought it reasonable action to drug me, lie to me, and keep me away from my newborn child?"

"No! I most certainly would not," Jake stammered, hurt by what Aderyn had suggested.

"Of course you wouldn't, Jake." Aderyn softened, taking his hand. "But if you think that Evron should be pardoned completely because of the few respectable things he has done since, you are saying as much," she contended.

"We all need to calm down," Keelin begged. "We should not be arguing amongst ourselves."

"Keelin is right," Frayne said softly. "Jake is just thinking through his confusion and the shock that we are all feeling right now."

"I just don't believe it," Jake tried to explain. "I mean, how can this be true? Avery, we practically grew up in his home."

"There is more."

The unemotionally made statement instantly hushed the room and turned everyone's attention back to the four friends. Terran had moved in front of Sage, Douglas to her side. Sage was grateful for the distraction from the quarreling adults.

"There is more to tell you," Terran repeated, his smooth, low voice soft and clear. Everyone took their seats once again, looking unsure whether they could take any more. "Yesterday, when Sage and Douglas came to tell me and Anila—though she wasn't able to be there—what had happened with Nayana, it was right when the big storm came in. Sage and I found a place in the forest to keep dry and not be overheard. Two people approached along the trail. We couldn't see their faces, but Sage knew who they were before they spoke. It was grandfather and the man that was in the woods when I was hurt."

Sage knew that her father's friends didn't know her very well yet, and when she had been talking, a few of them were listening as if she were only a storyteller narrating a fairy tale. Now, the fairy tale became much more real—coming from Terran, whom they had all watched grow to a young man. Their furrowed brows and drawn faces revealed their pain. There was no way they could have prepared for what Terran would tell them next. Frayne rested his elbows on his knees and lowered his weary head into his hands, listening to Terran recall the brief discussion he and Sage had overheard. For the first time, Linaeve's control seemed to fail her. Her placid face was replaced with watery eyes and a trembling chin.

"There could be more, then," Keelin thought out loud. "They may be planning more attacks."

"Yes, it does sound that way. What are we going to do about it—about Evron?" Hannah demanded again.

"Nothing yet," Avery said to everyone's surprise. "We don't know who the other man is. We can't do something about Evron and take the chance that this person will keep on attacking—or that he'll disappear and never be brought to justice."

"So we do nothing, Avery?" Aderyn asked. "Do we dare wait until someone else gets hurt—or worse?"

"For now, we must go on as usual. I fear that people *will* get hurt, especially if Evron knows we suspect him of treachery," Avery stood and turned to his friends. "If Evron found out about Nayana, her life would most certainly be at risk. If he learned the whereabouts of the book, he would hold information that generations of Seers thought valuable enough to write down—some of which he believes will aid him in gaining more power. We need—"

"What exactly is in the book?" Keelin interrupted.

"So far, there isn't much that fits clearly with the happenings we have seen," Avery said, being intentionally vague. "It is possible the book will yield nothing helpful to us. Even so, there is enough information without it to have concern for the safety of our people."

Still tearful, Linaeve stood and walked gracefully over to Sage, drawing the eyes of the entire room with her as she moved. She wrapped her arm around Sage's shoulder and pulled her close. As Sage felt the attention of the adults in the room turn from Evron toward her, a great weight lifted from her, and her eyes began to refocus.

"We are all growing very tired, and emotions are running high." Linaeve's voice was warm and comforting to Sage. "I would like to suggest that we all make a commitment that none of what has been said here tonight will leave this room. We can, for a short time, go on as if we are unaware of Evron's vileness.

This will give us each time to frame ideas on how better to approach the issues we have begun to discuss. We can talk more when we are all together again for the fall Council sessions."

Suddenly aware of everyone's eyes on her, Sage lowered her gaze to the floor. She was grateful to Linaeve for stepping in when she did, especially knowing she had been close to passing out, just as she had at her grandmother's shop the day before.

"You are right, as always, Linaeve," Aderyn said with great respect. "Your words have always been soft spoken and few but, like the mountains, they are powerful."

"I thank you, Aderyn," Linaeve said with a bow of her head. "Are we all, at least for the moment, in agreement, then?"

Everyone, including Hannah, raised a hand in agreement. After a few minutes of quiet conversations, Aderyn and Jake left for their tent. Frayne and Linaeve prepared to leave as well.

"I think you should come to Ashtyn by the river," Frayne told Terran in a purposefully lighter tone. "It would be fun, and with so many people heading back tomorrow, there shouldn't be anything to worry about. Avery and I will meet you there mid—well, probably late—morning." He chuckled, looking at the late hour. "Ready, Avery?"

"Yes, I will be right there," he replied. Then he turned to Douglas and Sage. "It was a hard night. I'm sorry for that, but you have one more thing to take care of before you turn in."

Sage and Douglas looked to where Anila sat in the same place she had been since returning to her home. Terran was with her now, though they were not talking. She was lost in her own thoughts. They turned back to their father, understanding what it was they had left to do.

It was Terran who led them up to the rooms.

"Anila," he started in a whisper. "We have something more to share with you."

"I know," she said.

She walked past her bedroom to the room at the end of the hallway. The room they entered would be where the two boys would be sleeping for the night. It was an enormous space, taking the entire top portion of the tree. Part of the oak's trunk and its branches jutted through the floor in several places around the room and up again through the arched ceiling. Large windows surrounded the room, which was set up as an office and library. Bookcases filled the walls between the windows, and four comfortable reading chairs were grouped together, with an oversized ottoman shared among them. There was an ornately carved oak desk near one wall, with a large, detailed map of the national park on the wall behind it. The map was neatly shaded in different colors, marking the four communities and tagged here and there with red tacks.

Anila walked straight to the chairs and waited for her friends to join her. Sage sat in the chair next to her, Terran and Douglas across.

"I listened to everything you said, Sage," she began. "I'm sorry about what happened with your grandparents. It's really unfair. I also heard you telling me that I have a part in what is to come."

"Anila, I didn't ..." Sage faltered. The whole time in the living room she had been thinking of how difficult it would be to tell Anila exactly that.

"No, not in so many words you didn't," Anila continued. "It was the part about the legend and how similar I am to it. You didn't talk about the other legends, just Ambara—and me. You didn't mention the eagle, either," she smiled. "I don't know why the eagle is so important. It just is."

"Yes," Terran agreed. "I think the eagle's return is important, too."

"We don't know all the pieces yet, Anila," Douglas stated. "You won't be alone—no matter what happens. We'll be there."

"Through thick and thin," Sage added.

Anila and Sage walked down to her bedroom. All of the lights that had been glowing in the trees and on the walkways had gone black for the night, but enough moonlight still filled the room for the girls to pull on their pajamas and get ready for bed. Sage lay down on the bed made up on the floor next to Anila's bed.

"I'm sorry about you having such a part in whatever is going on," Sage said.

"Don't be," said Anila. "If it's true—all of this—then it is a great honor, and I will be proud to be a part of bringing my people back."

"Still ... I hope I'm wrong, Anila," Sage told her.

Anila dropped her hand over the edge of her bed. Sage reached up and took it in her own.

"I'm glad you're here," Anila whispered.

As Frayne predicted, they didn't even rise until mid-morning, but were loading the kayaks on the river with plenty of time to arrive in Ashtyn before the noon hour. Most of Oakley had already emptied out, with very few tents remaining on the outside edge of the town center. There were people visible on the trail, and Sage could also see there were a few kayaks already drifting gently down the river.

"We should split up," Anila suggested to Terran. "You and I know the river and the rapids, but Sage and Douglas don't. It would be better if each of us were in separate kayaks, don't you think?"

"Yeah, good thinking," he agreed. "You and Douglas ride together; Sage can ride with me."

While Terran began shuffling backpacks around in the boats, Keelin and Hannah stepped forward.

"It was wonderful to meet you both," Keelin told Sage and Douglas.

"Have a wonderful school year, and we will be looking forward to seeing you again in the springtime," Hannah said. She shook their hands before the four friends stepped into the kayaks.

"Do *not* walk back without Terran," Keelin told Anila sternly as he pushed the boats away from the bank.

"It will be a short trip downriver," Terran called out. "Should only be about ten minutes, unless other people get backed up unloading in Ashtyn. Most of the way will be like this." He indicated the river at Oakley, which was gentle and deep, with no obstacles to guide the boats around. "Just before we get to the mill, there will be a small rapids area, where Anila and I will need to guide the boats through the rocks. It will still be rocky the rest of the way to Ashtyn, but only along the banks."

Even though most water sports were off her favorite to-do list, Sage had always loved canoeing and kayaking. Whether just flowing along with the current or the strenuous activity of rowing, she found it enjoyable. There certainly was not much work to do on this trip so far. The waters moved gently, winding through the forest with the trail almost always visible to them, with people smiling, waving and yelling out greetings. The shadow of the mix of large oak trees and ash disappeared as they curved around a bend into the bright sunshine. It took a moment for their eyes to adjust, and all of them tried to block the glaring reflection off the water.

"The rapids are just ahead," Terran called out, shading his eyes with his hand.

Anila slipped her kayak back behind Terran and Sage, so their boats could maneuver the rapids more easily. The mill and the spinning water wheel were ahead on their right, and the rocks Terran had talked about at the start of their trip jutted from both banks. The water was picking up speed. White foam from the rapids was on all sides of their small boats. Terran knew the way safely through the large rocks jutting from the river, and after a few sprays of water, they were in calm waters again. Sage turned back to see Anila skillfully guiding her boat along the same path Terran had taken. Then, she and Douglas rowed up alongside Sage and Terran again.

There were many people ahead at the clearing in Ashtyn, but no other boats were left to be unloaded. Ahead of them, Sage could see Frayne and Avery walking to the water's edge, looking for them upriver. Avery smiled and waved as soon as he spotted the kayaks.

"He's here, Terran," Sage whispered above the river.

"Who's here? The mystery man?" he asked, scanning the crowd for anyone he did not recognize.

"No. Evron is here. See him standing behind those trees? I don't even think our fathers know he's there," she answered. She talked without looking in Evron's direction, trying not to draw his attention.

Terran waved over to Anila and Douglas, trying to get their attention, but before he could signal them, something large and black moved between the boats from behind them. All their eyes followed it as it moved downriver toward the unloading area.

"That was a serpent!" Douglas called over to Terran. "What's it doing this far from the lake?"

"I don't know. It would have had to come up through the rapids closer to the lake, and those are a lot worse than the ones we just went through." Terran's voice was edgy. "There was one up this far in the early spring, too."

"Here it comes again," Sage said. She pointed as it sliced between them, causing a wake that rocked their boats. They were close to their destination, and now Frayne and Avery were both aware of what had just passed between the kayaks. The four friends began to guide their kayaks toward the rocky river-bank. Once again, the serpent, moving faster than before, came between the boats. It lashed its tail violently, striking both of the boats and separating them. Sage and Terran were nearly tipped completely over as they were thrust toward the rocks, and Anila and Douglas's kayak pitched from side to side near the opposite bank.

Shouts and cries began to draw crowds along the shore. Avery's voice pierced the din of the crowd, calling for them to get in quickly. Sage and Terran began to steer their turned boat to the bank again. On the other side of the river, Douglas and Anila had regained their balance quickly and were already rowing back. But as they reached the center of the river, the serpent passed underneath them, raising their kayak out of the water and letting it fall hard against a nearby rock. Both passengers were thrown from the boat in the deepest part of the river. Screams erupted from the crowd that looked on helplessly, unable to do anything but watch the events on the river.

"Douglas!" Terran yelled in horror as he and Sage watched Anila struggle in the current. "Anila can't swim!"

Douglas had just reached the opposite bank when he heard Terran. He dove back in and swam with the current to where Anila flailed her arms, trying to stay above the water. He grabbed her arm, helping her move to his back so he could swim to the bank just down river from the clearing. Frayne and others ran to help Douglas and Anila out of the water and up the steep embankment.

The other kayak, carrying Terran and Sage, had come to a stop at the rocks, just yards from the usual drop off area. They had not gotten out, watching fretfully to make sure Douglas and Anila were safe. When she was certain they were fine, Sage turned to Terran, and they smiled at each other with relief. Avery and a few other townspeople were making their way along the rocks to their boat. Terran held out his hand to help Sage climb from the kayak. She stood, reaching her hand upward, but another blow struck the small boat, shattering the far side and sending both Sage and Terran backward into the water.

Evron had slipped forward to the edge of the rocks. "What is going on here?" he asked with authority.

"It's back!" someone screamed, pointing into the water.

Terran pulled himself onto the closest rock and turned to search for Sage. She was safe, kneeling on a rock just behind him to his right, and she could see him relax a little. He reached behind to help her stand and move on the sharp, slippery rocks.

"Watch out!" Avery screamed, but it was too late. Her legs were whipped out from underneath her by the serpent's tail, slamming her face down into the sharp rocks.

"Noooo!" Terran screamed.

CHAPTER 20

Nine Months Away

Terran lunged to catch her. Sage could see him out of the corner of her eye just before she struck the rocks. But he was not fast enough. The blow felt as if it had split her head open, and for a moment, she lost consciousness. Limp and woozy, Sage slid from the rocks into the river. Terran jumped back into the water, struggling to reach her before the currents pulled her away. He raised Sage's head above the surface, then gathered her limp body in his arms. She could feel him fully for the first time, and he was frightened. Sage wanted to look at Terran, wanted to show him she was going to be fine. Her eyes opened briefly, but she was too weak to turn her head. Sunlight was all she could see as it streamed through the trees above her. She closed her eyes again. The taste of blood filled her mouth. She could feel its warmth streaming from her nose and through her hair.

"I see it!" a voice called out.

Terran had gotten almost all the way up the rocks and was fighting to keep his balance on their slick surface while carrying her. Screaming began on the river's edge, and Sage knew this meant a serpent was once again close to Terran. She could sense her father getting closer, too, frantic to reach the spot where the two of them had been pushed back into the water.

"Go! Return to the lake! You do not belong here!" she heard Evron bellow.

"It's— It's turning back," another townsperson yelled.

A smattering of cheers broke out when Evron's orders to the serpent were apparently obeyed. Avery reached them and helped Terran balance with Sage in his arms as he climbed off the last of the rocks.

"Sage!" Anila screamed out as Terran made his final step safely onto the riverbank.

"We must get her to my house, Avery!" Frayne directed. Terran, now safely on solid ground, began to move much faster. She could hear each elf gasping or murmuring as they parted to allow them to pass.

"You're hurt, Terran," Douglas said. He sounded like he was jogging beside them. "Let me take her for you."

"I have her," he said.

"Then let me help you."

"I said, I *have* her!"

"We don't have time for this! It would be better not to move her again, Douglas," Avery barked. "We need to get through faster!" Sage started to hear Douglas and her father just ahead of them, clearing an opening through the last of the crowd.

"Anila!" Frayne called out. "Run to the house and have Linaeve prepare a space for Sage. Tell her I've gone to get my sister!"

Sage was shivering. Even with Terran holding her she felt cold, drenched from the river and fighting the onset of shock. Her right wrist throbbed. *It all happened so fast*, she thought. *Did I try to use it to break my fall?* She was still too weak to open her eyes or respond but she wanted to remain conscious. Sage forced herself to pay attention to everything around her, the sound of the gravel on the path beneath Terran's feet as he moved swiftly along it, Douglas and her father ordering people to clear the path ahead of them, and people catching their breath or crying out when they caught a glimpse of her. They were afraid; she knew that, yet there was laughter. Someone was laughing.

"Take her to your room," she heard Linaeve direct very calmly.

Sage couldn't bear the pain from her wrist or her head any longer and she couldn't concentrate on staying awake. She was so cold. The pain was growing more intense, and she wanted to give in, wanted to sleep.

"I did the best I could on her wrist, Avery," a woman's voice said. "She'll need to stay in that splint for a couple of weeks yet. I mended her nose, and although the bruising will take some time to fade, it shouldn't give her any trouble."

Sage's eyes felt heavy and swollen. She forced them to open, seeing only light and some fuzzy shadows.

"Hi there," Anila spoke softly, her voice unsteady.

"Dad. She's awake," Douglas whispered.

Avery moved to the end of the bed. There were blurry shapes around her. It took time for her to finally focus on them.

"Ah … good. She does have a mild concussion, Avery. You should check on her a few times tonight," Jason's mother instructed. "But she is doing remarkably well, considering."

"I can't thank you enough, Ophelia," Avery said. He walked her out of the bedroom.

Sage eyes were beginning to focus; she could see Anila more clearly now. She was sitting on a chair next to the bed on her left side, holding her hand. Her face was pale and tense, yet Sage's eyes fixed on Douglas. He was more worried than she had ever seen him—but somehow relieved, too.

"You've been out for quite a while," Douglas said with a shaky voice. "Jason's mom is amazing. She said you were very lucky—and really tough."

"We've been so worried," Anila told her. Sage could tell she was trying hard not to start crying.

"I don't remember what happened after Terran … Terran?" Sage asked in confusion.

"Here," he said. He moved to where she could see him. "I'm right here."

He had been standing on her right side, back behind her, where she could not turn her head. Being careful not to jar her, he sat on the bed near her knees and gave her a forced smile.

"Thank you … for everything," she said sincerely, looking into his eyes. "You carried me all the way here even though you were injured."

"I'm fine. Just some scrapes and bruises," Terran assured her. "How much do you remember?"

"I remember waiting in the kayak to make sure Douglas and Anila were safely on the shore," she scrunched her forehead in thought. "I remember the serpent hitting the boat when we were trying to get out and tipping us backward into the water. Gosh. It seems like it happened so long ago. I don't remember how I fell. I had just gotten on a rock. You were in front of me. You reached back to help me get to my dad … and I fell. The next thing I remember was looking up at the trees when you were carrying me. People were afraid, and—I heard it very clearly—someone was laughing. I am sure someone was laughing at me."

Terran looked up at Douglas and Anila. "Was it the man? The one from the forest?" Terran asked hopefully.

"I didn't hear anyone laughing," Douglas said slowly, looking at the others.

Sage thought harder. "No," she said. "I don't think any of you could have heard it. I knew it like I know when someone is sad or angry—or frightened." She looked at Terran, who nodded his head in understanding. He grinned at her and took her hand in his. He wasn't frightened any longer. "It wasn't that man, Terran," she continued.

"I know who it was," he sighed. "I was just hoping, that's all."

"Evron?" Douglas questioned. "Evron was there when it happened? I only saw him after Anila and I were already out of the water."

"That's what I was going to tell you when the serpent separated our boats. He was hiding in the trees *trying* not to be seen," Terran explained.

Sage winced when she tried to use her hands to push herself to a sitting position. Anila leaned forward to help pull her up. "Does he have power to talk to the serpents?" Douglas asked, placing extra pillows behind Sage's back.

"He must, because he was the one that sent it away," Anila figured.

"I think he is capable of doing a lot of things," Terran suggested. "Things that others have either lost the ability to do or just haven't ever learned."

They heard footsteps near the door and stopped talking until they knew who was on the other side. The door opened, and Avery peeked into the room. Sage was sure he had remained strong during the ordeal. But it was obvious to her that he was struggling to maintain his composure now that he knew she was fine and had had time to think.

"How are you feeling?" Avery asked quietly. He was carrying a tray with tea for Sage and lemonade for the others.

"Better now," she told him. "I'm sorry, Dad."

"It's not your fault. It's not …" he began, his chin trembling a little as he looked at her.

"Yes, it is," she asserted. "The attacks were directed at me—both of them—and we all know that's true. I put everyone in danger just by being there today … by being here." The others in the room tried to disagree and console, her but she continued without paying any attention to them. "I didn't think we had anything to worry about today, and I let my guard down. I should have been paying more attention to—" She stopped, suddenly aware they were being listened to.

She raised her eyebrows in an attempt to silently signal them. Everyone stared at her. She opened her eyes even wider, angling her head toward the door. Still, they stared at her. The door to Terran's bedroom opened.

"Attention to what?" Evron asked. He acted as if he had been sitting in the room all along and was simply waiting for Sage to finish what she was saying.

"My surroundings," Sage said. She spoke very calmly even while the others were fidgeting uncomfortably. "I should have paid more attention to my surroundings, given the circumstances, sir."

More than anything, she wanted Evron to believe she was not shaken by the events of the day. She didn't want to give him the satisfaction of knowing that she had been terrified by what had happened on the river. "Douglas told me what you did, sir," she said as respectfully as she could manage. "I want to thank you for calling that serpent away before it could have knocked Terran—and me—down again."

She flashed him a disarming smile through her own nausea, but Evron had already seen the expressions on the faces of everyone else in the room. He seemed to know more was being said about him than she was telling him now. Another wave of anger hit her.

"Yes," Evron replied, drawing the word out slowly. He looked at Sage skeptically for a long time before he spoke again. "It was the least I could do to prevent any *further* injuries. You are a fortunate young lady." He kept his eyes locked on Sage, scowling at her distrustfully as he said, "A word, Avery."

Avery walked out of the room and into the hall. He closed the door behind him but purposefully did not latch it. Sage and the others sat very quietly, listening closely to decipher the muffled conversation.

"Your daughter is right, Avery," Evron said coolly. "She was clearly the intended target when Terran was injured, and I don't believe it can be any more obvious that she was the target once again today. The townspeople are talking. They see her presence in the elf communities as dangerous and unwelcome."

"But not Douglas, too?" Avery asked incredulously. He appeared to be unruffled by Evron's accusations.

"He has not been the focus of two attacks in just a matter of days," Evron fumed. Sage felt Evron force himself to calm down before he began speaking again. He spoke now as if he were offering friendly advice to Avery. "After I ordered the serpent back to the lake, I did my best to abate their fears. Still, it would be of paramount importance for her to leave as soon as possible. She looks as if she is doing quite well and could easily—"

"She will leave when she is able to walk without assistance," a smooth, calm voice interrupted. "She is going to rest a while longer before I will allow her to make the walk back to the cabin."

There were heavy stomps on the stairs and a slamming door. A moment later Avery and Linaeve entered the room. Linaeve walked to Sage and checked the bandage on her head. She briefly looked into each of Sage's eyes and felt her head for fever.

"Drink your tea, dear," she told Sage. "It will help you heal more quickly."

"Thank you," Sage said appreciatively.

Linaeve smiled at Sage and gently rumpled Terran's hair on her way back to the bedroom door.

"She's really great, Terran," Sage said.

"Yeah. And she can put Evron in his place, too," Douglas added in a whisper.

Linaeve packed Sage some herbs for tea and handed her backpack to Terran. Frayne gave Terran and Anila clear instructions before they left Ashtyn for the cabin.

"It is getting late, and I don't want either of you walking home tonight. You will stay at the cabin until Keelin and I arrive tomorrow," he told them.

"Thank you for taking such good care of me. It was a lot to ask of you, just having met me this summer, I mean." Sage knew that both Linaeve and Frayne were risking some backlash from Evron by having her in their home.

"We always take care of our family," Frayne told her. Linaeve slipped her hand through her husband's arm and smiled at Sage. There was complete agreement between them. Avery and Douglas shook hands with Frayne and Linaeve.

"I will see you at the fall meeting, Avery. And I'll look forward to seeing you both again after your school year ends," Linaeve said to Douglas and Sage.

With Sage taking her father's arm for support and the others walking slightly in front of them, the group made their way through the town. Some of the townspeople simply moved out of the way when the group passed; others rounded up their children and hurried back to their homes or even the opposite way. They were afraid, and Sage knew Evron had not truly done anything to ease their fears. *He's the hero right now*, she thought. *So the townspeople will believe anything he tells them.*

Avery took the lead when they went down the steps to the bridge. The boys stayed close to Sage as they descended in case she felt her balance waver. Just after they crossed the bridge, their formation changed again, and Sage couldn't stifle a chuckle. She had her own private guard marching about her. Avery was slightly ahead of her, Douglas slightly behind. Terran and Anila stood on either side of her.

"Mom is going to freak out when she sees you," Douglas said, poking Sage in her ribs.

"Ow! That's really not funny," she replied.

The walk proved to be tiring for Sage. When they started out, she didn't think she would have any trouble with the relatively short distance to the cabin. Now, she found her energy fading, and as they neared the split in the trail, she became woozy. When her legs faltered a little, Sage spread her arms wide in an attempt to catch her balance. Douglas ran up to hold her from behind as Terran and Anila each grabbed an arm.

The wind blew violently, and the ground shook threateningly beneath their feet, startling everyone into action. The boys spun around defensively, scanning the forest in all directions. The birds and other animals of the forest had begun screeching with the wind, and the water from the river splashed up to the trail behind them with the rumble of the earth.

"Is everyone all right?" Avery asked over the now quieting animals. "I think it was just a small earthquake, but we should be aware. Who knows what could be in store for us." But whether it was a small earthquake or an impressive demonstration of Evron's formidable powers, nothing else happened on their way to the cabin.

Adel was waiting on the porch for them, not seeming the least bit concerned about the late hour of their arrival. "I have beds made up for you," she told Anila and Terran. "I want you to go lie down right away," she ordered Sage after giving her a quick examination. Douglas and Sage looked at each other and then to their father, who had an equally bewildered look on his face.

"Who are you?" Douglas asked. "And what have you done with our mother?"

"Ha ha," Adel smiled at him. "Let's get her in the house."

Without further explanation for her unnaturally serene manner, Adel and Anila helped Sage up the stairs and into the cabin. They settled Sage comfortably on the couch. Spread on the table beside her was an assortment of first aid supplies from bandages to slings. Adel calmly looked under the bandage on Sage's head and, deciding that it did not need changing, she turned her attention to the others in the room, who were still staring at her in disbelief. The fact that Adel was not freaking out, as Douglas had expected, mystified her family.

"I went to see my mother this morning," she started. "I figured with everyone up late last night or still returning home from the celebration this morning, it would be safe. I wanted to see her again—alone—before we left." She waited for an argument, but no one questioned her need to learn more about her mother. She sat on the couch next to Sage and continued her explanation. "I was getting ready to leave Nayana's shop, thinking I would be home around lunchtime before you arrived. That's when Nayana saw it happen—probably as it was happening. She said that there had been another attack and that Sage was hurt. She told me that Sage was being well taken care of and would return home with her friends later this evening. That's all she could see, and she assured me that worrying about it would not bring you home any faster. So, I did what she said. I came home and prepared for any possible injuries—and guests." She laughed. "Knowing Sage was in good hands and would still be able to make the trip home tonight was enough information for me to maintain my sanity. I decided to save my worrying for when you all filled me in on what happened."

Everyone took turns telling parts of the story, beginning with the celebration. Adel showed only a little concern when told about Evron approaching Avery once again. That changed when she was given all of the details about the attack. Sage listened closely as Douglas, Anila, and Terran shared what it was like after she had lost consciousness. It was hard for her and her mother to hear, and Sage knew it was even harder for her friends to relive it.

"I had to leave the room for a while," Avery confessed. "It was too painful to watch you going through that—awake or not. But they— They stayed with you the entire time. Wouldn't budge from your side."

Anila smiled at Sage through her tears. "Through thick and thin," she said.

Sage fell asleep shortly after eating a late dinner with her friends and family. When she woke the next morning, she felt remarkably better. She could even place a small amount of weight on her wrist with no twinges of pain. The wound on her head had healed enough that it could be left without a bandage, covered only by her hair. Her face was still bruised around her nose, but as Ophelia had told her father, it wasn't giving her any trouble. Final packing and loading occupied the morning hours. Even with Sage taking it easy, they were soon ready to leave for home. Sage pulled her grandmother's book from her duffle bag and smiled. She took it to the porch, where Douglas, Terran, and Anila were sitting, waiting for Keelin and Frayne to arrive. She opened to the poem she had not yet been able to examine closely, the poem that had caught her eye with a line about the Child of the Wind.

"I haven't had a chance to show any of you this yet," Sage said, taking a seat next to Anila. "This is what started putting pieces together for me—that is, if I'm right. I have really only read this verse," she said pointing to the third stanza.

"Kind and beautiful. Powers beyond her knowing. The Child of the Wind," Anila read aloud, smiling at the idea of a poem being written about her.

"Haiku," Douglas blurted out. "Kind and beau-ti-ful …" he mumbled counting on his fingers. "Yeah, I'm pretty sure it's supposed to be haiku."

Sage hadn't thought of that before, reading each verse as an individual poem. They all looked down at the four stanzas on the page and began to read.

> **Green, growing wisdom**
> **Roots spread, seek knowledge and truth**
> **She is Nature's choice**
>
> **Powers newly found**
> **Spirit of the serpent guards**
> **Dark waters will shine**
>
> **Kind and beautiful**
> **Powers beyond her knowing**
> **The Child of the Wind**
>
> **Heart brave as the bear**
> **Loyalty unwavering**
> **Powers of the Earth**

Sage, her heartbeat quickening, looked at the first one, the second, and then the last. She looked up at her friends, all still awkwardly trying to read from over her shoulder or upside down. Slowly each of them finished, looking silently at the others, wondering. Sage knew they all understood. She shut the book.

"Well … umm," Sage finally managed to mutter. "Maybe we should wait a little while before telling our parents about this one."

Movement in the forest caught their attention. Frayne and Keelin stepped off the trail toward the cabin. The four friends stood and exchanged looks with each other once more. But this time it was not because of a shared secret and not because of a shared worry. This time the friends exchanged glances because they knew they would be saying goodbye to each other for almost nine months. Avery and Adel spoke with Keelin and Frayne for a few minutes before letting their children know it was time to leave. Anila approached Sage as Terran and Douglas said their goodbyes.

"I'm so glad you're going to be all right. So is Terran," Anila began after a quick check over her shoulder to see that Terran was out of earshot. "You should have seen him yesterday. He held your hand the whole time you were being treated and wouldn't let anyone take care of his cuts until Ophelia was finished with you. He even talked to you about all the fun we had together this summer, just in case you could hear him. Terran is my best friend, Sage. I love him very much, but in case you didn't already know, our feelings for each other end at friendship. We're family to each other and will never be anything more." Anila leaned close to Sage's ear and whispered. "It couldn't be any clearer who holds his heart." Anila stood straight again and smiled tearfully at Sage, who felt her cheeks flush. "Send letters with your dad when he comes for meetings, okay?" They hugged, and Anila tried to sound cheerful. "We'll write back about everything that is happening here."

"I will, Anila. And I feel the same way you really feel right now," Sage told her.

"I already can't wait for next summer," Anila said sadly. Then she turned away and walked to Douglas.

Terran had already finished saying goodbye to Douglas and was waiting a few feet away for Anila to finish talking with Sage. He stepped forward with his hands in his pockets. Their friendship had grown strong over the summer, and now she could admit she felt more for him than just that. Sage's cheeks warmed, and her heart began beating wildly as he smiled at her.

"It's going to be a long winter without you and Douglas around," Terran said in his normal, genuine manner.

"How do you know it will be any different?" Sage teased. "We've never been here during the winter."

He laughed. "It just won't be the same, that's all."

"I suppose that after this summer there is nothing that could ever be the same again," she said. She lifted her eyes to look directly at him.

He clumsily put his arms around her, seeming nervous for the first time. "I'm really going to miss you while you're gone," he said and then released her. It was a short embrace, and Sage found herself wishing it had been longer. Terran kissed her on the cheek when they separated and quickly turned his eyes to the ground.

Sage waited for him to look up again before replying. "I'm going to miss you, too, Terran."

"Everyone ready?" Avery asked his long-faced family.

They all climbed into the car and were ready to shut the doors when they heard a voice yelling from the direction of the forest. Avery jumped from the car and joined Keelin and Frayne in a defensive stance, waiting for whatever might come at them.

"Wait! Wait!!" the voice shouted again.

Sage started laughing and got out of the car. "It's just Lamar, Dad," she called out.

Lamar ran from the forest and up to the drive. He stopped in front of Terran and Anila, who were now joined by Sage and Douglas again. He was panting for breath, bent over at his waist with his hands on his knees.

"I almost didn't make it," Lamar wheezed, standing up again. His eyes stopped on Sage. He looked at her from head to toe and raised one of his eyebrows. "What happened to you?" he asked. He frowned, knowing he had missed something important.

"Long story! I'll fill you in later," Terran answered for her.

Lamar nodded to Terran and turned to Douglas. "I didn't see you yesterday, but I couldn't let you head home without saying goodbye," Lamar told him.

"Anila suggested we send letters with my dad when he comes for meetings," Douglas told him.

"Not to me you won't," Lamar laughed. "We stick to home when it gets cold, and nobody has ever wanted to brave the icy water to visit us."

"Yeah, right," Douglas remembered. He didn't try to hide his disappointment. "So … I'll see you next summer."

"Can't wait," Lamar replied. They shook hands in their usual way, bumping fists at the end. Then Lamar reached out, giving Sage a very careful hug.

"I'm fine, Lamar," she chuckled. "Really."

He shrugged his shoulders and got a mischievous gleam in his eyes. All of a sudden, he was hugging her tightly, raising her off of the ground, and shaking her in the air until she begged through her laughter for him to stop.

Once again, they piled back into the car and this time started down the driveway, waving out the windows as they left. They were on their way home. Home was the city, more than seven hours from this wonderful place. Home was where Sage had spent nearly sixteen years thinking she knew who she was. Home was where her friends, her school and her life had always been. Those things were still there for her, but her future was in the forest, and it had just begun.

They neared the town of Grace, and Sage's thoughts turned to Nayana. She still couldn't see herself calling Nayana Grandma, though that might come in time. Next summer, Sage thought, we will have more time to get to know her, more time to ask questions. Nayana needed that as much as Sage and her family.

"Mom?" Sage got up the courage to ask. "You don't have to say if it is too private, but I was wondering what you whispered to Nayana that day in her shop just before we left."

They could see her shop now, and a woman in a bright flowing gown, beaded necklaces, and matching scarves stood in the doorway. Nayana knew they would be driving by, and she was waiting for them. Avery slowed the car down just enough to see her clearly as they passed. Again, the family waved out the windows. She smiled at them and waved until they were beyond her sight.

"I told her that there was nothing to forgive," Adel smiled and rested her head back against the car seat.

It was cruel and unfair for Nayana to have lived so long without the two people she loved most in the world. Evron had taken away what he himself was not able to have with her. Now he wanted something else, and no one knew what he was willing to do to get it. Sage knew it would not be easy to figure out Evron's true goals or his plan for attaining them. She was certain, however, that there were more clues waiting for her and her friends to piece together and even more discoveries still yet to be made.

About the Author

Rachel VanZandt grew up smelling cereal baking in Cereal City—Battle Creek, Michigan. After years as a middle school band director, Rachel left teaching to raise her oldest daughter. She soon discovered a love for entertaining her daughter with rich tales of adventure, friendship, and valor. A move to Florida, three additional children, and several dogs later, Rachel's love of storytelling has not changed. In her free time, Rachel enjoys reading, playing in her craft room and gardens, and spending time with her friends and family.

www.ingramcontent.com/pod-product-compliance
Lightning Source LLC
Chambersburg PA
CBHW060325260626
47160CB00007B/2682